Moons Rising

by

Blythe Ayne

Moons Rising
Blythe Ayne

Emerson & Tilman, Publishers
129 Pendleton Way #55
Washougal, WA 98671

www.MoonsRising.BlytheAyne.com

Book and cover design by Blythe Ayne
Art Nouveau graphics are in the public domain.

Moons Rising

www.BlytheAyne.com

Paperback ISBN: 978-1-947151-12-3

[1. FICTION / Science Fiction / Genetic Engineering
2. FICTION / Science Fiction / Steampunk
3. FICTION / Fantasy / Urban] I. Title.
BIC: FM

First Edition

Moons Rising
by
Blythe Ayne

DEDICATION

To everyone who believes
In the Perfect Power of Love

Before the Beginning

Keeper A kept her eyes on the 3-D projection of a brilliant lavender light jetting upward in the night sky. She leaned forward slightly, back ramrod straight, her perfectly manicured fingers curled around the arms of her enormous chair. The ceiling-tall metal shutters, locked tight, made her massive office even darker than the nearly moonless night.

As she watched, the brilliant light within the beam of the Aurora Borealis advanced faster and faster. A funnel of ballooning darkness appeared below, hurtling toward the glowing pastel light. Keeper A couldn't see what transpired inside the funnel when the darkness encountered the light, but she knew a fierce battle raged.

An explosion suddenly disrupted the funnel. She held her breath. As the dark smoke cleared, the brilliant lavender light burst through. Eventually, the horizon of the little satellite moon, Pink, filled the view of the 3-D projection, as the bright lavender light landed on its surface in a radiant bubble. She heard a faint cheer rise up, as if the very sound followed the enthralling light.

The door to Keeper A's office flung open, and a nervous, wiry, tiny man, dressed in a bright yellow body suit, came into her office. As he focused on getting to the desk in the room's darkness, he blurted out, "Did you see…?"

"*Get out!*" Keeper A commanded in a low, dangerous voice.

The tiny man raised his eyes to the 3-D, watching the lavender bubble burst upon the surface of Pink. "*Oh! How* do you have this view on Pink before even the news bots?"

"*Get out!*" Keeper A's voice rose a notch.

"Right." The intruder retreated as he'd come, daring to glance again at the glowing lights above Keeper A, pulling the door shut with a solid thud as he exited.

"*Idiot!*" Keeper A whispered. She returned her attention to Heart, the runaway Darling Undesirable, secure upon her stunning, intrepid, winged clockworks horse, Equuleus, as they moved from the midst of the ballooning lavender light. Alive.

Instantly, the feed went black, the few minutes of her exorbitantly expensive space bot's near view of Pink, drained. She sat in the darkness, pegging together many bits of information that would have shocked almost everyone who knew her.

Chapter 1

Heart tried to adjust to the endlessly pink environment, to the profound stillness, to the lack of responsibilities. She tried to adjust to the eternal twilight, with no true daylight, no real night. But she missed her garden, her flowers. She missed her precious friend, Eye.

If she just knew she'd see him again, she could endure anything. But what was the likelihood of that? It appeared she'd remain on this small moon forever, while Earth loomed overhead in the sky.

She loved Equuleus devotedly, and she came more and more to adore Father Inventor—*her father!*—but she'd never been so isolated. Coupled with nothing meaningful to do—such as care for crippled and broken children, as she'd done at the Darling Undesirables Facility at Long Prairie—began to wear on her.

She sat with these brooding thoughts, book open, staring out at the pink and lavender hills. Equuleus came up and nuzzled her shoulder.

"Enough of this dark reflection, Heart. Let's explore!"

She reached up and patted him. "Explore? To find what? Pink upon pink—and then we'll find—more pink."

"You never know. We might find a flower, or—something."

"Or something."

"Well then, humor me. I need to stretch my wings."

Heart plopped the book without ceremony on the little mahogany side table. "Why didn't you say so? That's something else altogether. Let's go!"

She didn't bother to tell her father they were going out. He'd been relentlessly busy, rarely uttering a full sentence to her. He seemed unable to focus on her whenever she tried to talk with him. She feared he regretted bringing her here, and, politely as possible, ignored her.

Equuleus started off in a lazy canter after they exited through the double airlock of the front door.

"What about the wing stretching?" Heart asked.

"Ah, if it's flying you want, it's flying you shall have!" Equuleus broke into a full run and lifted off the pink terrain.

"*Yes!*" Heart's mood rose from the doldrums as they flew into Pink's sky. "This is exactly what I need!"

"*Me too!*" Equuleus banked and spun, pulled in his wings and dropped, then turned over and over in a series of cartwheels. Heart stuck like a burr.

Exhilarated, they finally came to the ground. Heart jumped down and they wandered to a small hillock, sinking down to rest. She moved over to lean against Equuleus, contemplating Earth overhead. "Do you ever ... do you ever miss Earth? I mean, do you ever miss being on Earth?"

"For myself? Not really, Heart. Through you, yes, I feel it through you. But for myself, all I need is you, and I'm happy as a clockworks, bio-matter horse can be."

"And being here with our father, too, who brought us both into being. But ..." Heart paused, and could not go on.

"But what?"

"I feel he doesn't—it seems he wishes—I mean, he's always acting like he's impossibly busy. It's as if I'm ...."

"*No, Heart!* You're not in his way. He loves you. But he's working diligently on something of great importance."

"You know about this?"

"Well, sort of."

Stunned, Heart sat up and faced Equuleus. "You know something I don't know? I didn't think you even *could* keep secrets from me."

"Ordinarily, I can't. But Father has needed to engage certain of my integrated bio dark matter components, that are unique to me. Although I'm aware of the project in general terms, it's moot, as

I *cannot* tell you. He has it locked away from even my access."

"Oh! That doesn't sound right. Why would he hide things from us? From me? *Why?* If you're certain he's not regretting that I'm here ...."

"He's not! What he's doing is *for you*. And for all the mechanical, clockwork and bio beings."

Heart nodded. "But will you promise to tell me anything that comes through if you *can* remember it?"

"I will, Heart."

"*Hey!*"

Heart and Equuleus leapt up from the ground.

"*What was that?*" Heart whispered.

"*Hey!*" a squeaky, high-pitched voice demanded, "under your feet."

Heart and Equuleus looked down, where, right between Heart's feet, the furry long ears of a lavender rabbit peeked from a rabbit hole.

"*A rabbit!*" Heart stepped back. "Where'd you come from?"

"I *live* here. A more relevant question would be, where did *you* come from?"

Heart pointed to the sky. "Earth," she said simply.

The little lavender rabbit looked skyward. "Earth! Ah ... *sooooooooo* beautiful! I love Earth. Truly, truly." The little rabbit's hyperbole made Heart and Equuleus chuckle.

"Is there something funny about Earth?" the rabbit asked, indignant.

"No," Heart tried to stifle her giggle but failed.

"Then logical extrapolation would only leave the probability that you're *laughing at me!*"

Equuleus snorted, the last straw for Heart, and she burst out in an unseemly guffaw. "No. Sorry. I mean, yes. Yes, we're laughing—not *at* you, just, you know, you're so cute! And so indignant, and—you're, *ahm*, well, *you're a rabbit!* We're charmed."

"Oh, well then," the rabbit's tone calmed, "that's all right then." Her little lavender front paws appeared at the edge of the hole and she pulled herself out, brushing off a couple bits of pink with her long ears. She extended her paw to Heart, "I'm Violet. I'm very pleased to meet you, Heart."

Heart took the offered paw. "I'm delighted to meet you, as well, Violet. But—how do you know my name?"

"You two have been sitting over my head jabbering away …."

"True," Heart agreed.

"I'm not a dummy …."

"Clearly not! I imagine you're the smartest rabbit anywhere."

Violet bowed slightly. "Thank you. Much appreciated. Though I suspect on Earth there are other brilliant rabbits."

"Why would you say that?"

"It seems logical."

"Ah, well, though you may be right, I can tell you that from my experience, I've never seen another rabbit such as yourself."

Violet hung her head, her ears flopped forward, dramatizing her sadness.

"Oh dear, now what?" Heart asked.

"I know," Violet sat on the ground and crossed her furry, lavender legs, "I know I can be very contrary at times. Although it's lovely to hear I'm the most brilliant rabbit anywhere, it's also very sad to imagine I'm the *only* one."

Heart sat next to Violet, and Equuleus joined them. "I understand. I know what it's like to be one of a kind. It's the same for me."

Then Equuleus quietly whispered, "And the same for me, too, as long as we're making confessions."

"*Equuleus!*" Heart exclaimed, "I didn't know you were lonely ...."

"Well, now that you've come into my life, I'm not lonely anymore. But, there *are* those times when one thinks, *ummmm*, it'd be glorious to fly with another winged gear horse. Not hugely important, but the thought comes to mind on occasion."

"*Oh!*" Heart put her arm around his neck and hugged him.

"All those years in that showcase, waiting for you to come, Heart," Equuleus continued, "now and then I'd dream of flying with another creature such as myself."

"Well," Heart said softly, "That's a lovely dream, I trust you still have it."

"Mixed feelings. A poignant pleasure."

Violet hopped closer. "Yes. I have dreams of digging tunnels with other rabbits. Sometimes it seems so real. But when I wake up, this is my reality." She waved her paw about. "Don't get me wrong, I love my home—I love Pink. But those dreams of being with other rabbits ...."

Heart patted Violet, nodding. "I have strange dreams—I can never fully remember them—of flying through the Universe, and feeling so, *so* un-alone. Truly strange dreams."

They reflected upon their private dreams until Heart broke the spell. "But, we're not alone—we have each other!"

"*Yes!*" Violet hopped up and down. "We have each other."

A beeping sound issued from Equuleus.

"What's that?" Heart asked, frowning.

"Father installed a communication module on me." He paused, listening. "He's calling us back to the castle. That's what we get for not telling him we were leaving."

"We'd better go." Heart stood. "It's been wonderful meeting you, Violet. We'll come visit you now and then, if you'd like."

"*Like?* I await the moment. Time will drag without meaning until I hear your dulcet voices again," Violet's squeaky-sweet voice trilled.

Laughter overtook Heart and Equuleus again.

"Really!" Violet demanded. "*What. Is. So. Funny?*"

"Hmmm, it's hard to explain." Heart leaned down and gave Violet a big hug. "You're just so adorable!"

"Good enough, I guess. As long as you're not laughing *at* me. I have my pride, you know."

"Of course!" Heart jumped on Equuleus. "Goodbye, dear Violet, until we meet again!"

Equuleus took a running leap and left the surface of Pink, then he circled above Violet three times before heading back to the castle. Far below, Violet waved her paw and ears, calling after them something they couldn't hear in that comical little pontifi-

cating tone of voice, making them laugh all the way
to the castle.

10 – Moons Rising

Chapter 2

"**F**ather's message says he has dinner waiting for us." Equuleus landed with a soft *"swoosh!"* at the front door.

"That's unusual."

"Rather."

As they entered the dining hall, Heart noticed the light from the wall sconces muted into a mellow gold. Two places on the side of the table near the fireplace were set with muted golden plates and cups and dinnerware.

Everything glowed in a mist of gold.

"*Oh! My!*" Heart sighed, drinking in the beauty.

The door behind them slid open and her father came up to them. "Do you like it?"

"It's stunning," Heart said. "What's the occasion? Ought I to have changed into something more formal?"

"No, dear Heart, not at all." Her father led her around to the two place settings. The fire crackled, adding its golden flowing light to the room.

He patted Equuleus on the forehead, who settled down in his place by the fire, relaxed but attentive. Then her father pulled a chair out and gestured Heart to be seated, after which he sat beside her. Then he rang a little golden bell. A clockworks butler appeared from the kitchen, carrying serving dishes.

"Oh! Father, a clockworks friend, how lovely!" She turned to him. "Hello," she said as he dished up green beans for the two of them.

The butler didn't say anything.

Heart looked at her father, bemused.

"I'm sorry, Heart, he's only clockworks. He has no dark matter or bios."

"Oh!" Heart said, disappointed. "What a pity. I'm not used to clockworks that are *only* clockworks. But he seems to be quite intelligent, coming when you call, and gracefully serving us food."

"His computer program makes him quite clever in his specific duties, but he's limited beyond that."

"What's his name?"

"Why, I haven't named him," Father Inventor said, acting surprised. "I think you'll have to name him!"

"You've done that on purpose."

Her father smiled at her warmly. "Perhaps."

"So ... *hmmm* ... what's his name? Let ... me ... think."

The butler stopped and turned to look at Heart, his clockwork eyes making direct eye contact with her. A frisson rushed through her, and the strangely familiar look they exchanged stopped her breath. "*Ohhhh!*"

His gear eyes sparkled. He knows more than he's letting on, Heart thought. "I am going to name you, *HelperFriend*." She paused, feeling quite pleased with herself. "Yes, it's HelperFriend!"

The mechanical eyes twirled in a twinkling dance, catching the firelight, and reflecting the sprinkling, golden light about the room like tiny fairies.

"Well, I like that very much, and clearly Mr. Butler likes it as well," her father said.

Equuleus made a soft neighing sound.

"Yes, and Equuleus," he added.

HelperFriend returned to the kitchen.

"Oh, Father! The dinner, the clockworks man—everything is so, *so* lovely. You've made me very happy!"

"Mission accomplished! Shall I pour you some tea?"

"Yes, please."

Heart watched as her father made a small ceremony of pouring her tea. A cozy warmth rose up in her. She glanced over at Equuleus, feeling her heart in him responding with the same warmth.

"But—Father, this feels like an occasion."

"No occasion, other than being in the moment. I *know* I've been neglecting you. I have too many projects, too much to do. I've been planning to have this dinner for some time, with poor Mr. HelperFriend hidden away in a closet, waiting for me to bring him out and put him to good use.

"Every day, which, of course, is rather metaphorical here as there are no days, but, as every metaphorical day flew by, I'd say to myself, I'll do it soon.

"When I discovered that you and Equuleus left the castle without even telling me, without even a note, I realized I've neglected you so badly you felt I wouldn't even miss you, and that you ought not bother me."

"That's true," Heart said softly, looking down.

Her father patted her hand affectionately. "*So!* The time had long passed for me to give you some undivided attention. And to bring a helper onboard for you to direct as you please—to reach books off the top shelf in the library, to help you plant a garden, or what-have-you. Anything you might wish you had another pair of hands to accomplish."

"*Plant a garden!!*" Heart flung her arms around him. "*Oh, Father!*"

He giggled a shy, schoolboy giggle.

"Is it possible? Is it at all possible that I could have a flower garden here?"

"Sure. You and HelperFriend can build a greenhouse, anywhere you want it."

"Would it not be lovely to have flowers along the walkway to the front door?"

"It would indeed, Heart. Very lovely. But please promise me you will not be sad and depressed anymore. I know it seems like I'm off in my own space, without hardly knowing you're here, but that's not true. Yes, I'm working furiously on several projects, but you are *always* on my mind."

"I believe you. I believe you now, anyway. I thought you regretted my coming here."

"*NEVER!*" He appeared to surprise himself with the force of his denial. "Never," he said again, tenderly. "*You* are the reason behind everything I do."

"Equuleus said something like that."

He turned to Equuleus, "Really?"

"Only because I told him," Heart went on, "that I thought you regretted my being here. He said that much of what you're doing is *because of me*." She paused, then probed, "Whatever it is that you're doing. I'd be most interested to know."

HelperFriend returned with steaming bowls of vegetables, disrupting the moment.

"Not to worry, my own Heart. It's nothing other than boring math and the like." He changed the subject. "So, Mr. HelperFriend, big day for you! You've been named, and are likely to help plant a flower garden on a synthetic, plant-less moon, off-world from one of the most verdant planets in the Universe. I guess I'll have to increase your programming."

HelperFriend seemed to understand exactly what Father Inventor told him, and, much to everyone's surprise, he carefully set down the bowls, then danced and twirled up and down along the far side of the table.

"Where did that come from?" Father Inventor, asked, clearly shocked.

HelperFriend snapped his metallic fingers, and fabulous music came on from everywhere and nowhere.

"Amazing! Let us be in the moment!" Heart's father stood and extended his hand to her.

"*Yes! Let's!*" They joined HelperFriend, twirling and whirling about the room. Equuleus rose from his cozy space and flew straight up to the ceiling, adding the sparkling glimmer from his wings to the golden glow below, while HelperFriend spun faster and faster, until he looked as though his dazzling, twirling gear eyes wound completely around his head.

*　　*

After dinner, HelperFriend went to wherever he stayed. Then Heart's father kissed her on the forehead and took himself to his cot in his little room at the far end of the castle, and Heart and Equuleus went up to her rooms.

Because of the delightful but unusual dinner, the amusing little rabbit, Violet, had surprisingly slipped Heart's mind. But now she recalled the funny, furry, adorable little creature. How rich her life suddenly became—two new friends! A brilliant, amusing, lavender rabbit, and a dancing, eye-twirling, clockworks man.

Even if her father didn't share with her information about the projects he was working on, she now had something to work on herself. *A flower garden!*

Please let it be true, she wished silently. Let it be true that I'll be able to have a flower garden here on Pink, where I've not seen one single hint of vegetation anywhere.

She and HelperFriend would build a greenhouse. Father must have brought seeds from Earth, or he wouldn't have suggested it.

She jumped back up from bed, running through her mind all the things she needed to make a greenhouse. Invention became her cause! She would build a plant-safe structure on an environmentally unfriendly moon.

She scurried down the back stairs in search of HelperFriend. After dancing and enjoying the sumptuous dinner, she and her father had their heads together over cups of tea, and Heart hadn't even noticed that HelperFriend subtly stole away, taking with him the plates and serving bowls and dinnerware, leaving them with a steaming pot of tea.

But—where had he gone? Back to his little closet her father mentioned? If so, that would never do! He'd become a friend, and had a name, and he danced when even her father didn't know he had it in him. He made them laugh, and dance, and fly, in a cozy golden glow. HelperFriend must have his own room, and he must have his own things!

Heart entered the kitchen. Everything hummed and sparkled in perfect order, white as angel wings, as far as the eye could see. White tiles, white appliances, white cupboards, white floors, stretching out—white, white, white.

Heart had only been in the kitchen once since she'd been on Pink, when her father took her and Equuleus on a tour of the entire lavender castle. She now suddenly felt as though she interloped somewhere she ought not be, tiptoeing around the great, open expanse of the kitchen. Why had her father constructed this gigantic kitchen for himself, with no one here to appreciate it?

She thought she'd find one little closet, and in it, HelperFriend, standing like a floor mop, inanimate. Instead, doors she hadn't previously noticed, lined the walls. As she opened each, a bright, white light came on, displaying various cleaning and who-knew-what sorts of objects. It looked as though her father possessed at least one of each appliance or device related to kitchens or cleaning.

Then Heart gasped with insight.

These were her father's inventions! He'd built this castle more as a repository for his creative work than as a home. A spectacular museum!

The realization made her instantly homesick for The Museum of Scientific Improbabilities and Unpredictable Oddities.

"Oh!" she sighed. She pulled out a white chair and sat in the middle of the white kitchen, most of its many doors now standing open. She recalled the first

night she'd been at The Museum of Scientific Improbabilities and Unpredictable Oddities—the magnificent dance of the clockwork people, the clockwork moon working its way across the rotunda of the museum. And—*Equuleus!* The first time she talked with Equuleus, *her own heart*.

"Well," she said aloud to herself, "it's sweet to remember that time, but look at me now! I despised living at The Darling Undesirables Residence of Long Prairie, and now I'm free. Equuleus and I are together, no one can touch us! I'm with my adorable father, I have two new friends, and—*I'm going to plant a flower garden!*"

But this thought of new friends brought on a sad pain, and her ceaseless worry about her life-long best friend, Eye.

What was he doing this very moment?

Her thoughts were interrupted by a sound that seemed to come from the back of the closet she'd just opened. It sounded like voices ....

It sounded like *a lot of voices!*

Chapter 3

Poised, Heart didn't move, listening. Voices? Raised and agitated voices. Her father must be listening to a transmission from Earth. But she'd never known him to do that, and, more mysteriously, the voices sounded very close.

The raised murmur dropped, then stilled altogether. Heart saw a door at the end of the room open, and out stepped HelperFriend.

He moved toward her as if he knew she stood there and—he was smiling! "Hello Heart," he greeted.

A bit shocked, Heart stood up. *"Oh! You're talking!"*

"Yes. Father Inventor augmented my circuits. I've been perfecting my voices ...."

"Perfecting your voices? Is that what I heard?"

"Perhaps. Do you like this voice? Or how about this one?" HelperFriend raised the pitch of his voice nearly an octave and increased its volume. "Do you like this one?"

"*Yikes!*" Heart covered her ears. "No. That is *not* a preferred sound! Back to the other, beautifully modulated voice, if you don't mind."

HelperFriend lowered volume and pitch. "I don't mind. I don't think I *can* mind. I can only do as you or Father Inventor direct me to do."

Oh, well," distracted and a bit disconcerted, Heart continued to wonder if the sound of multiple voices could have come from the clockworks man before her. "I'm sure you'll develop likes and dislikes over time."

"All right. I will do my best to develop likes and dislikes. It's a bit difficult because I don't understand emotions. Cooking dinner, practicing voices, easy enough but ...."

Heart interrupted him. "I'm not giving you a *directive* to have likes and dislikes. I'm only suggesting it might be the natural outcome of increased experience."

"I see," HelperFriend said, seemingly thoughtfully. "No, that's untrue. I don't see." His eyes whirled and he appeared distressed.

"There!" Heart exclaimed. "You seem unhappy. If there's something you dislike, you'll have a *feeling* you don't like."

Though his face was made of whirling gears, HelperFriend's frown revealed his unmistakable confusion. "Why would I *want* to have a feeling I *don't want*? That challenges logic. Totally incongruous."

"Here's how it works—when you realize there's something that gives you a feeling you don't like, you move away from it, and toward something that gives you a feeling you *do* like!"

"Oh, goodness! Couldn't I have the feeling I *do* like without going through this business of experiencing a feeling I *don't* like?"

"Well, of course. That's the whole point of the emotional learning curve. To discover the feelings you like. For example, what did you feel at dinner, when you suddenly started dancing?"

HelperFriend thought very deeply. "I—I don't know!"

"Why did you do it?"

"Because, *hmmm*, because—no, I don't know."

"But it was wonderful, and fun, and made us all so happy that we joined in and danced with you."

"Yes, and I made the music."

"And you made the music! Why?"

"It—just—seemed—right. Somehow. But—strange, wasn't it? You're right! Clearly odd behavior. Why would I do something completely different from serving dinner, as instructed?" HelperFriend hung his head. "I'm broken!"

Heart jumped up from her chair. "You are *not* broken! You have within you a core of emotion. Of feeling. You acted spontaneously because you somehow knew it would make others happy. Making them happy would feel good. And it did, didn't it?"

"I don't know, Heart."

"Well, I think it'll become clearer over time."

HelperFriend hung his head even further. "May I go back to my closet now?"

"Ah, poor HelperFriend. No. We have things to do! I'm going to plant a garden. But first, I have to ... I mean, *we* have to, build a greenhouse."

"A 'green' house? Will that go with Pink?"

Heart laughed. "Yes, green and pink are lovely together. But, more importantly, what we're going to build will have an environment flowers can grow in."

"Flowers." HelperFriend looked around him as if a flower would suddenly appear to let him know what they were talking about.

"That's all right, my friend. You don't have to know *everything*."

"*Oh!*" He perked up visibly.

"Did you really think you must know everything the moment I mention it?" Heart took him by his metallic hand and wandered back through the kitchen, closing all the doors she'd opened along the way.

"It's my directive to help you," HelperFriend said. "But how can I help you if I don't know what you're talking about?"

Heart chuckled at his impeccable logic. "Excellent question! You will help me simply by helping me. If I say, 'could you bring that bucket over to me,' and you don't know what a bucket is ... "

"I *do* know what a bucket is," HelperFriend said, cheering visibly.

"That's very good, but I'm just giving an example. So, if I ask you to bring the wanogtic to me .... "

"What's a wanogtic?"

"Nothing. I made it up, to explain my example. Anyway, if I ask you to bring anything to me that you don't know what it is, you simply ask, 'what's that?'"

"I did, and you said it's not a real thing. So how can I bring it to you? How, Heart, how can I bring unreal things to you?"

They stepped out of the kitchen into the dimly lit

hall. Heart turned to him and put her hands on his shoulders. "You're very literal, aren't you?"

"Am I?"

"Yes."

"Well, that's good."

Heart giggled, "You are *so* frustrating and charming!"

Equuleus came around the corner. "What's so funny?"

"I'm very literal, and Heart says that's frustrating and charming!" HelperFriend's eyes spun, beaming.

"I see," Equuleus looked at Heart for clarification.

"It's as he says."

"Wait! You're talking!" Equuleus extended a wing around HelperFriend's shoulder.

"I am. I am indeed! And learning. Heart is teaching me it's good to feel bad because ... *ahm* ... because. Hmmm, well, I've lost the logic of that, but, anyway, we are going to make a *green* house and it will go beautifully with Pink. We're going to grow flowers. I don't know what flowers are, but it seems like they might be somewhat like a wanogtic."

"What's a wanogtic?"

"It's nothing. I asked. Heart said if she asks me to bring her something, and I don't know what it is, to simply ask her what it is. Which I did, I asked her what a wanogtic is and she said it's nothing. I still don't comprehend how I am to bring her something that doesn't exist. But I'm sure she'll make it perfectly clear, eventually. Eventually."

"I hope I'm there when it happens," Equuleus said, slightly sardonic.

"All right, enough of this unreal chatter about unreal things," Heart moved down the hall. "We have work to do. A *real* project. Growing flowers on Pink. It needs to be done!"

Heart led the way, heading for the front entrance. "Father said there is some sort of structure that looks like a hill, outside the castle a ways, where we'll find building materials and 'everything I need for a flower garden,' were his precise words."

"Yes, yes, he told me to show you." HelperFriend pushed a finger to his temple and a 3-D map appeared in the space before him. "Here's the front entrance where we are. Over here, this is the hillock he mentioned."

"Let's go!" Heart gestured about her to make sure all the door locks were sealed. The three of them could tolerate any environment on Pink, but not so for her father, who was fully bio. Then, once she and Helper-Friend were in the double baffle, she waved her hand over a series of buttons, and the front door slid open, Letting them through, followed by Equuleus.

Stepping outside, the strangest sensation passed through Heart as her bios closed down and the dark matter took over her breathing and everything else that kept her alive in Pink's environment. It happened automatically, but Heart still liked to attend, at least intellectually, to the process.

"Is everything all right?" HelperFriend asked, coming up close to her, looking into her eyes and reaching a hand out to touch her throat.

"I'm fine! What are you doing?"

He jerked his hand back as if he'd been stung. "*Sorry! Sorry!* I'm—ah, well, I don't like to say this ...."

"Say what?"

"I'm programmed to keep you ... to make sure you ... to ... you know."

Heart frowned. "What are you babbling about?"

"He's programmed to make sure you stay alive," Equuleus said.

"*Oh!!*" Heart recoiled in shock. "Really?"

"Well, yes. Equuleus said it most accurately."

"Goodness!" Heart shoved past the two of them. "Goodness! That's disconcerting to hear. And I was in such a pleasant mood."

"Please observe that I didn't want to tell you," HelperFriend said, hurrying after her. "I felt—*see, a feeling!*—felt it inappropriate to tell you. I felt you might not like it. I don't even know how I knew that. It just came to me."

"Right," Heart continued to stomp toward the pink hillock.

"Be nice, Heart," Equuleus said, coming around to fly backwards in front of her. "He only did as programmed. It doesn't make sense to be angry with him."

Heart stopped. "I'm not angry with him." She turned around. "I'm not angry with you. I'm, I'm upset ...."

"You're feeling something not good and very strong," HelperFriend recited, "so you can know it when it happens again, and so you can know what a good feeling that big would be like, by contrast, and move toward it. That's what you taught me." He nodded, obviously self-satisfied, his eye gears twirling brightly.

"Oh, you! Clearly, you're going to teach me more than I'll ever teach you. All right now, let's pay attention to what we're doing. And what we're doing is building a shelter for flowers."

"A shelter for flowers," HelperFriend said.

"A shelter for flowers," Equuleus echoed.

At the hillock—much larger than it seemed on HelperFriend's 3-D map, he pointed to the outline of a nearly invisible door frame, big enough for Equuleus to fly through with wings fully extended.

HelperFriend found the access pad on the side of the entrance, then entered a string of numbers nearly 40 digits long.

"What is that?" Heart asked, completely mystified.

"The code to open the door." HelperFriend gestured as the entrance slowly slid to the side.

"But, why so many digits? Who's going to break into this *hill. On Pink?* I mean! ...."

"Is it strange?" HelperFriend asked. "Isn't everything like that? How do you get into your room?"

"I open the door. With one hand. No code."

"Well! That's not very secure!"

"Secure from *WHAT*? We're on Pink. A tiny, synthetic moon, off world. A million miles from nowhere. Just us."

"Where's 'Nowhere?'" HelperFriend asked. "A million miles, yes, that's far. We're probably safe from any problematic creatures on Nowhere."

"*Arg!*" Heart cried. "'Nowhere is not a place. It's hyperbole. Figurative language. Meaning, why all this concern for security?"

"Hyperbole." HelperFriend paused, cogs clicking. "Definition: 'exaggerated statements or claims not meant to be taken literally.' Are you giving me another example, Heart? Is 'Nowhere' like 'wanogtic'?"

Equuleus snickered. Heart shook her head no but said, "Yes, my dear HelperFriend. The only reason I can see for security here on Pink is to assure that any-one fully bio does not accidentally come in contact with the lethal environment of Pink. My father is the only bio being on the whole moon."

"You're bio."

"Not fully."

"True, true. You're dark matter, and a bit of clock-works, and, you know *dark energy*."

"*I know what I am!* But that's off the subject."

"Is it?"

"I'm talking about—wondering aloud about—what we have to be secure from?"

"That I don't know. No. I don't know." HelperFriend bowed deeply and gestured to the opening before them. "The door's open."

"So I see."

The three of them stepped inside—bright lights immediately sparkled on.

"Wow," Heart whispered softly.

"Why are you whispering?" Equuleus whispered back.

"I don't know. I feel reverent, I guess. It's sort of overwhelming ...."

As far as Heart could see, the ambient invisible lighting came on, in rolling, sparkly brilliance, reveal-ing mountains of building materials. *"Oh! Wow!* Are we ready?"

"Yes!" Equuleus and HelperFriend said together.

"Well, come along then."

They moved into the interior of the gigantic space. Heart looked back, trying to keep her bearings. Where she felt certain the open door must be, she saw no opening. In every direction appeared smooth walls— or maybe not even walls. There was just *space*.

"I can't see any walls!"

"That's right!" HelperFriend agreed.

"What do you mean, 'that's right?' That's strange."

"It's another invention. Not to worry, I have my map."

"But what's the point? ... Oh! I see, if someone were where they ought not be, they'd not readily find their way out."

"Precisely!"

Heart nodded. "Great invention—and as long as you can take us out, we're good. All right, then, let's get at it." She looked around. "Look at these long, curved beams. Hundreds of them! Let's look for shorter ones." They wandered deeper into the hillside, the light becoming brighter around them as they moved, and dimming behind them.

"Here! These are good, shorter curved beams and short straight ones. They're all right here. This pile of materials is perfect! And—what's this?" She stepped behind the piles of beams and tugged at a gigantic, yet neatly folded stack of malleable material.

HelperFriend came by Heart and pinched the material between his fingers. "It's non-woven material, in a kind of stasis."

"A material that's in stasis? I don't understand."

"It would seem that there's a means of triggering it to an organically active state. There's something that will cause it to do *something*—I'm not sure what—under certain circumstances."

"Could this be my flower seeds? Yet another invention of my father's?" Heart moved further into the space behind the stack of short beams. "And another mound of pliant—*stuff*. Non-woven material. See how odd it looks in the pinkish light, sort of muddy. I'll bet if we unfold it, it'll begin to look green. I think this is the material to go over the structure of these beams, and this other pile of material is dormant flower seeds." Heart turned and hugged HelperFriend.

"Oh, it's so lovely, so amazing, is it not?"

"So—you're happy?" HelperFriend asked.

"Happy is not a big enough word. I'm stunned. I'm moved. I'm grateful. And more than those feelings wrapped up together, I know I am *loved!* My father put this all together, not knowing if it'd ever be used, on the chance that I'd want to make a flower bed. Just on the *chance!*"

"He was right, though," HelperFriend observed. "So, a pretty good chance."

"Still! It's love, dear HelperFriend. Love. Pure and simple."

"If you say so. I'm learning. This pile of materials is what love is." He made a whirring sound, recording the information.

"No, HelperFriend. These materials are not *what love is*, they are symbolic of my father thinking about me in a loving way, and then doing something he believes will make me happy. That thought, and this action show how he feels—which is love."

HelperFriend whirred frantically. "Very complicated reasoning."

"It'll get easier. Truly, it will. But for now, let's begin to take these building materials to the front entrance." Heart started to shoulder some of the materials before her.

"Should we not summon a hover raft?"

"A hover raft?" Heart and Equuleus said together.

"That's what they're here for." HelperFriend dialed a combination on the inside of his left wrist, and, immediately a huge flat surface zipped to them, and hovered, humming.

"*A hover raft!*" Heart exclaimed. "Excellent!" She began to carry the beams to it.

HelperFriend's strength came into play as he carried the remaining beams in one trip to the hover raft. Then Heart and HelperFriend loaded the green non-woven material on the hover raft.

Last, but certainly not least, Heart insisted that she, herself, carry the organic material she believed contained her sleeping flowers. She placed it gently on top of the other materials.

"I'm getting off easy," Equuleus declared. "I thought I'd be loaded down for several trips. This hover raft is the best invention yet!"

"A great convenience, no argument," Heart assented. "All right, dear HelperFriend, take us out of this strange maze. I will explore it more thoroughly some other time."

HelperFriend projected the map of the interior of the hillock before them as they returned the way they came. The lighting shut down to the total black of the deepest Earth cave as they moved.

"Kinda spooky," Heart whispered, looking over her shoulder into the impenetrable dark.

"Agreed," Equuleus said.

The wall before them slid open upon Pink's eternal twilight. Heart, Equuleus, HelperFriend and the hover raft emerged, while the giant door slid shut with a slight "*shush!*" behind them.

Chapter 4

They made their way to the front of the castle, where Heart paused. "I must think."

Equuleus, HelperFriend and the hover raft remained at attention to the side of the front entrance, as Heart paced back and forth, considering the walkway, the entrance, and how much space Equuleus, with wings fully extended, needed to access the front entrance.

She considered the view of the flowers, from various rooms in the castle. "Oh!"

"What?" Equuleus trotted up to her.

"What if the greenhouse materials are opaque, and the flowers can only be seen inside the greenhouse?"

"That would be sad for Equuleus," Equuleus said. "It would have to be a very huge greenhouse for me to be able to go traipsing through it."

"May I approach?" HelperFriend called from his station by the hover raft.

Heart looked at him quizzically. "May you approach? You don't have to ask such a question. Come here immediately."

HelperFriend hurried up to her. "I didn't know. It seemed that as you were thinking and pacing, you wouldn't want me interfering."

"You're not interfering. What do you have to say?"

"The greenhouse materials," he gestured to the hover raft, "will be quite translucent when activated."

"That's all I needed to know! Less ceremony, dear friend, and more direct interaction."

"Yes. Yes, of course. I shall keep that in mind."

"Now, then, let me get back to considering what will go where." Heart returned to pacing, visualizing how best to situate the greenhouse. HelperFriend moved with her in a lockstep.

Heart stopped. "I must ask. What are you doing?"

"You told me to 'come here immediately.'"

"Oh, you are *sooooooo* literal!"

"I am that!" HelperFriend swirled his facial gears into a big smile. "Very literal. Perfectly literal. Very good. Excellent!"

"Slightly less literal, at times, may serve."

HelperFriend's grin disappeared. "Oh. Wrong again! Literal is *NOT* good."

"It's not bad, HelperFriend. Just—use your own logic. Like right now, does it seem as though I need you to be in lock step with me, or might it be all right if you simply stood by while I planned out the greenhouse?"

"Let me think." Gears whirred. "All by myself, I'm going to say you do not need me to step with your every step to think about the greenhouse layout. Is that close?"

"You're right on target. *Brilliant, HelperFriend!*"

His gears twirled.

"I'm ready now, let's build! HelperFriend, bring the hover raft over here. Equuleus, if you would stand here, to mark this point. This is one end of the greenhouse. Anyone from those upper-level windows will be able to see the flowers at this angle."

Equuleus stood at the point she indicated.

"Then," she moved in a line twenty feet away, "this will be the other end. I'd like to have two greenhouses, one on each side of the walkway, but I don't suppose the non-woven materials will lend themselves to that."

"Two equal greenhouses," HelperFriend said, speaking into his wrist.

"What are you doing?"

"Instructing the directions that belong to the materials to do as you wish."

"Instructing the directions that belong to the materials to do as I wish?"

"Yes. As soon as you tell me to begin, I will sort out the materials, and, with very little labor, they will essentially construct themselves. Within each structural part is a robotic chip, magnetically attracted to the appropriate connection. All you need do is look at the plan, once it's to your liking, hold the components in turn and they will align and lock. *Soon! There!* Your House of Flowers!"

"*No!*" Heart exclaimed in awe.

HelperFriend jumped back, dismay in his features and stance. "No? Oh dear! What's wrong with that?"

"I didn't mean 'no' like no I don't want that, I meant 'no' like, that's incredible! Like it's unbelievable ...."

"*You must believe it!*" HelperFriend insisted.

"I do believe it—I believe you. *I do*. It's just amazing. *Awk!* Enough chattering, let's see it in action."

HelperFriend showed Heart the plans, then how each beam was identified, then how to activate each beam to sequence the construction.

"If you'd like, we can separate the two structures, one here, and the other there, and build them in tandem."

"I would like that very much!"

"Makes me wish I had hands," Equuleus said, quite droll.

"You do not."

"True."

"Besides, you get to watch! In fact, Equuleus, stand back and record our building the greenhouses. It'll be fun to watch!"

"Good idea." Equuleus removed himself to the distant end of the walkway, while HelperFriend and Heart sorted out the greenhouse materials in separate piles along each side of the walkway.

Heart turned to HelperFriend. "Shall we begin?"

"We shall!"

Heart picked up the first straight beam and the first curved beam. With a thrilling magnetic click, she felt and heard the two beams unite. *"Oh, wow! Powerful!"* She looked across at HelperFriend. He'd continued to lock beams together, but paused.

"Let me catch up with you!" The two of them worked their way along the twenty feet of the walkway. The perfect alignment and the magnetic power that flowed through the beams as they locked in place was thrilling. She sensed an intelligence within the growing little building itself.

Soon they came to the far end of the two structures, beam by beam, to the last magnetic, locking, click.

Heart stood back to admire the structural under-pinnings of the two buildings. "Beautiful!" she sighed.

"Quite lovely," Equuleus agreed.

"Let's continue."

"Yes," HelperFriend agreed. "Let us continue!"

The two of them returned to the hover raft.

"Will we have to cut the materials?" Heart asked.

"No. Wait until you see this!" HelperFriend moved the muddy-colored material to the ground. "Take this corner," he handed Heart the material. "I'll take the opposite corner. Now, with me, billow it up."

"All right." Heart mimicked HelperFriend's gesture perfectly. Much to her surprise, in response to their small gesture the fabric soared above them, opening out to its full size. From the muddy, unattractive color it transitioned to a delicate, gorgeous green. "*Oh!* HelperFriend, Look! Look Equuleus, look at the color!" A rush of joy and sadness surged through Heart. Earth green. In her hands. "*Oh, my,*" she whispered.

"Now move backwards until it's taut," Helper-Friend said.

Heart backed up, slowly. The billowing, glorious green material became flatter and flatter until taut.

"Perfect!" HelperFriend called, twenty feet distant. "When I give the command, 'According to Plan,' give the fabric a sharp snap at the same moment I do."

"All right!" Heart stood poised.

"*ACCORDING TO PLAN!*" HelperFriend intoned.

Heart gave the material a sharp *snap!* It divided precisely down the center, with barely a sigh, and fell, feather light, to the ground.

"Amazing, HelperFriend. *Astounding!*"

"I thought you'd enjoy that." HelperFriend joined Heart. "Now to put the skin on the skeleton." He took hold of the opposite corner of Heart's half of the materials. "Align along the side of the structure," HelperFriend said, returning to the far end.

Heart aligned the material along the bottom end of the structural beams. "I'll again give the command, and as I do so, billow the material over the structure."

Heart nodded.

"*ACCORDING TO PLAN!*" HelperFriend flicked the material upwards, Heart perfectly matching his gesture. The material ballooned over the structural beams, then settled upon them. As it settled, it adhered as if a vacuum suction inside the structure hugged the material to the beams.

Heart gazed in awe at her translucent, pale green, greenhouse. She saw HelperFriend through it at the far end, his facial gears twirling and whirling.

"So beautiful, HelperFriend! *So beautiful!*"

"Let's finish the other one."

"Yes!" She hurried to the other half of the material.

They carried it to the long side of the second structure, then billowing it up, HelperFriend said, "*ACCORDING TO PLAN!*" The green material fell into place and adhered to the structure, just as the first one had done.

Heart stepped back, looking at the two fabulous greenhouses, nearly overcome with emotion. Equuleus came to stand by her, and HelperFriend joined them. She put an arm around each. "Look at what we did!"

They heard a tapping. Looking up, they saw Father Inventor at a third story window, grinning and clapping in delight.

"Thank you!" Heart called to him. "Thank you, Father!"

He nodded, and mouthed, "Love you!" then turned from the window.

They paused in silence for a few lingering moments.

"Shall we plant some flowers?" she finally asked.

"We shall!" HelperFriend said.

Heart and HelperFriend returned to the hover raft. Heart patted the small pile of material left upon it. "Do we divide this in the same way?"

"No, it's already in two pieces. Before unfolding it, we'll carry it into the greenhouse." HelperFriend picked up the flower material and carried it to the greenhouse. "Would you open the door, please, Heart."

Heart looked in surprise at the door that appeared from nowhere. "Where did this come from?"

"Oh, it's part of the plan. Finishing touches. There's a two-door baffle at each end of the greenhouses."

"*Extraordinary!*" Heart opened the outer door and held it while HelperFriend came through carrying the flower material. When HelperFriend entered, the door closed with a sealing "*click!*"

"Let's separate the two," HelperFriend said.

"All right." Heart watched as HelperFriend gently unfolded the top layer, and the two separate pieces became evident. He adroitly separated them.

"I'll take this one to the other greenhouse." When he returned he said, "Now, we lay out the flower bed. We'll unfold it carefully."

Heart nodded, making her movements match his. Once they had the material stretched out, Heart could see the myriad seeds embedded in the translucent, slightly viscous material. The seeds were laid out in a beautiful plaid pattern. Surely something in her would burst with delight, she thought as she studied the design.

"Now what do we do?" she asked.

"We'll leave the flowers to germinate. Before too long, we will need to bring in a bit of earth. Not much though, and you will get to water your flowers regularly."

"*Earth?* Where are we to get that?"

"There's some on Pink. Not to worry, Heart. Father Inventor thinks of everything. Let's spread out the other flower bed."

"Yes." Heart exited the front doors, while Helper-Friend picked up the other flower material and went through the back. They met in the other greenhouse and spread out the flower bed.

"You seem very quiet, Heart." HelperFriend studied her intently.

"Ah, my dear clockworks friend! You see right into me." But she said nothing more. Crashing in upon her joy, she'd become awash with a deep sadness.

Chapter 5

Heart felt a growing anger with herself for mystifying and disappointing HelperFriend. Even if he didn't know how to name "disappointment," Heart saw she caused him to experience it.

She excused herself from the wondrous greenhouses and HelperFriend and even Equuleus. In her room, she contemplated the experience of her hands in dirt, here on Pink, and the connection to Earth.

When HelperFriend said there was earth on Pink— *earth!*—it knocked her completely off her equilibrium, took her away from the joy of the greenhouses and all the wonders of her life on Pink. Everything dematerialized in a flash.

Earth. Home. To walk with the Earth underfoot— happy and sad, good and evil, right and wrong, kind and cruel, beautiful and ugly, sane and insane, whole and unwhole, known and unknown, loved and unloved. *HOME.*

She missed it. She hadn't previously realized the intensity of her homesickness. She thought she only missed Eye and Swen. And Martha, and Key Man, and Peter.

All true. But it hit her hard to consciously realize she missed *Earth*, the sun, the rain, the earthbound flowers and trees, the green-blue-yellow-night-day wonder of it.

Would she ever walk on Earth again? She quivered to imagine she might not.

"*I will!*" She affirmed to herself. "I *will* walk upon Earth again. Perhaps I must remain a resident of Pink, but I will visit my home, I swear it!" Oh, if Father heard her, he would be so worried. She would keep her promise to herself—*to herself!*

But this horrible, lonely feeling made her wish to crawl out of her own skin. Or become unconscious. Couldn't she just not think for a while? Not feel?

"Trying to run away, Heart," she addressed herself aloud, "doesn't remove anything. You only move away from something you must return to. What can you do, *in this moment*, to change your frame of mind?"

Instantly, Violet came to mind. "Oh, my new witty little friend! Yes. I believe she will help me leave this dark mood behind." Heart recalled the picture of laughing with Equuleus at the personable little rabbit—the most completely natural, down-to-their-core, laugh they'd experienced since landing on Pink.

She ran downstairs in search of HelperFriend and Equuleus, to apologize to HelperFriend, and to get

Equuleus to join her in tracking down Violet. They might not be able to find her!

She found Equuleus pacing around the greenhouses.

"Why are you pacing like that?"

"I'm trying to figure out what about the last few minutes of putting these greenhouses together caused you so much distress."

"I'm over it now. Well, sort of. When—when HelperFriend told me there's earth, real earth, from Earth, here, on Pink, I recalled the times I spent with Eye, tending our flowers, our hands in dirt. I became flooded with a fear I might never be on Earth again. That thought hadn't crossed my mind since we've been here.

"But then I thought about the richness of my life here, and I set the sad negatives aside." She hugged Equuleus. "As long as the two of us are together, I'm content. Right now, though, I need to apologize to HelperFriend for hurting him, even if he may not quite understand what I'm saying."

Equuleus nodded. "He went rushing off soon after you left, saying Father was paging him."

"Good enough. I'll do it later, then. What do you say to us finding our new friend?"

"Violet? I say, let's go!"

Heart jumped onto Equuleus, and they swirled and soared above the castle and the new greenhouses.

"The flowers are in a plaid pattern," She said to Equuleus. "Father knew one day you and I might fly above the greenhouse and see the gorgeous plaid patterns."

"That will be stunning!"

"Stunning—and perhaps informative."
"And perhaps informative," Equuleus agreed.
"Now, where is that witty little Violet?"

Chapter 6

The sheer freedom of the flight made Heart's spirits soar. Everything would work out. She lived *here,* on *Pink,* with Equuleus and with her father—such a miracle! And she had new friends, Violet and HelperFriend.

Life glowed!

Equuleus flew close to the pink terrain below, trying to recall where they'd met Violet.

"Don't you remember where we were?" Heart asked.

"No," Equuleus confessed. "Strangely, I didn't map it, like I ought to have. I'm sorry, Heart."

"That's all right. We were distracted by Father calling us back to the castle, which he's never done. We'll find her, even if we have to grid the terrain and go over it inch by inch. I seem to remember that ground feature." She gestured into the distance at three small hills, clustered together.

"*Hmmmm,* I don't recall them."

"Really? That can't be good." Then Heart heard a small noise through the whoosh of wings. "What's that sound?"

They looked down and saw lavender ears wiggling and little lavender paws waving wildly. *"Heyyyyyy!"* a tiny, tinny, squeaky, voice rose up to them.

Heart waved back. *"We found her!"*

"Ahm ... technically, she found us, Heart." Equuleus banked and whirled with a flourish, coming to a soft landing a short distance from Violet.

She hopped out of her rabbit home. "Well, it looked like you would fly right by! Just leave me altogether, flying by without even bothering to say hello."

"No way!" Heart protested.

"Where are you going? What are you up to?"

"We've come to visit you. We're a bit chagrined to admit that we couldn't remember exactly where we were when we met you."

"Well, you were *here*—right in this very spot." She gestured to her hole. "There's exactly where we met, while you chattered away above me."

"True, Violet, it's as you say. But that doesn't mean we were clever enough to mark it, distracted by my father calling us back to the castle."

"Hmmm," Violet muttered. "Not extremely flattering, but understandable, I suppose."

"Again, apologies. We've marked the spot now, haven't we, Equuleus?"

"Indeed!"

Mollified, Violet nodded. "Very good. Yes, that's acceptable." She relaxed, leaning back with her paws behind her head. "So what's the occasion of your visit? What do you want from me?"

"Want from you? Nothing! Other than the pleasure of your company." Heart sat down by Violet. "I realized, as I'm so far from Earth, I'm lucky to find a new friend. Equuleus agreed. So, here we are, hoping to get to know you better."

"I'm happy to get to know you better, too," Violet said. "I've thought about the two of you quite a lot since our first meeting, and hoped there'd be a chance encounter one day. But I'd never imagine you'd come specifically to visit me. Goodness!" But then, for no apparent reason, Violet began to whine.

"Is something wrong?" Heart reached out to pet her, but hesitated. Equuleus sat down on the other side of Violet, leaning his muzzle close to her.

"Yes. Something is quite wrong. There's something I must tell you. I'd hoped I wouldn't have to, but my conscience won't allow it. I must confess."

"Confess? What in all the worlds would you have to confess?" Heart asked, mystified. She looked at Equuleus. He shrugged.

"Well ... I ...." Violet stood and turned her little lavender back to them, "I must tell you that I ...."

"*YES?*" Heart and Equuleus exclaimed together.

"I ... I'm not ... not fully bio. I ... I'm not a 'real' rabbit."

Equuleus snorted while Heart laughed outright. "Oh my planetary stars, is that a confession? *Is that all?*"

"It's enough, is it not?" Violet glanced back at them. "*We know you're not fully bio!*"

Violet turned to face them. "You know I'm not fully bio? How? How do you know this?"

"First of all, *we're* not fully bio, and we intuit others like us."

"Well, him," Violet flicked a paw at Equuleus, "obvious. But you, Heart, you aren't fully bio?"

"No. I'm a mashup of Father Inventor's brilliance. Mostly bio, but also part mechanical, part dark matter, part dark energy ...."

"Dark energy? Not possible!"

"Many of my father's inventions are entirely not possible. But here I am, just the same."

"Oh!" Violet whispered, pulling back, looking at Heart with widening, round, stunned eyes. "You're," she whispered in an awed voice, *"you're the daughter!"*

Heart shrugged. "I'm not entirely comfortable with that, Violet. I'm not fully bio, and he is. So, I can't fully be his daughter. But he did peg me together—in that way, he's my father."

"You're *The Daughter. Oh my.*" Violet's ears wriggled around as if they did not know what to do with themselves, but would prefer at the moment to run off her head and scamper off across the open landscape. *"The Daughter. Heart,* of course. Here on *Pink.* I'm very dense not to have put it together already. So—here you are, on *Pink.* I see ...."

"What do you see?"

"I'm contemplating an *Ourbook* prophecy. So—you being here means—*oh, my!*" Violet tugged on her wriggling ears with her paws.

"Means what?"

"I cannot say."

"Here we go again. You dare not influence me, etcetera, etcetera ...."

"That's right! But, never mind all that, continue telling me how you knew I'm not bio?"

Equuleus snorted again.

"Secondly, *you're lavender,*" Heart said.

"I'm lavender? No, I'm not."

"Ahm, beg to differ," Equuleus said softly.

Heart looked at him with a minuscule wrinkle in her brow. She reached out and patted Violet. "How would you describe your color?"

"I wouldn't. I'm no color. I'm white. I am a perfectly ordinary white rabbit."

"Goodness, Violet, I must say 'no' to that description, in every regard," Heart protested. "You're most extraordinary, and you're not exactly white."

"I look white to me!"

"*Oh!*" Heart said with insight. "I understand—your eyes are adjusted to the pink environment. To you, you look white. To us, you look lavender. But, Violet, what color would you say the terrain is?"

Violet made a face as though Heart suddenly became inexplicably stupid. "Pink, of course. *We're on Pink.*"

"Yes. We're on Pink. I just thought you might have a color shift all across the spectrum."

"But we have no way of knowing what her pink looks like in comparison to our notion of pink," Equuleus observed.

"True."

"Babble, babble, babble. Please excuse me while I interrupt your inane conversation," Violet raised her squeaky voice. "Do you mean to tell me that, if I were on Earth, I would *NOT* pass as a common, biological, white rabbit?"

"No, Violet, if you were on Earth, you would not, in any way, pass as a white rabbit. You're not white, and bio rabbits do not talk."

"Well, why not?"

"Because they can't. I mean, I'm sure they have their own little rabbit language among themselves. But they neither understand nor speak human language."

Violet's ears thrashed about as she thought. "Earth rabbits only speak rabbit. *Hmmmm*, well—all right then, I can feign that. I can pretend I can't speak human. But I'm devastated that I can't pass at first sight. Little point in pretending I'm mute if I stand out by the way I *look!*"

"Does it matter? Are you planning to go to Earth?" Heart asked.

"It is my greatest desire," Violet answered, her ears curling around and framing her face. "*My greatest heart's desire.*"

"But—why?"

"I can't tell you."

"More *Ourbook* stuff, I guess."

"True."

"Although it gets a bit under my skin to have you tell me there are things you can't tell me—and, trust me, it's quite boring to hear that with regularity, I'll do what I can to see that one day you visit Earth. We may even figure out a way for you to pass as a fairly ordinary rabbit."

"Really? You would do that for me? I don't know why. I'm nothing to you."

"You're my friend, dear Violet, are you not?"

"I am! I'm your friend, you can count on me."

"Except to clarify what you think *Ourbook* says?"

"Oh, well, that's different. Entirely different. I'm not at liberty to mess with prophecy. As you may have already learned, one rabbit's idea about *Ourbook's* prophecy will disagree with another."

Heart chuckled, "I've certainly noticed that to be true among non-rabbits."

"I'm sure you have!" Violet fell silent, sighing deeply.

Heart noticed Violet's fixation on her sleeve. "What are you thinking, in such a concentrated manner, Violet?"

"I ... I'm studying your plaid."

"Do you like plaids?"

"Well, of course! But I'm wondering—and I don't know if I dare ask!—but I'm wondering if Martha and the nieces wove your garment. Your gorgeous, yellow and pink and white garment."

Heart looked down at her sleeve, "Wove? And, 'the nieces?' I don't know what you're referring to. Martha made three beautiful plaid outfits for me. Although this plaid looks yellow and *lavender* and white to me. But what do you mean 'wove,' and who are 'the nieces?'"

"*Whoa!*" Violet stood up on her hind legs. "I'd better be careful with *everything* I say. Never mind, never mind. If Martha told you no more than that she made these outfits for you, that's all that's important! I think I gotta go now!" Violet vanished down her rabbit hole in one giant leap.

"*Hey!*" Heart jumped up and put her eye to the hole, "Come back here, Violet! At least say good-bye!"

"Bye!" Violet called from a distance, already far below.

Heart sat back on her heels and looked at Equuleus, puzzled, then she leaned down to the hole again. "I thought you wanted to be my friend! Does this mean you don't want us to come around anymore?"

Violet's fuzzy head tickled Heart's nose. "No, that doesn't mean that."

"*Oh!*" Heart leaned away from the hole. "How am I to understand your abrupt departure?"

"Sorry, kinda rude, I know. But I gotta figure out how to keep my mouth shut. I'm going to mess with destiny if I keep babbling. Not good! Not good at all!"

"Don't worry, Violet. I put small credence in *Ourbook.* I've never read it, and it simply seems like a big distraction for a lot of people—er, people and all beings—to get confused about life. In other words, I'm not a big fan of *Ourbook,* so I don't think you can blow its esoteric what-have-you, cover, with me, and certainly not 'change destiny' by chatting with me about things you believe, and I don't.

"But I *will* tell you that Martha told me she wove the paisley blanket I was wrapped in when I was left as an infant on the doorstep of The Darling Undesirables Residence of Long Prairie. So, if she wove that, I guess it makes sense that she wove the plaids. I wish she'd told me herself that she wove this fabric, so I could properly thank her."

"You thanked her plenty when she gave you those outfits," Equuleus interjected. "I heard you exclaiming and thanking her all the way down the hall."

Heart grinned somewhat sheepishly. "I cannot deny my delight when I saw the beautiful plaid outfits. Given the weird growth spurt I experienced right then, the new clothes were even more wonderful because they *fit!* I was crowding out the seams of the outfit I'd worn for years, when I got to The Museum of Scientific Improbabilities and Unpredictable Oddities."

Violet's cheeks puffed out as she moved her little paws to cover her mouth.

"What is going on with you?"

"I'm going to explode. I'm simply going to explode, being witness to this conversation. *Oh! Oh!* I really have to go now Heart. Really," she muttered around her paws. "Otherwise, I'm going to babble or I'm going to faint, and if I'm going to do either, I need to do it in privacy." She ducked back down into her hole.

"Please, please, please come again," she called. "I wish I could invite you down here into my home, but you can't fit. I apologize that we have to meet out there, but please come again, soon. Mark your mind maps so you can find me."

"All right, Violet, we'll return soon, although I'm sorry that just about everything I say seems to cause you distress."

"*NOT DISTRESS*, Heart. *No!* It causes me great joy that I never imagined I'd ever experience. Who am I? What am I? Just a lowly little mechanical, bio, dark matter insignificant creature ... why have I been chosen? Why, it's so ...."

As Violet continued to babble, her voice became smaller and smaller until it faded altogether.

Heart looked at Equuleus. "Strange!"

"And yet not, Heart. I heard years and years of *Ourbook* when Martha read it to me while I all but atrophied in the showcase at The Museum of Scientific Improbabilities and Unpredictable Oddities. Violet's rant—not so strange."

"Equuleus!" Heart said in a voice of warning.

"I know, I know. You've told me to keep all that 'superstition' to myself. I'm just saying, I understand where Violet is coming from. I know how moving this moment must be for her. I know that now she'll be in her little lavender rabbit meditation for, well, who knows how long? A while, that's for sure."

"I see. Well, meditation never hurt anyone, so we'll leave her to it. But—if my presence causes her too much excitement, perhaps I ought to stay away." Heart frowned in disappointment.

"Not necessary, Heart. You and that amusing little creature have a spark between you, and, well, she's cuddly. You could use some cuddly."

Heart jumped up and threw her arms around Equuleus's neck. "You're cuddly!"

"I most certainly am not. I'm all metal and gears, and *big!* Violet is the *most* cuddly mechanical to come into your life."

"She is. However, that doesn't mean she *wants* to be cuddled!"

Violet's head popped out of her hole. "I'd love to be cuddled! But your horse is right, I must be about my meditation. Bye-bye. See you soon, I hope." Again she disappeared down her tunnel.

"I think she's truly gone this time," Heart stood. "But we have to watch what we're saying as much as she does, if she's going to eavesdrop like that after she seems to have left! Not that I have anything to hide, like she thinks *she* has to."

Equuleus stood, then rose up on his hind legs and pawed the air, whinnying loudly.

"What's that for?" Heart asked, laughing.

"Just felt like showing off for our little rabbit friend who, I'm fairly certain, has some sort of visual recording device out here."

"*Well done!* And, by the way, beautiful form." Heart leapt onto his back, and they flew high in the sky above Pink. Equuleus fully extended his wings. Heart, connecting with him where her heart resided, felt freely, happily, and fully one with her beloved clockworks horse.

Chapter 7

They winged their way back to the castle. As they flew over the flower beds, Heart was stunned to see lines of slightly darker green showing through the green canopy of the greenhouses.

"Equuleus! Look! The flowers have already sprouted!"

He flew near, hovering above the greenhouses, then landed smoothly in front of them, and Heart slid off. "I'll take a peek." She went through the double doors. Inside, the greenhouse air enveloped her with its warm and loamy scent. Again, Heart felt a rush of longing at her recollection of times past, when she and Eye would spend a lazy afternoon in sun and shade, tending to their cherished flowers.

She marveled at the tiny budding rows of green, valiantly raising up through the synthetic material. The little plants would soon need earth to support them as they gained height. She came back out of the greenhouse and stood by Equuleus. "I must ask Father where the earth is. The little flowers will need it soon."

"Are you all right?"

"Yes. Just—again, haunting thoughts of Eye, and those quiet days we spent with our flowers. No hint of our strange future—no clue at all! If someone a year ago handed me a 3-D of me at this moment, I would never have believed it! A little throw-away girl, a Darling Undesirable ...."

"A famous Darling Undesirable ...."

"Well, yes, but only because of my unique deformity—to not have a heart."

"Safeguarded in me," Equuleus said.

"Yes, safeguarded in you. I wouldn't have it any other way." Heart sighed. "Enough reminiscing, I must talk with Father about the earth for the flowers. I want to talk with him about Violet, too." She moved to the front door.

"What about Violet?"

"I'm curious about her bios, living out here on Pink. You know, except for her color, she looks bio. I'd like to know more about how he accomplished that. She's perfectly healthy in this weak environment."

"I imagine her clockworks are right under the surface of that lavender fur."

"I suppose. Of course, dark matter can tolerate virtually any conditions. But I'd still like to know more. When I step outside, I can feel all my bios and dark matter and dark energy shifting around in a millisecond. I wonder what it's like for Violet, who is in this environment all the time."

"There's a big difference between you and Violet, of course, because of your dark energy."

"True."

"Oh!" Equuleus stopped where he stood. "I see! You're thinking about Eye."

"I'm *always* thinking about Eye."

"And maybe Swen."

"Yes. And maybe Swen."

"You're wondering if there's any possibility of altering the environment so they might live here."

"Or at least visit. Spend some time together."

"Well ...." Equuleus looked off into the distance, "Maybe someday, Heart."

"Yes. Maybe someday. But not soon, I suppose." She waved her hand over the entrance lock. Inside they heard the foyer shunting the sealing locks into place. Heart shook her head. "Definitely not soon. It's enough for Eye not to be able to see, but to also be locked away in this beautiful prison is no choice."

They stepped inside and, sealing the exterior door, the inner locks shifted open.

"But he still might be able to visit," Equuleus said reassuringly. "Once he's a bit older and the social unrest has settled ...."

"Whenever *that* might be." Heart walked down the narrow hall leading to her father's workshop, Equuleus, with wings hugged tightly, following close behind.

"There might be a chance for Swen to come for a while, though," Equuleus observed. "As he's a hybrid, it might be possible to provide an adaption for him."

Surprisingly, the thought—the practical thought!—that Swen might be able to visit her, cheered Heart immensely. "It might be possible at that. If he would *want* to come and visit me."

"Of *course* he'd want to spend time with you. Remember how difficult it was for him when you left?

He only acted aloof those last few days, because he knew he must. For your sake."

"I believe you're right. I ...." Heart stopped short in the hall. "*Shh! Listen!*" She heard whispering coming from her father's workroom. "It sounds like someone one—or several someones—are saying, 'rabbit warren, rabbit warren ....'"

Heart turned around. She and Equuleus exchanged a look. Without enough space for him to turn around, he began to back up, tiptoeing his way back through the hall with Heart following.

Finally, they returned to the front room. Heart gestured for them to go upstairs to her rooms, while Equuleus gestured that they go back outside.

In the moment of hesitation, they heard Helper-Friend coming down the hall. "There you are, Heart. I'm looking for you! We need to get some soil on those flowers soon! They've germinated—they need a bit of dirt."

Heart nodded. "You're right, they've sprouted already. I wonder what's in that greenhouse environment to make them germinate so fast?"

"Hmmm," the cogs in HelperFriend's head turned. "I've been doing a lot of study on flowers, so I think that, although the seeds have been in stasis, they were ready to burst forth given the slightest encouragement. The moist warmth in the greenhouses is considerable encouragement."

"True. I want to ask my father about the soil. Is he very busy?"

"Yes, he's quite occupied—in addition to dealing with me, and my insistence on practicing my voices, which he has begged me to quit."

"Probably not necessary to practice your voices at this point."

"Right you are!" HelperFriend's facial gears swirled into a grin. "All righty, shall we retrieve the soil to put on the flowers?"

"Great idea." Heart exchanged a look with Equuleus, thinking, *Do you believe his story about his voices?*

Not for a moment.

Heart shook her head as HelperFriend shunted the foyer seals into place and opened the front door. *There are many others who need protection more than I do!* She pictured *The Wall* at The Periphery.

After they stepped outside, HelperFriend summoned a hover raft and gathered shovels and buckets from the side of the castle. Then he led them to the back of the castle, and further beyond over several small hillocks.

"Why are we going so far away, HelperFriend? Why isn't the soil close to the castle?"

"Let me look in my data banks for an answer, Heart." HelperFriend paused, the gears in his head visibly whirled and audibly whirred. "Here's the answer in a very old journal of Father Inventor's. I'll read it:

"Transporting materials to space station to construct a small moon. Today transported several container-sized loads of earth, that is to say, *dirt* to space station. I know, once I'm living on my little moon, I will need to keep this earth at some distance. The aroma will make me distractingly homesick. For the sake of all I've built, invented and created, I cannot allow myself to be emotionally hijacked."

"*Oh!*" Heart whispered. "*Poor Father!* So much more difficult for him than for me! He left everyone and everything, coming here, completely alone."

She moved away from HelperFriend and Equuleus, thinking, then turned to them. "We can't take the dirt to the greenhouses! It'll make him homesick if it's right at the front door. I can't be responsible for making him sad. He said himself, years and years ago, it would distract him from his work. I can't be responsible for that, either!"

HelperFriend came to her and put his gently clicking gear hand on her shoulder. "He would have asked us to put the flower gardens at some distance, Heart, if he still felt the same. He's lived here a long time—it's become home for him. More importantly, he now has you and Equuleus, it's not the same. But if we wait too long, the flowers will suffer."

Heart felt paralyzed. "What do you think, Equuleus?"

"HelperFriend is right. Father would have made a suggestion if he wanted—or needed—the flowers in any particular place. He left it up to you to place them exactly where you want them. Frankly, the front of the house is logical. And he has little to be homesick for, now that you're here."

"Still—I feel I must ask him."

"Do you want to send him a message?"

"Yes." Heart waited while HelperFriend connected with her father. "Ready when you are," he said.

"Ahm …." Heart became impossibly shy. "Hi, Father. Ahm, I want to ask how you feel about us bringing the earth soil to the greenhouses. I—I don't want to make you uncomfortable."

She waited far too long, it seemed, for an answer. Then his voice came through HelperFriend's sound receptors, clear as if he stood among them. "I see HelperFriend has accessed my historic database. But, my darling daughter, that ancient information has nothing to do with me—or us!—now. Nothing whatsoever! If I had the smallest reservation I would have said something before you began building the greenhouses.

"I want nothing more than to look out the window and see your glorious flowers blooming along the path outside the front door. It gives me great joy. I want you to be happy.

"Now get to work lazy HelperFriend, and get that soil to the flowers. They're hungry!"

HelperFriend jumped when thus addressed—coming from his own body!

"Yes, sir," he saluted.

"I don't know what to say," Heart finally said, after her father broke the connection.

"Tell us to get to work," Equuleus suggested.

"That's a good idea! Get to work you two."

HelperFriend hurriedly moved to a small hillock and waved his mechanical hand over it. The face of the hillock slid away to reveal a mound of earth filling it.

"Oh! that's a lot of dirt! More than enough for our little flower beds," Heart observed. "Let's load up the hover raft. I'm glad you brought shovels! I thought we'd find shovels on-site, but I don't see any."

HelperFriend shook his head. "Nor do I." He picked up a shovel. "We'll have the flowers feeling like they're on Earth in no time."

Heart grabbed a shovel and began to load up a bucket faster than HelperFriend.

"It's not a race," Equuleus suggested.

"Oh yes, it is," Heart argued. "As fast as those flowers are growing, they need dirt, and they need to be watered."

"True, true," HelperFriend agreed.

Soon the weighted-down hover raft, Heart, Helper-Friend, and Equuleus returned to the greenhouses.

HelperFriend and Equuleus worked out a system between them to rotate buckets of earth to Heart in the greenhouses, where she, most happily, worked away alone.

Hard at work, she replayed how her father had talked to her through HelperFriend's audios. *He called her darling!*—and not in the way everyone always said, "darling" on Earth, when they referred to a Darling Undesirable with that awful, prejudice-loaded *emphasis* on the "r" so that the word sounded like it had three syllables. Da-*r*-ling.

No, he'd called her "darling" like people did when they held someone truly *darling*. He said she made his life light and joy-filled. Everything she'd done so far in life was about making people happy, or safe, or contented. But most of all, *joy-filled!*

Heart took her time, nesting a mound of earth around every plant, talking to them with endearments, gently brushing the soil off their tender, green leaves.

Oh, so beautiful, these little, valiant, off-world Earthling flowers. Although Pink was not designed for terraforming, flowers now grew on Pink!

Heart looked up through the greenhouse overhead at Earth, ever-present above. That empty place in her chest tugged at the sight of home, while, happily, she cuddled little flower plants from home in her hands.

"Love to Earth," Heart whispered, bowing her head to the fragile plant.

Chapter 8

After placing the soil around each plant, Heart showered the flowers with watering cans of water HelperFriend handed through the baffle doors to her. She finally emerged from the second greenhouse, sighing a deep sigh of contentment.

"Excellent work, my friends. Now I must wash up for dinner, and I mean, *really* wash up!" She looked at the mud on the knees of her beautiful plaid pants, not the least bit upset. To the contrary, she found it a lovely sight.

"A different plaid for dinner!" She went inside, followed by her two cohorts.

After putting her outfit through the vibration-based autoclean, she did the same with herself, then pulled on the glorious gold, cerulean blue, and Kelly green plaid outfit—considerably more bold than the replaced lavender, pink and yellow. Standing before the mirror, she saw that the bold colors suited her very well.

She walked downstairs and into the hall to the dining room, when she heard her father and HelperFriend engaged in an animated conversation.

"It's all up to Xavier," HelperFriend said.

"I just hope he's ready. The time draws near," her father replied.

She stepped into the dining room. Equuleus appeared to be relaxing, curled up by the fire. Her father and HelperFriend fell silent, staring at her in obvious admiration.

"What? Why are you all staring at me like that? Did I grow wings?"

Her father came to her and gave her a hug, then led her to her chair. "Perhaps better, dear. You've grown in some other hard-to-express, but very tangible way. You *radiate* in these beautiful, bold colors."

Heart smiled shyly. "I don't know about 'radiate,' but I did notice how powerful this intense plaid is."

"Beautiful, beautiful!" HelperFriend said, filling the bowl at her place with a steaming soup.

"Smells fantastic, HelperFriend. What culinary miracle have you created?"

"It's a creamed cauliflower base, with lentils, rosemary, and turmeric. Delicious and so healthy for organic types."

Heart hadn't even waited for him to finish his description before half emptying her bowl. "*Wow!* I'm hungry, which, as you know, is rare."

"I love seeing you full of life and happy," her father said. He finally stopped staring at her and began enjoying his soup. "Oh, yes, HelperFriend, this truly *is* special! It goes on my 'favorites' list!"

"Mine too," Heart agreed. "So—who is Xavier?" She looked to her father, who couldn't hide the surprise her question sprung on him.

"Ahm, no one in particular."

"*Awk!*" HelperFriend commented.

"Well, yes. I mean, no, that's not entirely correct," Her father stuttered. "He's just not someone I can ... this is not the time to bring him up."

"You just brought him up!" Heart observed.

"And now," HelperFriend said, "the time has passed."

"All right. Not too strange. You don't want me to ask about Xavier."

"That's about the size of it," her father agreed. "Not right at this moment. But, he will come up in the not too distant future."

"Hmmm, well, I won't push. I guess I overheard something I ought not to have heard. I don't want to disrupt the lovely mood I'm in, right after having spent time with my precious, sprouting flowers."

Her father shared his enthusiasm. "I'm so glad you decided to put the flowers outside the front door. And the two greenhouses are charming genius."

"I don't know about *genius*, but thank you, Father."

HelperFriend waved his hand and an enchanting music filled the giant dining hall to its very corners like lilting butterflies, and, despite the strange response to

"Xavier"– whoever he might be, the rosy glow of love settled over the group.

Heart felt herself float into a mesmerized suspension, present, while at the same time leaving her physical body. Watching from the midst of the music, she understood, deep, deep within herself, that she had waited longer than she even understood for this delicate, ensorcelled moment—this moment during which, with all its beauty and simplicity, her previous life cleaved away from the life about to manifest. She felt certain it had something to do with the named, but uninvited, guest.

*   *

After dinner, Equuleus flew Heart up to her rooms. They entered, silently. Heart closed the door, brought up some dreamy music, and the two of them moved silently to the window, where they looked out at the forever twilight.

"Can you explain that to me?" Heart asked.

Equuleus wrapped a wing around Heart, making a private cocoon between them. "I'm not sure. Before you came into the dining room, they were talking quietly, I wasn't paying much attention, thinking about your lovely flowers. Then I heard the phrase, 'the launch.' That caught my interest. They spoke somewhat cryptically, I suppose on the off chance I might be listening. *Of course, I'm listening!*

"Father said, 'No one but Xavier,' and then, it sounded like he said, 'worried about,' then, 'distracted by Heart.'"

Heart gasped. "Since when am *I* a distraction?"

Equuleus shrugged. "Then, HelperFriend said something like, 'it's too bad we don't have time to build a team,' and that's when you came in, just as HelperFriend said, 'It's all up to Xavier,' and Father's reply, 'I just hope he's ready. The time draws near.'"

"What do you make of it?"

"I have vague images wheeling around in my mind. It hooks up to something I've been exposed to in an altered state. But I can't quite fully access it. I have a picture of a very strong, attractive, human-looking young man. But it's odd because I *feel* he's not bio. And, here's the even more curious part, somehow, he's connected to you, before Pink."

"How can that be? Is he a Darling Undesirable?"

Equuleus contemplated his vision for a moment. "No. No, Heart, he's not."

"*Most mysterious!*"

"Indeed, it is."

"I feel tired, Equuleus. Too much to process, I think I might actually sleep. But you will let me know if your shards of images make a more complete picture, won't you?"

"Of course, Heart."

She retired to her little cot, sleeping deeply and at length. When she awoke, she wondered what the purpose of all this sleep might be. What if she began to grow again? What would she do? There was no Martha here to provide her with lovely outfits.

She looked about for Equuleus. He was not in the room. He must be out flying, she decided. She loved to watch him, in the light gravity of Pink's sky, performing his breathtaking "sky ballet" as she'd christened it. His pure, guileless self-love as he moved into the pleasure of freedom, after so many decades trapped in a museum showcase.

Then she recalled her conversation with Equuleus after dinner, and the mysterious bio but *not* bio being, by the name of Xavier, along with the disturbing news that her father said she might be a distraction. Very troubling. He had immensely important issues to deal with, and certainly did not need her to be a distraction—for *any*one, in *any* way!

Then—and she couldn't imagine what the connection might be, if, indeed there was one, Violet's comment about Martha and "the nieces" came to mind, coupled with the information that Martha wove the plaids from which she made Heart's outfits.

Did that have anything to do with this mysterious Xavier? And who were "the nieces?" She'd meant to ask her father about it at dinner, but his behavior around the comment she'd overheard impinged upon her feelings of trust. Of course, he couldn't tell her everything. But the sense of specifically shutting her away had been the trigger for the discordant—but fascinating—experience of finding herself out-of-body, watching their activity, hovering above them.

Heart decided to visit Violet again, to see if she could glean more information. She went downstairs, shunted the front door seals, and stepped outside. Hoping to see Equuleus above, she looked up. But only the ever-present Earth hung over her, in the eternal twilight sky.

So! She would trek alone to Violet's home, now a pinpoint on her mind map. It'd be interesting to walk the terrain by herself, enjoying features as she went.

After walking for a while, however, passing one similar, pink, synthetic, hillock after another on what appeared to be a path, smooth and easy treading, the sensation of simply going around and around in the same spot became unnerving. Finally, a subtle shift in her surroundings let her know she'd made progress. Consulting her mind map, she saw Violet's little rabbity hole directly ahead.

She hurried up to it, dropping down on her knees. "Violet," she called into the hole, "are you home?"

Fluffy lavender ears immediately brushed Heart's face. She sat back on her haunches as Violet's head peeked up through the hole. "Oh! Heart! I'm so glad to see you! *Soooo* delighted to see you!" But she sounded far more anxious than happy.

"What's wrong, my little friend? Why are you so anxious?"

Violet visibly calmed. "No, nothing's wrong. I'm fine. I'm a silly rabbit. I get very hyper ... hyper ... hyper something."

"Just, hyper, maybe," Heart suggested.

"Yes. Just hyper."

"Would you—would you like me to hold you?" Heart asked, feeling a bit shy to be so forward.

"Oh! Heart!" Violet jumped out of her hole and leapt into Heart's arms, turning and snuggling, and nesting her nose into the crook of Heart's elbow. "How, how wonderful to be held."

"Yes," Heart said simply, feeling the warmth of the strange little mashup of a creature in her arms, soft and fuzzy and utterly like a "real" rabbit. But, Heart thought, Violet had emotions, Violet had thoughts, just like "real creatures." Was she not then, "real"?

"Are you happy, dear Violet?"

She turned to face Heart. "Happy is an impossibly inadequate word. Happy? Yes. Contented? Yes. Protected? Yes. Full of joy? Yes. *Yesyesyes!*" She snuggled down again. Heart rarely felt so invincible or nurturing. She could protect Violet, she could give Violet love. They relaxed in serene silence.

"But, Violet, I've found myself wondering about something you said when I visited you before."

Violet burrowed deeper, if possible, in Heart's arms. "Pay no attention to anything I say. I'm a babbling, mindless brook, knowing not whereof I speak."

"You know, and I know, that you know *perfectly well* 'whereof you speak.' Don't try to be coy with me, Miss Violet."

"Oh, I don't need to try to be coy. It comes quite naturally."

"So I've noticed. However, I want to ask you to tell me more about the nieces …."

"*Noooooo*, don't, please."

"I'm not going to. Because right now, I'm more curious about Xavier. Do you know who Xavier is?"

Violet sat up and faced Heart. "Oh, interesting!" She became busy cleaning her little front paws.

"*Well!?*"

"I was waiting for you to say more."

"'Oh, interesting,' is hardly an adequate response to 'do you know who Xavier is?' Is it?"

"I suppose not." Violet agreed. "Well, the short answer is, no, I don't know who Xavier is. But a slightly longer answer is, I have heard this name, echoing underground, and I suspect it's rather an important personage—whatever form he may be in."

"Whatever form?"

"Well, it seems he's human, but something tells me he's not. I know nothing more. I'm very pleased about that, because that really is all I know, and I don't have to hop back into my rabbit hole for fear of saying something I ought not. I'm very, extremely, exceedingly, extraordinarily, tremendously, immensely, vastly, intensely, singularly, decidedly, supremely, really-truly, mightily content right here, right now, and hope with all my hope-abilities that you do *NOT* ask me any question that I fear my response and, therefore, must leave."

"*Arg!* Little lavender rabbit, *you are exasperating!* All right, I shan't ask you any more troublesome questions. I agree that just being together is sweet."

"So sweet, yes, Heart."

Heart sensed Equuleus. Looking up, she saw him flying overhead, magnificent in the sky.

Gorgeous! she thought to him.

Shall I join you and the little rabbit?

Enjoy your flight, dear Equuleus. I'll walk back to the castle later.

"Will you two please be quiet," Violet twitched her ears.

Equuleus neighed. *We have no secrets from the lavender rabbit!* He looped a heart shape in the sky, then flew off.

"Finally!" Violet muttered. "That mind-talk is quite a bit noisier than audio, if you want to know the truth of it."

"*Interesting!*" Heart said. "You have some remarkable talents."

"Hearing stuff doesn't seem like a talent. But then, neither does the ability to talk. Anyway, that clockworks horse has had plenty of your undivided attention. I'm enjoying my few minutes."

Heart gave Violet a little hug. "It's just us."

Sometime later, Heart stirred, realizing she must get at her responsibilities, despite how wonderful it may be to sit and cuddle a fuzzy rabbit.

"I suppose," she said cautiously, "that I ought to be getting back."

"Oh, no," Violet whined in her highest of high-pitched voice. "*Noooo ....*"

"As delightful as it is to sit here with you, I need to take a look at my flowers. I need to talk with my father about inventing some means of circadian rhythm, arranging periods of light and dark, in the greenhouses."

"Flowers?"

"Yes. Beautiful plants, blooming in an array of colors and forms and aromas. So stunning!"

"I'd like to see them," Violet sat up in Heart's arms. "I'd like to see them very much!"

"I'm sure we can arrange that sometime soon. They haven't blossomed yet. Or maybe they have—the plants have grown at incredible speed. The greenhouses are quite a sight from the sky!"

"*Ohhh!*" Violet sighed. "Sounds sublime."

"It is," Heart agreed. "So, now I must leave you. But I'll be back before long."

"I have an idea," Violet winked at Heart then flopped an ear over one eye. Violet could not have known Heart's weakness in being winked at, but the added flair of the well-placed ear made her putty in Violet's paws.

"What's your idea, you little coquette?"

Violet paused for a moment. "*Tee-hee*, coquette! I had to look it up. Well, that's me, if given the chance. My idea is that you take me with you!"

"What do you mean?"

"*Take. Me. With. You.* Simple. You're already holding me. Just stand up and walk back to the castle without putting me down."

"But, why?"

"Because I want to be with you. Because I love you. Because I'm small and cuddly and you would enjoy having me around."

"All true—but, don't you have a life here? You have your little rabbit home. You have your life."

"There's nothing in my life. Every moment before now is as nothing. I can't remember a single thing I've ever done that made an impression on me like this time with you. If you're afraid I'll be in your way, I won't! I'll find things to do to that are helpful."

"I'm sure you would. But ... why do I feel hesitant? I think there's something I don't know. I think you ought to stay here, Violet."

"I don't want to. Does that matter?"

"It matters." Heart tried to picture Violet in her life's routine, but couldn't quite see it.

"Don't over-think it, Heart. Just take me with you, and if it's troublesome, I'll come back here and perhaps you'll visit me from time to time."

"Of course I'd visit you, you know that!"

"So, it's settled. You'll take me with you now, and I'll return to my dingy little hole if it doesn't work out."

"Oh my goodness, poor pathetic Violet," Heart laughed, standing. "Living in a dingy rabbit hole instead of a gigantic lavender castle. Or perhaps, to you, a white castle. Okay, I'll take you back on a trial basis. Trial for both of us, because you may not like it there in the least, it's big and built for Equuleus to move about fairly freely. It is, most certainly, not a cozy little rabbit home."

"I will find a corner to enjoy and to lay claim to, I'm sure."

Heart headed toward the castle while Violet prattled on. She adored the cute, chirping banter of her cuddly, affectionate friend. She tried not to get too attached to the notion of Violet in her regular routine. There could be a myriad problems, including her father insisting that Violet needed to stay living at her rabbit hole.

Before long, the castle came into view.

"There it is," Violet said, "Father Inventor's home. Glowing white upon the horizon."

"Or lavender, as the case may be, but, yes," Heart nodded. "Home."

"White," Violet argued. "Glowing white light."

"I sort of wish I could see it as you do, Violet. But it's also amazing and beautiful in its lavender glow."

They soon came to the near greenhouse. "Oh, look, the flowers have grown another couple inches. Some of them may be budding."

"Lovely," Violet agreed. "You must be sure to keep me from going inside."

"Why, Violet?"

"Something in me is wanting very badly to taste that tender green. I think it must be a genetic pull in my bio component."

"Oh dear, I didn't think about that. It's true, Earth rabbits are a hardship to household gardens! You are not to harm my precious and rare Earth flowers, promise me! It's the only thing I ask of you. Of course, if it's truly something beyond your ability to control, you will need to go back to your little rabbit hole home."

"In that case, not to worry, dear Heart, I have it all under control. I've set an internal alarm that will go off, disallowing me to enter the greenhouses."

"Good solution!" Heart waved her hand over the control panel at the front door and listened as the seals shut indoors. The outer door opened and Heart stepped in, with Violet in her arms.

The outer door closed, and as the inner door began to swing open, Violet said, "Something smells strange."

The inner door opened fully and the seals slid open. Violet began to writhe in Heart's arms, squealing pathetically, she turned red and died, in an instant, in Heart's arms.

Heart looked down at Violet in disbelief and shock, trying to understand what had happened. "Violet? *Violet?*"

But Violet lolled, inanimate.

Suddenly realizing that the precious creature in her arms was probably as incapable of living in a fully bio habitat as a fully bio life form could not live outside the castle, Heart ran furiously down the narrow hall to her father's private room that she'd only seen once, briefly, when she first arrived.

What she saw at that time was a cozy little room with work benches covered in a myriad of mysterious inventions, a wall of 3-D devices, and a simple little cot against the wall.

As Heart ran to his door with the lifeless and lolling Violet in her arms, she definitely heard voices.

Many, many voices, on the other side of the door.

Chapter 9

Heedless of anything she might find, Heart flung the door wide with such force it slammed into the wall.

Shocked out of her wits for a second time in but a few moments, she did not see before her a warm and cozy workroom. Instead, she encountered a cavernous space, stretching as far as she could see, until the curve of Pink, itself, fell away in the far reaches.

Even more shocking were the hundreds, if not thousands, of clockwork, clockwork-bio, and mechanical beings and creatures, all falling silent in an instant, reflecting their own shock at Heart bursting upon them.

A pin dropping would have been heard the entire circumference of Pink.

Heart, driven by her mission, looked around for her father. She finally saw him, off to the side at one of his workbenches, in a strange device, much like a man-sized bell jar, arm raised, in the middle of, apparently, instructing. He, too, had been silenced by Heart's completely unanticipated arrival.

"Violet," Heart cried. "Father, Violet!" She held up the limp, red creature, changing moment by moment into an unrecognizable and badly distorted form.

"Oh, Heart! She cannot be in a bio-supporting environment."

"I rapidly figured that out, Father. But you can save her. I know you can save her. Why didn't she know she couldn't be in the castle?"

"I never imagined she'd see the inside of it. I had the idea of a modest terraforming—for you, Heart. For you to come upon creatures and plants, so you would feel at home. But, with all my other inventions, which also need attention, I didn't get as far as I'd hoped I would before you arrived."

"But ... Violet, Father. Heal Violet. She's doesn't deserve this, because I didn't know, because she didn't know."

"Well ..." he clearly couldn't resist Heart's plea. "I cannot promise anything, Heart. It's a challenge to try to revive a reversed bio-mechanical. Bring her here." As they talked, her father glided in his protective environment toward a small glass chamber through the crowds of silent beings, who cleared a path for him as he went.

Heart dashed to him, but at sight of the little chamber, she halted, shuddering. It was all too like those at The Darling Undesirables Residence of Long Prairie—as no doubt could be found in every Darling Undesirables facility.

"*Oh!*" She stepped back.

"It's all right, Heart," Her father pushed buttons inside his bell jar, and the top of the little glass chamber slid open. He gestured for Heart to lay Violet down on its interior surface.

She did as he bid, and the chamber slid shut. He raised his hand above the bank of buttons and knobs in the bell jar, hesitating.

"Why are you waiting?" Heart asked urgently.

"I've not done this before. I must compute in my mind the reverse sequencing of Violet's bio-matter. Her mechanicals are fine, but that's of little import if the bios are beyond repair. I don't want to make it worse because ... well, I'm not going to say that out loud, but she must not have too much dark energy pulse. I must not under stimulate her bios, either, or she simply will not reanimate."

He slowly entered a sequence on the tabs, marked with mysterious scientific, dark matter, dark energy symbols.

As Heart watched, Violet very, very gradually shifted from the weird and wrong brownish-red to pale purple. The purple became more and more pale. Finally Violet returned to her proper color.

But she did not stir.

Hysteria nearly washed over Heart. How could she ever live with herself, having killed her little friend? Heart looked to her father with angst and pain.

"We must wait, Heart," he said. "We just have to wait. It could take some time for her to reanimate, if she's going to. The rapidity with which she regained her proper color is promising, but I don't know if she will reanimate."

Heart could hardly bring herself to tear her eyes from Violet, but glancing at her father, she became arrested by the thousands of mechanical, gear-driven, bio, or hybrid eyes riveted upon her.

Following her glance, her father said, "Heart, meet the residents of Pink. Residents of Pink, Heart."

"Heart ... Heart ... Heart," the creatures and beings whispered, echoing throughout the gigantic cavity.

Heart couldn't think of a single thing to reply, silenced by several forms of shock.

At that moment, Equuleus came bursting through the open doorway, ears pinned back, chest expanded, and, once he got through the doorway, his wings expanded upwards, scraping the ceiling. An intimidating sight! Heart had seen his battle stance before—poised to take action.

He saw Heart immediately.

"It's all right, Equuleus. I mean, it's not all right. I brought Violet into the castle. She begged me piteously to bring her with me. But neither she nor I knew she could not withstand the bio supporting environment inside the castle."

Equuleus came to stand by Heart and looked down at Violet. "But why can't she? I'm fine with it."

"Father explained that he designed Violet to live out on the surface of Pink for my enjoyment, I guess, while unable to live in any other environment. Whereas, you, dear Equuleus, like me, can pretty much go anywhere." Heart turned to her father.

"Will you be able to make her so she can be in both environments?"

"Yes, Heart, if she reanimates, I'll have to surgically implant some stem cells that will develop into bio-components to support her, and implant a chip that will sustain her and help her shift in multiple environments."

Equuleus and Heart stood over Violet, unmoving within the little chamber. "Please, Violet, please, come back. If you don't, I'll hate myself forever," Heart said.

"Don't say that," Equuleus whispered. "You can't hate yourself for not knowing something."

"I'll bet I can."

While the two of them stood there in concerned silence, all the residents of Pink, with the exception of HelperFriend, slowly backed away into the far reaches of Pink, and soon the cozy walls with sconces of flickering pink and golden-hued lights closed in and bathed the little rooms. The warm light also danced upon inert Violet under the transparent dome of the chamber, the flickering light making Heart think again and again that she saw Violet moving.

But she did not move. It was only the warm and animate light.

Heart and Equuleus stood vigil hour after hour, not speaking, other than an occasional mental exchange of hope or despair. Both her father and HelperFriend suggested Heart take a break, but she could not be persuaded to move.

The incredible sight of all the clockwork, bio, dark matter and hybrid entities crossed her mind from time to time, but, try as she might, she could not wrap her mind around the implications—beyond the implicit lies from both her father and HelperFriend.

Living the life she'd lived before coming to Pink, her trust was not easily won, and readily lost. She refused to give it any more thought in this moment. Right now she could only concentrate on believing she had the ability to will Violet to come back to life.

She kept going over and over in her mind her losses, her separations. The hardest, the biggest, would always be Eye, of course. Then Swen, who believed in her when she didn't believe in herself. Swen, who put up with her accusations of him being a spy. Who put his life on the line for her. Then add Martha, Key Man, and Peter, along with all the clockworks, especially Wonderman One and Wonderman Two, at The Museum of Scientific Improbabilities and Unpredictable Oddities. There was Jackson, Zack, Amdrona and The Mystic in The Periphery.

Her life seemed to unfold as nothing other than a continual and steady stream of losses, from the moment she'd been discovered on the doorstep of The Darling Undesirables Residence of Long Prairie, to this moment of standing over her sweet little friend, who only wanted to be loved, and in no way deserved to be lying, motionless, before her.

Equuleus stepped away when HelperFriend waved him aside with great urgency. Heart glanced at them with a small, but passing curiosity about what could be so urgent. Yet, only thoughts of Violet prevailed.

"Violet!" Heart cried when her gaze returned to the chamber. 'She moved! *SHE MOVED!"*

Equuleus and HelperFriend hurried to Heart's side.

"I don't see any movement," HelperFriend said, patting Heart on the back. "I'm very sorry to say ... *oh, say, yes, that little paw twitched, it did! I saw it!"*

"Get Father," Heart urged.

"Yes, yes, off I go, so right. Oh, this is a happy moment," HelperFriend sang as he hurried out the door.

"You moved, little rabbit, you moved. Please reanimate, my little friend."

Her father came rushing into the room, looked at the arcane readout on the wall and pushed several tabs, raising this, lowering that. "It looks good, Heart. It does. See here? This is brain activity, weak, but relevant brain activity. Please don't become over-hopeful, but it is promising."

"I'm not 'hopeful' at all. I completely 'believe.' Violet will return to us, better than ever, once you get the implants in her."

"Well, one step at a time, Heart. One step at a time." He became engrossed in pushing tabs and reading the output. As Heart watched him pull the strings of life, the vision arose of him as an adoring and thoughtful puppet master. Here she stood, herself the apparent pinnacle of his profound mastery.

Though she loathed to move, Heart backed away from Violet to let her father move about the transparent chamber. She longed to hold Violet, like she had by the rabbit hole, before this nightmare began. If she could just hold her, everything would be fine.

Then she heard a little squeak—a tiny, but very real squeak.

"Very good, little rabbit, that's a lovely sound." Her father glanced over his shoulder, smiling, at Heart. "I think we're going to make it!"

"How are you feeling, my dear little rabbit?" he asked.

"Where am I?" she asked in an exceedingly grouchy voice.

"You're in my home. Which is not suited to your makeup. You've been—unconscious for a while. But you're with us now, aren't you? I think there's someone you might like to see." He stepped aside so Heart could come up beside him. Violet reclined, one leg crossed over the other, wagging her foot and both of her ears, looking quite disgusted.

"Heart!" Violet jumped up and bumped her head against the transparent curved chamber. "*Ouch!* What is that?"

"You're in a, *ahm*, a health chamber. My father has to give you an implant in order for you to be able to go from environment to environment."

"Well, let me out!"

"I'm afraid you'll have to stay there for a while," Heart's father said. "It'll take a little longer for you to return to perfect health, and then I must augment both your bios and your mechanical chip. Just relax. Heart will keep you company."

He turned and left the room, while Equuleus joined Heart.

"You look wonderful," Equuleus said.

"You're not so bad yourself," Violet answered.

"I mean, given all you've been through."

"I'm not aware of having gone through anything. So I ought to look just the same."

Heart chuckled. "Oh, I'm so glad you're going to be a part of our lives, Violet—if you still want to stay with us here in the castle."

"Well, of course. Just because I passed out or something, which I don't remember, doesn't change my mind."

"Very good!"

Several hours later Heart, Equuleus, and Helper-Friend were in the throes of gales of laughter, witnessing Violet performing a ludicrous dance on her small stage, hunched over in the chamber.

"I see our patient is in excellent form!" Heart's father said, coming into the room in the midst of the gayety.

"More than," Heart agreed.

"Let me check her vitals. If they're strong, I'll do the surgery now, and she can be out of there that much sooner."

Heart, Equuleus, and HelperFriend stepped back while Father Inventor studied the information attached to the tabs. "You've recovered excellently, Miss Violet Rabbit. Now just lie back. I'm going to send a little something into your space that'll let you sleep very lightly. Then I'll put my hands in these gloves attached to the chamber. I'll give you an injection of stem cells, and make a small incision between your ears to implant this chip, and in about 24 hours, you'll be a new, improved version of yourself."

"I'm just about certain I cannot be improved upon," Violet protested.

"I agree!" He pushed a tab, and Violet immediately closed her eyes and appeared to be asleep.

Heart stood nearby, but she walked away when he began to make an incision on Violet's head. She knew there would be no blood, but she couldn't pull herself away from empathy for her precious Violet.

"All done, and in perfect order," her father soon declared.

Heart returned to her position by the chamber. "How long will she be unconscious?"

"Not long. She's not entirely out as it is. The hard part will be getting her to tolerate staying in there for a stretch of time yet. When she comes to, the chip will be in effect immediately, but the bios will take a while to settle in."

"I'll be stern with her!" Heart felt so happy and relieved, she would have crawled in the chamber with Violet if she could fit.

*   *

Violet did, indeed, put up quite a fuss when she regained consciousness, which Heart more or less deflected by asking her to do the dance she'd been doing before the medical procedures.

When Violet couldn't even stand up, let alone coordinate her little lavender feet, she conceded that maybe she needed to rest a bit. But then she began a serious argument in favor of being allowed to rest in Heart's arms rather than the cold, sterile chamber.

Finally, Heart's father acquiesced, allowing Heart to hold her, on Violet's strict promise to remain very still and quiet until he said she could move about. Violet nodded solemnly that she would obey. Heart took her in her arms and went across the room to sit on her father's narrow little cot that rested like a sliver against the narrow wall of the room.

"Even *I* have more of a bed than this," Heart said, "and I don't need sleep."

"Ah, well, my dear, sleep has always been an occasional necessary evil for me. With a mind like mine, things are always coming to the surface, and up I jump to make notes, to start an invention, or to solve a problem ... not real rest. A space to lie down is all I need."

Equuleus and HelperFriend, who had been having a conversation in the hall, came into the room when they heard Heart making little comforting sounds to Violet.

Heart screwed up her courage to ask her burning question. "Now then, Father, the moment has arrived for you to tell me what's going on. How is it there are all these residents I've never been told are here? Why have you hidden them from me? And, more to the point, *how* have you hidden them from me?"

"I didn't want to trouble you, Heart."

"Why would it trouble me to know there's a huge population of mechanical and clockwork beings on Pink? Why would it bother me? If you think I have a problem with mechanicals or hybrids. *I AM ONE!*"

"I know, dear Heart. I know." Her father replied, clearly flustered—not an emotion or behavior she'd ever seen in him. He could be shy, but never unsure.

"What are you not telling me? What's going on?"

"I think there's a lot of things going on," Violet said in a quiet little voice, ears twitching.

"I believe you're right," Heart agreed.

She looked at HelperFriend, who glanced away. "Umm-hum." Heart nodded. "Something is up. HelperFriend is acting as guilty as you, Father."

"Sorry, sorry!" HelperFriend said. "Can't help it, sir, her look is so penetrating. It simply does not allow for lies. Even partial ones. Even ones that are for her sake."

"I know, I know. Calm yourself, HelperFriend. It's all right. You've done well. Don't be hard on yourself."

Heart's ire rose. "Right. Don't be hard on yourself for successfully lying to Heart. Don't be hard on yourself for duping me."

"It's all been motivated by love, Heart. Please don't be angry with me. I'm always trying, and *will* always try, to protect you. From harm, from hurt. If you must be angry with me because of that, then be angry. I will apologize for lying, but I won't apologize for why I haven't told you everything. Nor will I apologize in the future for not telling you everything, if such an occasion arises.

"In any case," he continued, "there are simply things I've not told you because you had no need to know. But I've not told you a single outright lie."

Heart, wanting very much to tap her foot impatiently, didn't, because she didn't want to disrupt Violet, but she trusted foot tapping was implied in her frown.

"Do you really think it's in my best interest to not know, well, *anything?*"

Her father pulled up a little stool and sat by her. He studied her for a moment as she sat, stiff-backed, but gently holding Violet. "You're probably right, Heart. You're probably right. I can't help my fathering instincts. Maybe it causes me to make some less than best choices.

"But you're not a little girl! You're a brave, brilliant, intrepid, protective and loving young woman. You've become this amazing person all on your own. Without any input from me, without any parenting to speak of, and with minimal socialization in the Darling Undesirables Facility, where there is not a single child anything like you. Not that there's a child anything like you *anywhere*, but even less so there."

"That's not true, Father. Eye. I had Eye. He is not usual. He has all of those attributes you just named—brave, brilliant, intrepid, protective, and so much more loving than I am, that it's practically a different quality. And, Father, he's all that, and more—without eyes! He protected me to the best of his ability against all the onslaughts and oppressions of that place. He stepped between me and their oppression, time and again, interfering with them so that they couldn't crush me.

"Then, when I went to The Museum of Scientific Improbabilities and Unpredictable Oddities, and finally—*finally!*—met Equuleus, Eye showed his undying bravery, stumbling around in the Darling Undesirables line while Keeper D herded the group like little lost sheep, back onto the Darling Undesirables vehicle, so I could bond with Equuleus.

"And what horror did he have to experience because of his unlimited love for me? Keeper A had him put in a sensory deprivation chamber. The only thing he truly feared in *LIFE*, Father. The worst, *WORST* thing that could have happened to him.

"But he prevailed. And now, what? I don't even know how he is, or what's going on with him. I'm not fulfilling my own personal directive, my one and only desire, my one and only driving, compelling reason for being, to be sure he is away from that place and safe. I'm doing nothing about it. *NOTHING!*"

"Oh, my!" Violet said in a very, very small voice.

"Sorry, sorry, Violet!" Heart looked down at her recovering friend. "Are you all right? I'm sorry. Did I hurt you?"

"Goodness no, Heart. You have quite energized me. What passion ... I feel, well, I don't know what I feel. Very charged up, like I want to do something to help. But what could I ...." Violet glanced at Father Inventor and stopped chatting suddenly.

Heart looked over to her Father, shocked to see tears running down his face. *"Oh! No!"*

"Oh, Heart, I've made so many wrong choices. Well, not exactly wrong, I made choices that were the best of bad options. But I feel terrible about what you've gone through. I am so grateful that Eye came to be there, and that he gave you what I wanted to but could not, all that time. The love and the care and the protection. Here I was, exiled on Pink.

"I watched you as much as I could. I saw you had this bond with Eye, and thought it very sweet and charming of you to care for him. I never considered his care and love for you." He pulled out a handkerchief and wiped his eyes.

"Sorry, Heart and everyone. It takes an awful lot to make me even tear up the slightest, but this release has been building up for some time. I've been feeling so, so, so guilty for all the years I wasn't around. I don't see how you will ever forgive me ...."

"Oh, Father, no. There's nothing to forgive. You did everything in your power, and I had a life filled with luxury. But—I was so different, and what could the Keepers do? They had—and continue to have!—their hands full with all those sad, broken Darling Undesirables. I had better care than many children anywhere, yet I posed a relentless challenge to those responsible for me.

"But I had the blessing of Eye in my life. I was truly loved and had someone to truly love. I learned we are all the same, no matter how strange and different we may seem to be. The common thread running through every conscious creature is, well, consciousness!—the spark of life, which is *love*.

"Goodness, enough philosophy for now." Heart gently hugged Violet. "The serious point I'm making is that I will never be comfortable or relaxed until I know that Eye has the very best life possible, that he is safe and happy in a beautiful place, where he can garden, and study, and love, and talk with intelligent beings, people, clockworks, mechanicals, hybrids—whatever. Just so he is stimulated and being loved and has the opportunity to grow."

"In other words, from the context of everything you've said," HelperFriend observed, "you will not be happy until Eye is living with you."

"No. We needn't live together. As long as he and I each know that the other is safe and living a fulfilled life, we'll be all right. But right now, neither of us knows anything about the other. I feel him thinking about me, feeling toward me, trying to figure out if I'm all right, and what my life is like. I do the same with him. And it's difficult, so much has happened!"

Her father leaned over and brushed his hand across her forehead lovingly, "You're so amazing, sweet daughter! I give you my word, which I have rarely done in all my over two-hundred-and-fifty years of living, I will see to it that Eye has the life he desires and deserves. You're right, it may not be possible for the two of you to live in the same location for the foreseeable future. But he will be safe and happy."

"Thank you, Father," Heart said simply.

The calm reassuring knitting of love flowed through everyone in the room, along with strength of will, kindness, determination, caring and gratitude, that would serve each of them, as the future came roaring toward them.

Chapter 10

When that nearly mystical moment passed, Heart's father shifted gears. "So, my dear, clearly the time has arrived to apprise you of a bit of history, and what's on our near horizon, to the best of my ability."

He stood and began to pace up and down in the small room. "All the residents of Pink, a few of whom you saw when you brought Violet here …."

"A few!?!"

"Yes, a few … they are amazing 'folks' I'll call them generically, as they are so many different types of creatures and beings—let's just, simply call them 'The Folks'—they are all family among themselves, and certainly, Heart, welcome you into their midst. Since you arrived they've been after me to introduce you to them. I thought I operated from a better sense of wisdom. Right or wrong, that's different now.

"Anyway, The Folks, the incredible, amazing Folks, were, originally, heaps of junk that I hauled up here—load after load, mostly accomplished many years ago, before things got really crazy with The Purists on Earth, and before the decree of exile that removed me from legal residence on Earth.

"Of course, I constructed Pink, in particular, to be habitable for me to live on, should that event occur. The two little blue moons in the southern hemisphere are nothing more than something pretty to look up at, and Yellow, although the biggest of the moons I put into orbit around Earth, is also not set up for habitation, but I did construct it so that a habitat can be readily devised, if necessary. It appears it has become necessary.

"But I'm getting ahead of my own story." He returned to sit on the little stool, leaning toward Heart, clearly about to tell her something even he found hard to believe. "

"So I brought up here all those broken bits and rusted pieces of my inventions and clockworks, and machinery for two reasons: one, I thought that from time to time I might need a bit or piece for a new invention, and two, I didn't want any nefarious evil-minded someone taking anything I'd manifested and turning it into something dark and destructive.

"I shunted and dumped all that pile of what I believed to be waste into a giant cavern on Pink, and closed it up, mostly forgetting about it, because of my focus on you, Heart, and your life—how to make sure that you and Equuleus ultimately came together. I focused on constructing the Aurora Borealis that connected Pink to The Museum of Scientific Improbabilities and Unpredictable Oddities, making sure it would function properly to bring you and Equuleus here, should that day arrive.

"I hoped it would not. I hoped something resembling sanity would reign. *Ha!*" he exclaimed so explosively, everyone jumped. "Sorry. You know how it is, Heart, unswervingly believing in the highest, and forever being blindsided by the lowest."

Heart nodded. "I understand perfectly, Father."

"So, during that time, right here in the castle, adjusting the Aurora, watching you, was almost the sum total of my activities, except to begin to make a few creatures I imagined might give you pleasure if you ever came here. In fact, you're holding my favorite little creatures right now ...."

"That would be *ME!*" Violet squeaked, bowing her head and ears, making everyone chuckle.

"That would be you, Miss Violet." Heart's father continued, "But in all that time, an astonishing miracle was transpiring, unbeknownst to me.

"One day I heard sounds I didn't recognize. I put my bell jar on a hover raft, which I'd never bothered to even get into as nothing ever needed my attention away from the castle before then, and rode to the other side of Pink. There, I opened up the cavern door, and oh my eternal stars, what did I see?"

"What?" HelperFriend asked, sitting on the edge of his seat.

"You were there, HelperFriend!" Father Inventor said, looking at him curiously.

"Oh, yes! I was. Goodness, you tell a great story, I got completely caught up, I forgot I was there!"

"As I stood in the entry of the cavern, I saw that all those rusted, broken, bits and pieces had put themselves together. They cooperated unfailingly and had taken the puzzle pieces and assembled themselves into individual beings, with their united intelligence and love.

"They shined and polished one another up. They taught one another everything each of them individually knew.

"The moment I opened the cavern doorway, they all turned their attention to me, and fell to their knees, which I immediately forbade.

"Then I sat in my bell jar for hours and hours on end, having them introduce themselves and tell me their story, because most of them were not what I originally constructed. Many of them had originally been intended as entertainment devices in the homes of humans. But here, they understood they had a mission. They are focused on the preservation of Pink, and protecting you, Heart, and Equuleus, and my inventions, and ... my mind.

"Such an experience that defies explanation or even understanding, other than to say, a spark of intelligence, struck upon the flint of love will always take form."

"Oh, Father!" Heart breathed. "I'm at a loss for words … who could imagine such a thing? I'm so honored to be here with them. But how have I not heard them or seen them?"

"Well, other than when they come to this side of Pink for our meetings, they live and work inside the other side of Pink. Though Pink is small, most of the time they are still miles away."

"I've heard them a couple of times. And this one," Heart nodded her chin at HelperFriend, "lying to me about 'practicing his voices.'"

"*Awk!* No lie, no lie at all!" Immediately emanated from HelperFriend the sound of a myriad voices, identical to what Heart previously heard.

"*Oh. My. Goodness!*" she exclaimed. "But why? Why would you bother to do that?"

"That's sort of obvious—so I wouldn't be lying to you when I said I'd been practicing my voices, and so I could cover for them if they needed to be working on a stealth mission. Some of them can communicate telepathically. But others must make audible sounds and communicate in language."

"I see," Heart nodded. "My next question is, what is this 'rabbit warren' I keep hearing mentioned?"

"The interior of Pink is a maze of tunnels that we refer to as the 'rabbit warren,'" her father said.

"Rabbits are the best!" Violet interjected.

"No argument!" he agreed. "If you listen carefully, you will hear some designation appended, such as 12-X or 2-YP, and the like, that refers to a precise location within Pink. In each location, specific work is being accomplished. It's a kind of shorthand to name a location.

"Thus, everyone knows what's going on everywhere, and we can focus on the progress in detailed terms—where things are going well, where things need attention."

Very much her father's daughter, Heart needed to pace about to get clarity on the enormity of this information. She stood and tried to put Violet down in the chamber.

"*No!*" Violet squealed. "Just pace, I don't mind— I'm all right. But don't put me down."

"All right, all right!" Heart paced, while her father, Equuleus, and HelperFriend watched. "So … clearly you are preparing for something big. What would be that big? Another onslaught by the Purists." *Pace, pace, pace ….*

"So the purists have gathered forces and somehow advanced their abilities considerably, if you're concerned that Pink might be involved. You've not left the Aurora as a means of accessing Pink, although you left it to beautify the museum rotunda, and to cause wonder and awe in the visitors …."

"You've gained knowledge that somehow the Purists have advanced considerably—*in areas that go against their beliefs!*—to pose a threat to Pink." Heart paused, eye-to-eye with her father.

He nodded, smiling and frowning at the same time. "True, true, and true, dear, brilliant, Heart."

"But how? And why? They believe your knowledge, your science, your harnessing of dark matter and dark energy is a sin. So, they would have to commit sins, by their own beliefs, to be able—in any way!—to come here of their own accord."

"Also profoundly true."

"So what ....?"

"*OHHHH!*" Equuleus neighed with alarm and insight. "It's about—it's about your first incarceration, is it not?"

"Yes, Equuleus, you are correct. It's about my first incarceration, ever so long ago. One might say I now may be 'hoist by my own petard.' We all may be."

"I don't understand." Heart returned to sit on the cot near her father.

"The first time the Purists incarcerated Father," Equuleus explained, "after they gained a foothold in the so-called government, they had some of his own scientists, who worked beside him for years, and were, he believed his most loyal friends as well as co-inventors—the Purists had these very friends download and manifest a copy of your father's brain. This clone exists somewhere, in some data bank.

"As the Purists became ever more rabid in their 'Battle against Brains' as many non-Purists like to refer to their movement, Father Inventor's clone brain was lost and believed destroyed.

"But now, it would appear, this is no longer the case."

"Impeccable reasoning, dear Equuleus, perfectly accurate. One thing I know for sure, my clone brain has not been destroyed. I can feel, on occasion, its strange echo. But so far, I've not been able to pinpoint its location."

"Oh ... *oh* ..." Heart whispered, hugging Violet. *"This is truly very bad news."*

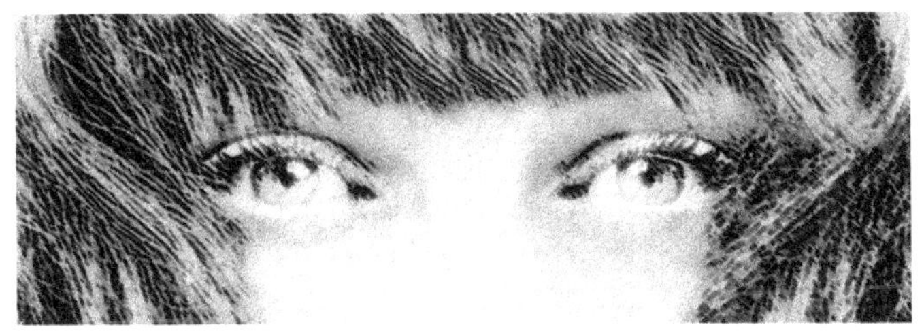

Chapter 11

Later, during a somber dinner, with Violet curled up by Equuleus near the fire, the two of them each munching on their favorite greens, Heart watched Violet thoughtfully. "Now, why haven't I wondered this before?"

"What's that?" Her father followed her gaze to Violet.

"With all the production of getting my flower garden put together—and I completely forgot the issue of light for the flowers in the ensuing excitement—but, anyway, with all the details involved in getting flowers to grow, I'm wondering where Equuleus's and Violet's greens come from?" Then she pointed at her own plate, "And where do these green beans come from?"

"We've several sources of edible plant materials. I brought tons of dehydrated flash frozen vegetables, reconstituted to original form by our wonderful HelperFriend."

HelperFriend bowed, gears whirling in a wide grin.

"I see. Well done, my friend."

"The flash frozen 'real' plant materials are reserved for anyone who has a significant component of bio, such as the two of us. Synthetic plant matter is produced by a contingent of Pink residents who are brilliant at invention. Many of them are not bio, but enjoy the community of meals, and so have created amazing synthetic plant wonders with but a little direction from me. Also, there are a couple of very small, carefully tended hydroponic gardens growing real vegetables."

"So what is Violet munching on?"

"Synthetics, with a bit of other components to keep her mechanicals running smoothly."

"So delicious, Heart. I've never eaten greens like these," Violet mumbled around a mouthful, greens sticking out every which way. "Well, I've rarely had greens at all, but oh, yum, these are amazing."

"That's because of the bios I injected into you, Violet," Father Inventor said. "You will not be adequately nourished by the same greens you had before. You'll start to 'run down' if you don't have these synthetic greens with what I call 'bio-boost.'"

"Good to know," Heart observed. "How can we make sure she has her own long-term supply of her particular food?"

"I already have a team working on preparing a good supply of nutrition for her. It's not much different from our dear Equuleus."

"I don't need much," Equuleus interjected.

"It's true, he doesn't. But still, the machinery can use some fuel from time to time. Dark matter is extremely conservative, as I'm sure you've already discovered, Heart. In your case, dark energy even more so, as it makes itself from itself."

Heart nodded. "If you mean that I can go days without eating, yes. But these are all details I ought to know about, shouldn't I? Even if I'm only on this side of Pink, it's good for me to know how to take care of things here. Which brings me back to my concern about the flowers, and the light they need."

"Not to worry, it's been attended to. The Folks who have the hydroponic gardens came a while ago and installed circadian lights. They're familiar with the needs of real plants, and have been quite successful with synthetic lighting."

"Oh! I'm so happy to hear this! Now, if only all our problems could be so readily solved!"

"Yes," her father said with quiet resignation, "if only."

A silence fell over the room, when suddenly HelperFriend jumped into full alert. "Sorry to interrupt your reverie, but … there's an, ahm …" he glanced at Heart and became entirely tongue-tied.

"A possible breach?" her father offered.

"Yes. A possible breach. A possible breach. Yes." He nodded energetically.

"Excuse me, I must check this out."

Heart leapt up from her chair. "I want to go, too."

"No, Heart, you must not."

"Why not?"

"For several reasons. But the most important one being, you are not yet 'marked.'"

"Marked?"

"Every entity that can move by its own power and with its own will has a chip implanted, to be able to move freely in the 'rabbit warren.' But you do not."

"*Oh!*" Heart said, crestfallen. "But—what happens if someone comes along who's not 'marked'—what happens?"

"It's not nice. The subterranean regions of Pink are designed to close walls around any unidentified moving form."

"*Sheesh!* What if I'd discovered the underground on my own and wandered in there?"

"It would have been most unpleasant for you—if you succeeded in doing so. Extremely unlikely. Everyone knows who you are, and they would have detained you, and called me. But if you'd wandered in without being detected, you probably would have wished you hadn't." He started to move from the room. "Anyway, I must go. Enjoy your meal, and I hope to return shortly." He passed through the door.

"What about Equuleus? Does he have an implant?"

"*NO!*" her father called back. "Do not send him beyond where the two of you have already been." She heard the door to his room slide shut, and knew he'd now become completely unavailable.

She returned to her seat and looked at Helper-Friend. "Well, aren't you going to go running after him?" she asked, unable to disguise her disgust.

"No. He didn't ask me to, did he? You are my primary objective, Heart. If he needs me, he'll call. But I'm supposed to be at your beck and ... *whoops!* Spoke too soon. Off I go!" And he, too, dashed from the room.

"So much for him being my protector, eh?"

Violet hopped up on Father Inventor's chair. "You have me, Heart. I'm here. I'm right by your side. Nowhere else I want to be. Nowhere else I'm going. Can I have Father Inventor's food?" She eyeballed his green beans with a glint in her eye.

"No, Violet. Not only might he come back to dinner, but I really have no idea what human food might do to you. So, no."

"Just a little bit. Not all of it. I'm sure it would be very good for me."

Heart reached over and picked Violet up and put her on the chair on the other side of her. "No means no, dear Violet." She looked at the place where Violet had been sitting by Equuleus. "Besides, look, you have plenty to eat."

"Yes. But variety is the spice of Life."

"Your life is plenty spicy without running the risk of something not being right for your system. I've had enough of saving your life for a while, at least."

"Oh, all right. That's a bit dramatic, isn't it? Save my life? *Humph!*"

"Not a bit," Equuleus spoke up. "We were careful not to shock you when you were so weak, but clearly you're in fine form now, and you need to know, Heart very much *indeed did* save your life!"

Violet let her ears fall over her eyes, then looked up at Heart. "Is this true?"

"Well ... since you ask directly, yes. Equuleus is telling the truth. I saved your life by running like mad to my father's room to have *him* save you."

"I'm an idiot. I apologize, Heart. I thank you, too! Oh, my, you saved my life!"

"Only after nearly causing you to die by ignorantly bringing you into this environment when neither your bios nor dark matter were attuned to surviving."

"But—I *insisted* you bring me here. I *insisted* you take me into your life. I *insisted!* You did nothing wrong, except to satisfy my little, silly whim."

"Not a silly whim, Violet. And now we're together, so the outcome is lovely." Heart looked toward the dining room door.

"You want to go to see what he's up to, don't you? You want to go to his room."

"Of course I do!"

"We could tiptoe, very quietly. He wouldn't even know we were there ...."

"Oh, you are the devil's little advocate, are you not?"

"I am!" Violet fairly trumpeted.

"I do feel like I have a right to know. Anyway, what could he possibly be keeping from me now, that I don't, at least broadly, know about?"

"Hmmm," Equuleus stood and stretched his wings as far as he could in the dining room, "emphasis on 'broadly.' There are details—*details*, dear Heart, that you are not ready to know."

"Nonsense." She stood, and Violet hopped off her chair. But taking in Equuleus's look, Heart sat again. "Perhaps you're right I wouldn't want to make Father angry with me. He has important things to attend to, which do not include me causing him worry."

"But the point is," Violet-as-devil's-advocate wheedled, "he won't know you're there. You're only interested in some information gathering. Which you're entitled to."

"Why do you care so much?"

"Simple. I want to know what's going on too! Besides, you're the one who keeps me safe. So the more you know, the safer I am."

"Makes sense. All right. I'll compromise. I'll go down the hall, but not invade his space. If I hear something, fine. If not, fine, I'll come back." She stood and Equuleus stepped aside as she left the dining room.

"Throwing caution to the winds," he remarked as she moved down the hall with Violet hopping beside her.

"Aren't you coming?" she called to him over her shoulder.

"But of course."

As the three of them approached the door to the inner sanctum, they silently tiptoed. Quiet sounds from the other side abruptly stopped. Total silence. Heart looked back at Equuleus, and as she did so, the door flew open. All three of them, even Equuleus, jumped.

"*Eek!*" Violet squeaked.

"My sentiments exactly," Heart said as her father swung the door wide.

"What am I going to do with you?" He looked more disapproving than Heart had ever seen him, as a frown grew on his features.

"Well, you might shrug and say, 'like father like daughter.'"

He shrugged. "Like father, like daughter. All right, you may as well come in. I've been going to introduce you to a few of The Folks. Not that now is the best time, but here we are, all together for once." He gestured for her to enter the room.

More beings crowded into the small room than Heart imagined possible. They gathered around a wall of diagrams and 3-D projections. Two of those present were very familiar.

"Wonderman One and Wonderman Two," Heart exclaimed. "When—*how!*—did you get here?"

"They are not the Wondermen you know, Heart," her father said. "They are others. The One and Two you know are still on Earth."

"Oh! Sorry! You look, ahm ... similar."

"We look exactly the same," one of then replied, sounding a bit defensive.

"Exactly!" the other one agreed.

"Ah ... yes, Exactly the same. I see that's how you prefer it."

"Of course! It would be very confusing if we looked different."

"Hmmm. If you say so. So what are you called?"

"I'm Wonderman One," one of them said.

"And I'm Wonderman Two," the other announced.

Heart could not stifle a giggle. "It's delightful to meet you. I, ah, I feel as though I already know you."

"Well, you don't," one of them noted quite solemnly. "But we look forward to you getting to know us."

"Excellent!" She looked toward her father, but he kept himself busy with something small. She had a feeling he enjoyed a good laugh on her. Well, she deserved it.

"Who else did you have in mind for me to meet?" Heart asked.

"I thought I'd introduce you to Xavier."

"Ah, finally! I get to meet the whispered, the clandestine, the mysterious, Xavier!"

"Xavier, where are you?" her father asked.

"Here, sir, I'm—I'm right here."

A very human-sounding voice came from a black space right before Heart's eyes.

"Well, materialize, my lad."

"Feel shy."

"Come on now, you've encountered more frightening life forms than Heart."

"Thanks," Heart interjected.

"More frightening, but never anyone or anything so intimidating!"

"Intimidating? Really, that's ridiculous!" Heart shook her head.

"You've never met you, live and in person for the first time," the disembodied voice said.

"Or if I did," Heart quipped, "I don't recall it. Really, Father, are you sure you want me to meet this invisible being who seems to be very weak? That is to say, in addition to being invisible."

"I'm not weak," The voice began to materialize into a young man who took form in the blackness before her. "As I said, I'm intimidated by you."

From the black fog, he moved straight toward her. If he continued on his trajectory, he would run into her, and it looked as though this might be his goal. But instead, he stopped two feet before her and saluted brusquely.

"Xavier, at your service." Then he fell to one knee, took her hand and kissed her fingers. "Your valiant—if you will have me—foot soldier." She could not resist gazing into his amazing green eyes.

"Oh! Oh, my." Heart took a step back, taking her hand with her. "I—ahhh—are you making fun of me?"

Xavier jumped to his feet. "No, Heart. Never, I wouldn't even know how to make fun of you. You're … you're *Heart. Heart!*"

"Yes, I know who I am. You needn't introduce me to me. You need to introduce me to *you*."

"Which I did. Your ever faithful servant."

"Yes. I got that part. But *why?*"

"Because ...."

"I know, because I'm Heart. Father, will you please intervene here. *Please!*"

"I don't think so, my dear. You brought yourself here, and so you must deal with the consequences. Xavier is the commander of my lead defenses. He's brilliant, charming, fearless. Except, of course, when it comes to you."

"*BUT WHY?*"

"Because you're you," Xavier said.

"He has followed your every move for, how long? About five years or so now."

"Six Earth years, seven Earth months and fourteen Earth days ...."

"There you have it."

"There I have what?" Heart asked, ever more bemused.

"I won't tell you my life's story right now ...." Xavier leaned as close to her as he dared without actually touching her.

"How kind of you," Heart answered, wanting to take a small step back, but holding her ground.

"But I will tell you that six Earth years, seven Earth months and fourteen Earth days ago, I saw the 3-D of you, when you said, 'stars!' were your favorite thing, and I fell in love. With you. At that instant."

"Oh, that's silly. Father, have you put him up to this nonsense?"

"Not nonsense, Heart," Xavier continued. "But, never mind. You needn't worry about my weirdness. I am a consummate protector. I tell my truth, and now I must get back to my station, the purpose of which is to protect you, so it's very important."

Xavier walked backwards precisely footstep by footstep the way he'd come, fading back to black.

She watched as he gradually but completely dematerialized, then turned to her father. "Adroit shape-shifter, but other than that, what was *that?*"

"Precisely as you see—and hear. Xavier has been undyingly smitten by you since the first moment he saw you on a newshound transmission, sketchy, bad transmission that it was, from Earth. I've nothing to do with it, except tolerate his occasional energetic babble about your wonderful traits and talents. All true, of course."

"But ... it's weird. How can someone be in love with someone they've never met?"

"The soul knows its own path, Heart. You cannot ask me about Xavier's deepest feelings and expect to get a meaningful answer. You must speak with the owner of the soul under discussion."

"Can't very well speak with a black wall, now, can I? Anyway, I've come to discover what you're hiding from me in terms of your work—not to hear about some being's infatuation with a newsreel I happened to be in, years ago. That's ridiculous."

"Nevertheless, Heart, Xavier bonded on you in that snippet. Furthermore, nothing you've ever done serves to make him like you less. You're always thinking of others."

Heart shrugged.

"Don't you find him the least bit charming?" her father sounded just a little disappointed.

"I don't have time right now to see if some hybrid is interesting to me."

"How do you know he's hybrid?"

"Isn't he?"

"Well, yes."

"I rest my case."

"But *how* do you know it?"

"The same as any creature that comes up to any other creature and knows it's the same sort of creature. Or that it's not."

Her father nodded studiously. "Is there anything unusual about him, in this psychic pickup you have of him?"

"You mean, aside from being completely weird and materializing and dematerializing through a dense curtain of black fog? No, he appears quite human, if that's what you're wondering. What's the urgency?"

"I need him to pass among humans without the slightest suggestion of being hybrid."

"He's going to Earth?"

"Yes. He's going to Earth. Sooner than we expected. Now then, you three, out from under my feet. I have serious work to do and you're a distraction. I shan't be back to finish my dinner."

"Can I have your green beans?" Violet piped up, hopping up and down.

"Let me think for a moment. Ahm, yes, you may have three—*and no more!*—of my green beans."

"Oh hooray. Let's go!" Off Violet hopped toward the dining room.

"I mean it Heart, don't let her have more than three."

"I'd better run after her. She's extremely willful."

"Like someone else I know," her father observed, as he closed the door behind her and Equuleus.

"He's not wrong there!" Equuleus observed as they hurried down the hall.

"No, I suppose not. Where is that little lavender rabbit? She can certainly move when it's something of interest to her."

"Again ...."

"I know ... like someone else you know ...." Heart dashed into the dining room, to see Violet sitting in her father's chair, with her little paws on the table, but, much to Heart's surprise, waiting patiently for her.

"My goodness—I expected to see you gobbling down those green beans as fast as you could."

"No. Because if I did, when you came in, even if I didn't eat three, you'd assume I'd gorged, and would take them all away from me. So I need you as witness. Anyway, I want to have a companionable meal with you. The green beans? Yes! But companionship is an even bigger yes."

Heart sat in her chair beside Violet. "You're a very interesting little creature, do you know that?"

"Of course," Violet answered, daintily picking up a green bean and beginning to munch on it." But it's quite nice to hear."

Heart chuckled, and began to enjoy her own green beans. "Delicious! So, what do you think of the green beans, dear Violet?"

"Well, to be honest, I prefer my own greens. They are more flavorful, but I suppose that's because they're developed for my particular needs."

"That's a big relief!"

Equuleus, curling up by the fireside, snorted an agreement.

"So I won't indulge in your bio food and perhaps harm myself, behind your back?"

"Something like that." Heart's mind wandered back to the interaction she had with the strange Wondermen, who did not seem at all sweet and endearing like "her" Wondermen on Earth. And ... even more to the point, the whole boggling, weird, jarring experience with this utterly humanoid looking young man, Xavier.

As if Heart had spoken out loud Violet said, "*Wow*, isn't that Xavier a cutie! I mean, I'm a rabbit, so there can't be ... you know, but I'm just saying. *Ummm-ummm-umm!* A tidy package, that young man!"

"Really? I didn't pay any attention, I became so nonplussed by, well, everything about how he presented to me. I think this is a convoluted way my father is 'punishing me' for going against his directive. To humiliate me. Fairly effective, I say. Fairly effective. I feel duly shamed. Not that that's going to change my behavior, but, I don't think it's the least bit funny to humiliate me like that in front of others. If I have to have authority over them some time, how effective is it to have shamed me?"

Equuleus cleared his throat, which Heart knew meant he intended her to listen to him with care. "Speaking of respect! Heart, what you just experienced was not put on to humiliate you. Xavier showed you his candid and guileless truth. If you don't accept it as such, then *you're* treating *him* with disrespect.

"Much like you, he can only tell his truth. Yet he is even more transparent than you. Quite frankly, I'm surprised you don't see it!

"Also, it's fairly obvious, he's high ranking in your father's 'leagues,' shall we say. If you humiliate him with disdain, if you treat him like he's less than who he is, then you run the risk of undermining—well, who knows what. Perhaps more than you realize. Think well about your attitude and your behavior. Treat this young man with the same respect you expect for yourself."

Violet applauded. "Bravo, Sir Horse, well said!"

Heart looked from Violet to Equuleus. "Well ... I must be wrong. *Hmmmm*, let me cogitate on that for a few moments, as it's not usual. *Hmmm* ...." She studied her plate without seeing it. If Violet and Equuleus were correct, why was she *so* wrong? If Xavier told his guileless truth, transparent and brave, why hadn't she sensed it?

"Because," Equuleus cut in on her thoughts, "as a Darling Undesirable, you lived with a constant mixed message: you're adored, you're unlovable. Society feels guilty allowing the Darling Undesirables to exist, but they want the search for longevity to continue, so you have a muddled picture of yourself as lovable and unlovable.

"For someone to simply come up to you and say, 'I Love You!' makes you look for their 'other agenda.' You think, 'you're saying you love me because why? Because you want some media attention? Because you feel guilty? Why?'"

Heart got up and moved to side beside Equuleus by the fire. "You're absolutely, one-hundred percent right, my heart-of-hearts. You're right. I need to—

well, I don't know what I need to do. How best to handle this? All right, I see I must be very respectful and kind to Xavier. But I didn't fall in love with him six or more years ago, I can't feel, or even act like I feel!—something for him I don't."

"Of course not. But I imagine if you simply said that to him, if and when the occasion arises, it will be quite acceptable. He told you his feelings, but it's obvious he's pragmatic. Your father would not put the trust in him that he has if that were not the case."

"Yes." Violet hopped down from the chair and jumped into her arms, and the three of them snuggled cozily together. "Yes, that's what I'll do, my wise friend. He's going to Earth, Equuleus."

"And? ...."

"Just—Xavier's going to Earth ...." Those words rolled around and around in Heart's mind. She couldn't shake the myriad images this piece of information stirred up.

The three of them—the gorgeous mechanical gear horse, the delicate and adorable bio-mechanical rabbit, and the beautiful, intrepid bio-mechanical-dark-matter-dark energy young woman—cuddled together, in peace and contentment, a moment that hung, poised, in the vault of timeless-time, sweet and precious.

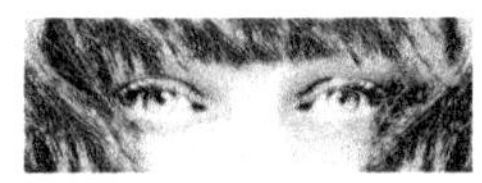

Chapter 12

Later, Heart went outside to check on her flowers, while Equuleus agreed to fly Violet up to Heart's quarters so she could become familiarized with the rooms, and to find a little spot of her own that suited her.

Heart didn't want Violet to move through the indoor and outdoor environments until her new bios were more fully integrated—the bloated, red Violet being a sight she never wanted to risk seeing again.

When she stepped out the front door, joy spread through her at the sight of the warm yellow light radiating through the pale green of the greenhouses.

As she moved into one of the greenhouses, she inhaled the wonderful aroma of the soil, the green plants, and the fragrant, budding flowers.

She leaned down to the rapidly growing plants, many tiny buds appearing on them, and a pale hint of colors soon to unfold, along with the heady, full-fledged scents of each. She cupped her hands lovingly around one little primrose, wondering how she could possibly leave her lovely flowers now, as they bloomed?

But—*how could she pass an opportunity to go to Earth?*

Oh, yes, she knew her father would not be sending her off to Earth. She knew she would have to stow away on whatever vehicle Xavier would fly to Earth.

She knew she would have to leave more than her flowers. She'd leave Violet and HelperFriend. She'd leave Equuleus, and her father.

In short, she'd be leaving everything that was now her life. Her new life—where she was loved, truly loved, and where, with each passing non-day, she had more to do, more to learn, and now, with the population of "The Folks"—many more beings to care about.

Why would she leave? She had many practical things to do here.

But—it was simple. She longed to see Swen, to have the conversation they never had, because he was protecting her, knowing she would soon leave for Pink when she had no idea this was in her near future.

They never had a chance to have a real, "good-bye for now" talk.

And ... she *needed* to see Eye.

As much as she spent hours and hours telling herself he was all right, it didn't matter. Even if he *was* all right, even if wildly happy, she, selfishly, needed to peek into his life—in person, for herself.

"It's hard, little primrose, it's a very, very difficult choice, either way. But the thing is, there *is no choice.* If a spacecraft is going to Earth, I'll be on it. Will I come back? It's hard to know. Will I see you blossom and bloom, dear primrose? I don't know. You say it's dangerous, it's foolhardy, it's unwise? Yes, I know. Equuleus will try to talk me out of it, I know.

"I see your logic, little flower, I must simply ask Father if I can ride along with Xavier. But I know his answer. I don't need any paranormal awareness to show me that outcome."

Heart drank in the whole developing pattern of plaid in her sublime and delightful greenhouse, then stepped out the back set of baffling doors and into the other greenhouse. Here the same extraordinary growth was in progress, a different range of colors, a different pattern of plaid, but the same loamy warmth rising through the air. The same welcoming little buds, raising their heads to the enriching, full spectrum light the "Plant Folks" had wisely installed. Not too bright, not too hot, not too dim, not too cool. Just—perfect.

Heart walked among her beloved flowers, knowing she was saying good-by. For now or forever, she did not know. In facing the possibility she might never return she realized that Pink, and everything it offered, had worked its way into her very depths.

It was an *option* not to leave. But not a choice.

She meandered through her precious garden, and when she came to the front doors, she turned to try to hold the aroma and the vision, physically. "Two homes! Two homes to tug at one's soul. Always wondering what's happening with one while at the other. Never quite comfortable. Never quite at home."

She left the greenhouse and went inside her father's home, slowly climbing the beautiful, sweeping, winding walnut stairs to her rooms, deep in thought and melancholy.

She took a deep breath before opening her door. Of course, Equuleus already knew what she planned. But she didn't want to show her hand to Violet, who would adamantly protest her leaving. When she opened the door she saw Violet on her bed, and Equuleus, before her, in a defensive stance.

"What's going on? Why aren't you settled in some little nook or cranny, Violet?"

"I don't want some little nook or cranny," she squeaked. "I want to be with you. Why would I settle on a remote corner of these gigantic rooms? It doesn't feel cozy, and more to the point, it doesn't feel safe."

"I tried to tell her she is perfectly safe here, but she won't have it," Equuleus interjected.

"Oh, well, it doesn't matter. Let her get comfortable anywhere. Over time, she might decide she needs a space of her own. I don't mind if she wants my bed as her space. You know I rarely sleep."

"That's my point. You rarely sleep, so, when you do, you don't need some fuzzy, energetic lavender ball of fur chattering at you or hopping about the bed."

This caused Heart's gloomy mood to disperse, and she laughed outright. "Well, you pose an interesting scenario, Equuleus. We must have an agreement between us, Violet, that you will not chatter or hop about when, on those rare occasions, I intend to sleep. If you feel so inclined, I will take it upon myself to set you outside my rooms altogether. Are we agreed?"

"Oh, goodness, I wouldn't want to be set outside your rooms altogether, under any circumstance. Goodness! Awful! Yes, we're agreed. When you intend to sleep, I'm inert!"

Heart laughed. "I don't think you'll need to go that far, but quiet and still would be perfect."

Someone knocked at Heart's door. Exchanging a look of surprise with Equuleus, as no one had ever knocked on her door since she arrived on Pink, she turned and opened it.

"I'm so sorry to interfere with your levity, dear Heart. I heard the laughter, it's very sweet ...."

Heart opened the door wide, "Then come in my dear HelperFriend and join us. Plenty of levity for all!"

"Oh thank you, that's very kind. But, unhappily, I must decline your invitation for the moment. Perhaps some other time, I would very much look forward to it ...."

"Then—is there an occasion for your visit?"

"Yes. Quite so. Quite urgent. Yes, Father Inventor requests the pleasure of your company."

"That's strange."

"Everything's strange right now, Heart, it's true." He turned and clanked and whirred halfway down the hall before looking back, clearly with an expectation that she'd followed him.

"All right. I'm with you!" Heart exited the room, Violet hopped onto Equuleus's back. While Heart followed HelperFriend down the stairs, Equuleus swooped with Violet down and around to the shining artistic mosaic marble inlay of Earth below.

"I want to talk with you, HelperFriend, about caring for the flower beds when we get a chance."

"Oh my, you don't need me to care for the flower beds. You're much better at it."

"Even so, I want to instill in you the procedure."

"Wouldn't it be better to have the Plant Folks attend to that?"

"Well, perhaps. But I don't know who they are. They installed the lights—which are perfect, by the way—when I wasn't around. Do you know them?"

"Oh sure. Of course!"

"Well, then," they arrived at the marble floor, joining Equuleus and Violet, "if I were in any way indisposed, you would tell them to attend to the flowers?"

"Of course I would Heart. But you're never indisposed. Why do you even talk like that?"

"Just covering bases, my friend. The flowers deserve to finally get to raise their little heads and not, in any way, have their full growth compromised."

"Sure. Yes, of course."

Equuleus gave Heart a studied look, slightly shaking his head, but said nothing.

"Let us hurry," HelperFriend said urgently. "Father Inventor is standing by, waiting for your arrival."

"Seriously?" Heart asked, incredulous.

"Very."

"Let us hurry then," she repeated, scurrying down the hall ahead of everyone.

When she opened the door to her father's room, she saw him in his bell jar, silhouetted in it, backlit by the light beyond. Heart could not see his expression, but his body language appeared tense.

She quickly turned to Violet. "Are you all right?"

"Perfectly fine," Violet answered. "Why do you ask?"

"The environment—"

"No problem. I'm perfect." She jumped up and down on Equuleus to demonstrate her point. "But something is bothering Father Inventor." Violet waved her ears in his direction.

"Yes, something is wrong."

"Something *is* problematic," her father agreed.

"What is ...." Heart stopped stock still, gasping at the sight before her. Flooded with the same feeling she'd had the first time she saw "The Tent" at The Museum of Scientific Improbabilities and Unpredictable Oddities—that sense of looking at something too big to be comprehended, too big to be believed. Rising up before her, a pure white, semi-sphere, making The Tent lilliputian by comparison.

"*Whaaaaat* am I looking at?" She couldn't help herself, she took a step back.

"This is part of the moon we will soon launch, that will be Yellow's moon."

"Yellow's *moon!?* Yellow *is* a moon."

"Yes, my dear. And Yellow will soon have a moon of its own. Pink will also have a moon of its own."

"With all that's happening on Earth, is decorating the sky with more moons the very best use of your genius?" Heart asked, stunned that she had the temerity to quiz her father. But, on another extremely pragmatic hand, she could not act as if this was utterly delightful.

"Brilliant!" Her father grinned at her. "*You are brilliant* ... and you're correct. The two moons will be connected by an invisible dark energy field that will repel anything and everything that does not carry a particular signal. It will be a shield protecting Pink and Yellow."

"Oh!" Heart exclaimed, taking in the enormity of the plan. "Fantastic, Father—speaking of brilliance!"

"Thank you, but I've certainly not accomplished this alone. Nor could I have. All the hard work and focus of everyone here has brought it into fruition. But we really, *really* must keep in motion."

"And you want me to do something?" Heart said, thrilled. "To be put to work, to contribute to such a creation as the moon's moons—that would be *so meaningful!*"

"Well, no, that's not what I have in mind. The work that can be accomplished here on Pink is essentially done. Now comes the extremely complicated project of launching Pink's moon and then ferrying Yellow's moon to Yellow. Many of The Folks here will immigrate to Yellow and colonize it. It's not bio-friendly, but the non-bio beings can build a home, a lab, and a workspace for themselves."

Greatly disappointed at not being recruited to do something constructive, Heart asked, "So—why have you called for me?"

"I know you won't like to hear this, but I need to show you a newshound 3-D recording. I hate to show this to you, as I know it's the only thing that has deeply frightened you ...."

"*The bots!*" Heart whispered.

"Yes, dearest, the evil bots. Like I say, I don't want to show this to you, but—I must. You need to be aware of what's going on."

"I don't need to see them to know they exist."

"I know, but you need to see this new iteration of the bots." He turned on the 3-D. As the light dimmed, bots began to fill the air around her, and Heart could not help crying out. Equuleus moved a step nearer to her. She reached up and put her hand on his muzzle, but other than that, she stood stock still, taking in the scene that emerged around her.

The bots' long tentacles swirled in darkness, a faint light emanated from their bodies, their pale sickly appearance belying their astounding strength.

These bots were even larger and more horrible looking than the ones that had accosted her. A deep repugnance welled up in her at the bulging, repulsive, purple vein-like growths upon their surface, recalling the unspeakable feeling of their touch as their tentacles wrapped around her when she escaped the Darling Undesirables Facility at Long Prairie.

As she watched the 3-D, she tried to get her bearings, but couldn't quite comprehend what she saw. Then, off to the edge, there hung Earth, the tiniest edge of it, a curve of its surface in the bottom corner of the 3-D. From that clue, she realized the bots had flown far out into space, beyond Earth's atmosphere, where, previously they could not have survived.

Heart then reasoned that the bots were making their way to Pink. But as she watched, one by one, they crumpled up and fell from flight, until soon nothing populated the space between Earth and the device observing the event, other than distant stars.

The 3-D faded and the room lights came back up.

"The bots are on their way to Pink," Heart said simply. "They've discovered your brain clone and are putting it to use improving the bots stability in space."

Her father nodded. "So it would seem. Those bots were practically halfway here."

"Where did the 3-D come from?"

"Oh, I have a number of dark matter 3-D recording mechanisms roaming the space between my satellite moons and Earth, especially, of course, Pink. We're extremely vigilant. At this moment, the greatest hope we have is the shield that will be produced by the moons' moons," he waved his hand at the partially completed moon. "At the same time, we must keep track of what the Purists and their scientists—a sentence I never thought I'd hear myself say!—are doing."

"Yes," HelperFriend nodded as if his gear-infused head would pop off. "'Purists' scientists,' an oxymoron."

"Not any longer an oxymoron, apparently," Heart shuddered, still feeling a chill at the sight of bots swirling around her. "I agree with HelperFriend. If they think it's fine to alter life forms, such as they are doing with bio-bots, what is their problem with you, Father? Is it not hypocrisy to the last degree? Why come after Pink? We're completely out of their life. Just leave us alone! We don't go poking around in their business."

"That may not be precisely accurate," her father said quietly.

"What are you saying?"

"All The Folks here and I have a rather significant agenda to *very much* interfere with the game plan of those in power. Though they pretend to be Purists, they are nothing other than greedy, greedy ...."

"Greedy whatever they are," HelperFriend said, clearly agitated. "Greedy, greedy, greedy ...."

"So ... what are your plans that have them coming after Pink?"

"Two major, world-changing plans. I know you're familiar with *'The Cause of All Beings.'* The first part of the movement's agenda is to free the people on the other side of The Periphery so they may come and go as they please, eliminating the stigma against them as criminals. As you saw, Heart, they are good and moral people, incarcerated because of their white hearted beliefs in *Ourbook*. They live simply and care for one another. A paradigm worth imitating by anyone."

"I agree. But they're content there. I doubt, if you took *The Wall* completely down, they would even bother to live on the other side. I'm sure they're safer with *The Wall* there. It's not so much a case of keeping them in, as keeping what is truly bad, out!"

"No argument, Heart. However, they deserve to have the stigma removed and not be considered criminals. They deserve, if they do cross *The Wall*, to be able to move about freely."

Heart nodded. "I couldn't agree more, having had my own life-threatening experience with *The Wall*, as you know. And what is the second thing you intend to do to rock the Purists collective self-serving boats?" Heart held her breath with the profound desire that her father might say what she longed with every fiber of her being to hear him say.

"You know what that is, Heart. That every Darling Undesirable live in a home with a loving family, and that, eventually, these unloving experiments cease."

"*Yes*," Heart whispered so softly, she hardly heard herself. "And even more ...."

"What more, my precious daughter?"

"That each and every Darling Undesirable be given what they are missing. Except me, of course. I'm an unusual case," She hugged Equuleus's muzzle. "My heart belongs in Equuleus, and that's as it should be. But that Darling Undesirables without arms get arms, that Darling Undesirables with partial brains get complete brains, that Darling Undesirables with wing nubbins who desire nothing more in life than to have wings, get wings ...."

"You mean Butterfly," her father said. "And that any Darling Undesirable without eyes ...."

"Get eyes. Yes. That is my true goal, Father."

Her Father beamed—if his vest had buttons, they surely would have popped off. "I'm so proud of you!"

"Nothing to be proud of, Father. I will never turn my back on the Darling Undesirables."

"Nor will I," affirmed her father.

"*NOR WILL WE!*" a huge cry went up. Without Heart even noticing, The Folks had quietly arrived while she talked with her father. Silent and attentive, filled with love so tangible that some began to cry. Soon bio, mechanical, clockwork, dark energy beings filled the air with affirmations of love and protection for the sad malformed bio children on the beautiful planet, looming over them in their sky.

"To the Darling Undesirables," a valiant, distant voice called.

"*To the Darling Undesirables!*" all-as-one roared.

Heart looked toward the single voice who cried out. Atop the gigantic curve of Yellow's moon, far in the distance, a tiny-yet-intrepid figure waved hugely, smiling.

Even at the distance, Heart made out Xavier, grinning broadly. Making, never mind the distance, eye contact with her.

The realization washed over her that he would play a significant part in accomplishing the goals that would subdue the power of the evil minds on Earth.

More power to him! She thought as she discovered herself, somewhat to her own surprise, smiling broadly back and him and, yes ... even waving.

Chapter 13

When the emotionally charged moment calmed down, and all The Folks went back to their various stepped-up duties, Xavier—*somehow!*—swung down from the moon's moon, and joined Heart, her father, Violet, Equuleus and HelperFriend.

"Xavier and I need to do some planning, now with the new urgency upon us," her father said. "Are you all right, Heart, after being surrounded by the 3-D of the bots?"

"I'm fine—not a fun experience, but maybe I ought to subject myself to the viewing every now and then, as a form of aversion therapy. I need to get to a point where they don't make me want to run, shrieking from the room."

"You were far from running, shrieking, from the room, Heart!" Xavier protested. "As real as a 3-D appears, you stood your ground."

"How do you know? You were over there on Yellow's moon."

"We have 3-D surveillance devices giving us a view of everything that goes on in Father Inventor's space. First directive, 'Protect Father Inventor.'"

Heart looked at her father, eyebrows raised as if to say, "Really?"

"Don't give me that look, young miss!" he reprimanded. "It wasn't my idea. Even though, objectively, there is wisdom in it. But I suspect the 'directive' came initially from the same mouth that just now repeated it. Am I right?"

"I can't seem to recall who first said it," Xavier answered illusively. "The Folks discussed at length directives and the like, as we needed order and organization. We all knew that. Then someone suggested we start with issues of protection, and work out from there. It doesn't matter who first said it—it only matters that everyone agrees."

"*Here, here!*" HelperFriend cheered.

"Well, I also agree. My father must, under any and all circumstances, be protected," Heart nodded. "Anyway, go ahead and get to the business at hand. Just ignore us, we're three little bugs on the wall."

"All right, strange bugs," her father laughed. "Yes, Xavier, let's get to work, we must change some plans and rearrange our calendar."

While her father turned his back on her and her entourage, Heart acted as though she didn't hear a word, but, of course, she listened intently, focusing on the details that particularly mattered to her: 1. When would Xavier leave? 2. What would be his mode of travel? and 3. Where would he land on Earth?

She sat on her father's cot, petting Violet, with Equuleus on the floor by her side. HelperFriend more or less hovered around the periphery of Xavier and her Father, ready to be of help.

Heart found herself watching Xavier's profile. *Hmmmm* ... he was, as Violet observed, "cute." About her same height, thin but muscular. She hadn't noticed before when he shape-shifted, it had been so disconcerting, that he had freckles. *Freckles!* Endearingly bio. Almost as endearing as being winked at.

His eyes were alight with listening to her father, giving him feedback, completely involved in their discussion—green eyes dancing, even in profile, with a mop of hair that looked like the only thing resembling a comb it had ever seen was his fingers. Not a bad thing, Heart decided.

No, his attention was not absolutely, completely on her father's conversation, as he dared to glance back at her and give her a wide, impossibly wide, grin that said, *"Ha-ha! I see you looking at me!"*

She looked away quickly, frustrated with herself for letting her guard down. Well, this energy certainly went into a realm different from anything she'd ever experienced.

And all new learning experiences deserved to be explored.

When she'd gleaned a very important piece of information from the conversation—which was, the location of the spacecraft Xavier would travel to Earth in—she stood and, with Violet and Equuleus in tow, exited the room.

Her father glanced at her as she passed through the door, and she waved. He nodded. Xavier turned his grin on her, and *oh my goodness, no*, Heart almost said aloud ....

He winked at her!

*   *

Agitated, Heart hurried up to her rooms. She already had too much to think about, without this ... this *person* winking at her. Feeling full of static electricity, Heart paced up and down the hall in front of her rooms, the view of the stunning marble inlay of Earth below, always a visual she treasured—now seemed to taunt her.

Are you going to Earth on a very small spacecraft, with this person, this person who disrupts your concentration? Who—who *winked* at you? she asked herself.

"What's wrong, Heart?" Violet asked, clearly worried, hopping alongside her, up and back, back and up.

Equuleus stood quietly at the end of the hall, watching Heart. "Not to worry, Violet. She's sorting out her options. Taking in information. Making decisions."

"Is that it, Heart? Is Equuleus right? You're just making decisions? Nothing too alarming?"

Heart nodded, but said nothing.

"All right then. I'll relax." When they came to the end of the hall, Violet stopped off with Equuleus, and the two of them silently watched Heart integrate her thoughts, gradually slowing her pacing.

"See?" Equuleus said to Violet. "She's coming to conclusions. She's figured out how to make puzzle pieces that don't seem to fit—*fit!* The pieces that will never fit, she's abandoned. She now has a picture. Now she'll begin to take action."

"Right." Heart entered her rooms, looked around as if she'd never been here before. Yes, she'd puzzled pieces together, but no, she had no certainty about what now developed.

The first—and biggest—conclusion she'd come to was that, yes, she would have to be in close quarters with Xavier, and she would simply have to keep her mind focused on her plans, no matter what sort of distraction he might pose.

The same for him! He had a very important mission on Earth, and must not be distracted by her presence. Perhaps she could hide altogether, and Xavier never even know she'd stowed away.

But then—how would she fulfill her mission to see Eye? If she depended on Xavier to help her get to Swen and then to Eye, thousands of miles apart, that would obviously interfere with his mission. That would never do. But perhaps she could induce him to simply drop her off at The Museum of Scientific Improbabilities and Unpredictable Oddities. Like—what?—he was some sort of public transportation?

She really ought to jettison the whole idea.

But—she couldn't. When would she *ever* have a chance to go to Earth again? She must take advantage of the opportunity. Once on Earth, she would figure it out. She'd done it before, when she first left The Darling Undesirable Facility at Long Prairie, before she knew—well, before she knew *anything!* She knew quite a bit more than nothing now ....

"*Hmmmm* ..." she mused aloud.

"What, Heart, what?" Violet asked, hopping up to her. "What does your '*hmmmmm*' mean?"

"I just came to the conclusion that I know more than nothing."

"Well, of course, you know more than nothing! What an idea! Goodness, all that stomping up and down and thinking, and the conclusion is, 'I know more than nothing.' Good grief, that doesn't seem very productive!" Violet's squeak raised into a nearly un-hear-able range.

Equuleus snorted.

"I'll have none of that from you," Heart said to the two of them with fake sternness.

"Just stating an opinion," Equuleus said.

"*Hmmmm*," she said again.

"Violet hopped up on the bed. "Enough '*hmmmming*,' Tell us what you're stuck on, what you're trying to sort out. Maybe we can help you."

Heart sat on the bed beside Violet and scratched her between her ears.

"*Ohhhh!* I love that, Heart," Violet said, closing her eyes and relaxing her long, lavender ears down the sides of her body.

"You're so adorable, little Violet. I appreciate your concern. But when I have to make big decisions, I have to go through it all on my own. I have my rough plan sorted out now, though. I need to learn some concrete details, and then, put it all into motion."

Violet looked at Equuleus. "What's she talking about?"

"I know, but I may not tell."

"No, you may not," Heart agreed.

HelperFriend appeared at the open door. "Sorry to bother you yet again, Heart, but Father Inventor would like you to join him for dinner."

"Really? With all that's going on?"

"It's sort of a farewell for Xavier. There will be a few others in attendance. The Wondermen and a few of The Folks you've not been introduced to."

"Fantastic!"

"I'll see you soon, then?"

"We'll return with you."

They made their way to the dining room where music played, the fire in the fireplace sparkled, and the light from the wall sconces glowed pink. Along with her father, Xavier, Wonderman One and Wonderman Two, and several other fascinating residents of Pink occupied the room.

A tall, beautiful mechanical woman with a small mechanical dog that followed her everywhere, yipping at her heels, dominated the scene. She wore a gear-tight outfit of shiny black, with a high collar, cinched waist, and leggings, through which her gear works showed. Her movements were strangely jerky and graceful. The smile on her gear face captivated and warmed Heart.

A very small man-like creature, about two feet tall, carrying a mysterious box, whose shape and color changed continually drew her attention like a magnet.

Two rather bio-looking children, almost identical, held hands no matter what. As they moved, the clockworks showed beneath a thin layer of skin-like material.

When Heart, accompanied by HelperFriend, Equuleus, and Violet, stepped into the room, the congenial chit-chat stopped. All eyes turned to her.

The beautiful, tall mechanical woman made came up to her. "Oh, Heart! It means so much to me to get to meet you. May I shake your hand?"

"Of course," Heart said, extending her hand.

Her father joined them. "Heart, I'd like to introduce you to Lady Gervi."

"So pleased to meet you, Heart, as I say. Allow me to introduce my little dog, Yippie."

"I see he lives up to his name," Heart observed.

"*Tee-hee*," Lady Gervi tittered. "He does. Hush, Yippie, we can't hear ourselves think!"

The dog whined as his gear eyes looked up at his mistress with keen understanding.

"Oh, all right!" She stooped over and picked him up. "He's so spoiled! But he's quite intelligent. Although he doesn't have a speech chip, he understands perfectly well what's going on. He knows who you are, Heart."

Heart smiled at the little gear dog, and became aware of it looking at her with great anticipation and expectation.

"Yippie, this is Heart!"

The dog nodded most enthusiastically, and extended its paw.

"Oh, my goodness!" Heart exclaimed, taking his paw. "I'm very pleased to meet you, Yippie!"

The little dog nodded some more, and began to make a series of sounds as speech-like as possible, without actually being words.

"Oh, well," Lady Gervi tittered, "he's giving you all sorts of accolades you're very used to hearing from everyone. Thank you, Yippie, that's very sweet. I'm sure Heart appreciates your endearments."

"I do! Thank you, little friend," Heart smiled at the odd little dog as Lady Gervi put him on the floor.

"Why not acquaint yourself with that lovely lavender rabbit, Yippie?" Lady Gervi suggested.

"Oh, forgive my rudeness," Heart turned to Violet, who had hopped off Equuleus's back. "This is my dear friend, Violet. Violet, Lady Gervi and her little dog, Yippie."

Violet curtsied to Lady Gervi. "Yes, I'm familiar with your name, but we've never had occasion to meet. It's a pleasure to meet you."

"Perhaps you and Yippie can enjoy one another's company?"

"Well ...."

Heart could clearly see Violet resisted this suggestion, altogether. She stooped over and picked her. "That's an excellent idea, Lady Gervi. But first, let me introduce you to Equuleus."

Lady Gervi nodded with a royal expression to Equuleus. "Oh, yes, Equuleus! The Keeper of the Heart. I am your devout admirer."

Equuleus bowed deeply in return, muzzle to extended hoof, wings pointing to ceiling, remaining mute. Meanwhile, Violet whispered in Heart's ear. "That's a dog, Heart! A mechanical dog, but a *dog*, nonetheless. Am I to keep *a dog* company? First of all, dogs are forever enemies of rabbits, and secondly, I'm *Violet*, and that is a mere dog."

Heart nodded, smiling, and whispered back, "I understand, Violet." Then aloud she asked, "Who else is joining us that I've not previously met, Father?"

The little man and two children had come up behind Lady Gervi. She stepped aside to allow them to come forward.

"This is Geometria," Her father said. "He's a mystic, tracking the sacred geometry involved in everything we do. The shapes and sizes and dimensions of every project."

"Hence the amazing box," Heart observed.

Geometria extended his free hand. "Yes, hence my Sacred Geometry box. It ceaselessly contemplates all the dimensional details of any situation. Not only objects and the space between them, but also, the dynamics between people and other beings."

As he spoke, the box became a pyramid, shifting from a pale green to bright white. "Ah!" Geometria exclaimed. "Not a complete surprise, but very nice, just the same. The sacred geometry box is noting that you and I form a pyramid, and that your purest energy comes from your fourth chakra, the heart. *I know!* Your heart is in Equuleus. But in non-physical terms, you are all heart, as shown by this beautiful green–becoming– white light. Excellent! That's the energy within the pyramid between us. Pure, very high, spiritual energy."

Heart did indeed, feel a pull all around her, as if her entire energy field cleared. "Oh! Lovely, Geometria, thank you!"

He bowed, then brought the two children forward. They looked shyly up at Heart. "Heart, this is Mira and Plaisir, two of our eternal children. They keep us remembering where we come from, and not to overthink things. Well—they do a lot more than that, too."

"Pleased to meet you, pleased to meet you," they said, all jumbled up together, each offering her free hand to Heart.

Heart warmly took their hands. "I'm very pleased to meet you too, Mira and Plaisir. It's lovely you will be joining us for dinner."

"Will there be candy?" Mira asked.

"I don't know!" Heart looked around to see if she could find HelperFriend. There he was, right beside her. "Oh! HelperFriend, will there be candy for the children?"

"There's candy for everyone!" He cried out and a giant cheer raised in the room.

Laughing, Heart hugged the two little girls. "All the children, large and small, get candy at dinner! Now, what do you think of that?"

"*It's fantastic!*" they exclaimed in unison.

Yippie, not to be outdone, joined in the general merriment, and the clockwork children bent down to play with the doggie, while HelperFriend made gestures in the air, and the music increased in volume and tempo.

Suddenly HelperFriend seemed to be everywhere at once, in lightning speed bringing bowls and plates and platters and dishes, spreading out a buffet feast—something to suit everyone. True to his word, HelperFriend set up a table in the corner, heaped with brightly colored candies and piles of light and dark chocolate.

Heart, still holding Violet, looked at the delights in every direction, set Violet on Equuleus, already munching his own stack of colorful straw-like "candy" by the fireplace.

She hadn't yet talked with Wonderman One and Wonderman Two, and just the slightest bit didn't much want to, given how belligerent they'd been before. When, suddenly, with hands full of colorful candy, the two of them began to dance a wild and stunning dance, juggling their handfuls of candy, back and forth between them, dancing on their hands while the candy hung impossibly long in the air, then spinning on their backs. They called to one another in an ancient-sounding language, and they *actually smiled!*

Everyone circled around them, mesmerized, food and candy forgotten, the Wondermen's unbounded joy contagious, running through everyone. Soon others called, imitating the language, whether they knew it or not. Heart didn't know it either, but she, too joined in, dancing and calling, the strange language seeming to know its own way through her vocal cords.

Heart noticed that when the room reached a joyous chaos, Wonderman One and Wonderman Two stepped aside, watching the fun they'd created with beatific smiles. She, too, stepped to the side, to watch. The Wondermen came up to her, smiling and joyful. "You must make fun where you can find it," one Wonderman said.

Heart nodded.

"If you cannot make fun, you cannot make anything," the other Wonderman commented.

"I believe you're right," Heart agreed. "I'm so glad you joined us tonight!"

"So are we. We will share this night forever and forever with all the residents of Pink, and any future off-world residents. Recorded, forever inside of us."

"That is so lovely, Wonderman One and Wonderman Two."

"Yes. There are but a few of us who can withstand this human environment. But all the others ought to at least see and hear it."

"And make your own party!"

"Oh yes," the two Wondermen looked at each other as if she'd suggested a new idea. "And make our own parties!"

They went to the center of the room and danced again. Heart filled a plate with the beautiful food for bio-based beings, then looked around for Violet, no longer on Equuleus. She finally saw her in the corner with the children and Yippie, the four of them deep in conversation, appearing much more grown up than anyone else in the room. Heart watched as Violet touched her forehead to Yippie's, unmistakably bonding.

She shook her head with a small crooked grin. How wonderful when anyone—even a clockworks rabbit!—put down prejudices, and got to know the "other"—who was, ultimately, rarely very different.

Eventually, Father Inventor went to the front of the room, gesturing to HelperFriend, who waved his arm, and the music abruptly turned off. Everyone looked around, a bit stunned, but when they saw Father Inventor quietly standing at the head of the table, they quickly found seats and the energy in the room instantly changed from merriment to attentive.

Amazed, Heart responded as well at the rapid shift in temperament. She looked about for Geometria, and saw him, solemnly holding his sacred geometry box, now a blue-gray, solid cube.

Her father looked around the room, taking in each and every one of them in turn with an affectionate look. "My dear Folks, this has been an evening of fun and celebration—and why not? We've accomplished so much—*you've* accomplished so much! I'm immensely proud of every one of you.

"You always look out for one another, you always care for one another. You have, in fact, *built* one another. But the time we've been preparing for is fast upon us, sooner than we thought. So we not only must step up our inventions and production, but we must also stand by, while one of ours bravely leaves us upon a secret mission to ensure our efforts are productive."

"*Xavier, Xavier* ..." whispered the gathering.

"Yes. Our own, brave, Xavier." The room lights, the sconces, and the lights above dimmed. In their midst appeared a 3-D, showing Xavier's little spacecraft, sitting within Pink. Heart glanced over to Equuleus, watching as closely as she. "This is a simulation, but you all know, it will be his little spacecraft's first flight," her father continued.

Heart saw that Xavier's spacecraft looked very much like any vehicle one might see on Earth's Dark Energy Highway. *Brilliant!* He would be able to roam around on Earth, completely undetected.

As the simulation showed Xavier's vehicle entering Earth's atmosphere, Heart's father continued, "Xavier will take his spacecraft to Earth. The spacecraft that he built with his own hands, and by his own brilliance, that fits him like a glove, that can fly faster than almost anything.

His mission is to set resonating devices in strategic locations on Earth that will unite the protective shield from Earth to Pink's and to Yellow's new moons, which we will launch soon after his return."

Then the simulation showed the little ship landing—Heart gasped—at *The Museum of Scientific Improbabilities and Unpredictable Oddities!*

First problem solved! Well, she reminded herself, not quite the first problem. The *first* problem would be how to stowaway on Xavier's spacecraft.

"The rest of the details are, of course, strictly confidential, known only to Xavier and myself, to protect all of you, if anything were to go awry."

"Nothing will go awry," Lady Gervi spoke up in the darkened room.

"That's right, that's right," whispered affirmations filled the room. Even Yippie seemed to be growling agreement, who, Heart noticed, sat at her feet by Violet.

"That is our prayer," Father Inventor agreed. He nodded to HelperFriend. The delicate pink light of the sconces came up softly, giving a glow to the room and everyone in it.

"Please, continue your feast and enjoy the party. Xavier and I must excuse ourselves. We have last minute details to solidify, and then he must get some sleep, to satisfy his bio components."

"Sleep well," everyone called after him as he and Father Inventor left the room.

Xavier didn't even attempt to make eye contact with Heart, and she now realized that, in all these festivities, they hadn't exchanged one word. Why did that make her feel a bit angry, she wondered? In any event, if she succeeded in stowing aboard his spacecraft, she would get her fill of him.

And he of her, she reminded herself.

Part II

Chapter 14

As soon as she could reasonably escape the party, Heart nodded to Equuleus. First, she left, then he followed as discretely as possible. Neither of them would be easily missed, but she had to let that be as it may. She didn't trouble herself with Violet, still utterly engaged in conversation with Yippie to the extent that when Heart stood up to leave, Violet didn't even notice.

When they came into the rotunda of the foyer, Heart jumped on Equuleus and he flew up to her rooms. They entered and she shut the door firmly.

"Not a good idea, Heart. Not a good idea at all."

"I have to go, Equuleus. *I must!* Can you imagine what I would be like if I stayed here, knowing I may have let the one and only chance to go to Earth, and have a real talk with Swen and to see Eye, and to make sure he's all right, go by? Maybe even plan his escape. I can't stay here. *I cannot!* I've been trying to argue myself into it. But—there's just *no choice.*"

Equuleus looked at her for a long moment, then sighed so deeply, all his gears spun. "No. I guess not. No. You couldn't. You're right. You *must* go."

"That's settled. Now then, to the next issue—how do I get on Xavier's spacecraft? A dream come true would be if I could ask my father if I could go with Xavier, and he said 'yes.'"

"That will never happen!"

"I know. That will never happen. So I must stow away. But if I have to go through Father's room to get to the spacecraft—I don't know how I'll pull it off. Is there any other way to get to it?"

"Nothing practical. Given that you must leave virtually immediately, the only choice is to go through his room, and you know what that means."

"I'll have to shape-shift. Which I've never done on Pink. I don't even know if I can here. I feel terrible doing it to avoid, and worse, *to trick*, my own father."

As you've noted before, Heart, *you are his daughter*. He's done many things historically to save people—or various sorts of beings. And that's what you're doing. You must release any guilt, it could be your judgment."

"When did you get so wise?"

"I have always been. Perceiving my wisdom is not a measure of my wisdom, but yours."

"Oh my, dear Equuleus, don't make me think so hard right now!"

He laughed. "Right. Plain and simple for the moment. And here it is. One: gather things you will surely need. Two: get down to Xavier's spacecraft."

"Doesn't get any simpler than that." Heart tore around her rooms, gathering up one thing then throwing it down, picking up something else, and finally ending up with a few things in a small backpack. "That's it, I guess. Can't think too clearly right now. But, Equuleus, did you see? He's going straight to The Museum of Scientific Improbabilities and Unpredictable Oddities! Right, straight there! I couldn't ask for more."

"No, Heart, you really couldn't," Equuleus agreed. "Right now, become calm, and let me put in your mind a map of two things. Exactly where Xavier's ship is at this moment, and the layout of his tight little ship on the inside. I've highlighted two places where I think you might successfully stow away."

"Is there anything at all I can jettison?"

"Jettison?"

"Yes. I am weight. If he does a careful check on weight, there I'll be. If there's something I can toss, and, if there's a small variance in weight, he'll not give it much thought. He's in a hurry, I don't think he's going to go crazy to discover where a small bit of weight is, but a notable difference …."

"Let me see." Equuleus checked the interior of Xavier's spacecraft, then chuckled.

"What's funny?"

"Xavier apparently has a sweet tooth. He has a load of candy from the dinner, conveniently placed right by the best location you can stow away in. If you set that out, it weighs over half of what you weigh …."

"*Sheesh!* He's not going to keep those pretty teeth!"

"Ah, well, his teeth aren't bio. Anyway, if you can set it out—without being seen!—that's your solution."

"Got it. All right, my precious friend, I'm on my way."
'Shall I go down with you?"
"You might, in case I need any unforeseen help."
They stepped out of her rooms.

"Just a minute ...." Heart ran around the landing to the window to take one long and loving look down at her flowers, now resting in darkness inside their greenhouses. *"Love you ..."* she whispered to them, then hurried back to Equuleus. "The flowers ...."

"I'll remind HelperFriend to get the Plant Folks to water them and talk to them."

"Yes, please."

They tiptoed down the winding carpeted stairs to avoid the clatter Equuleus' feet made upon the marble when he flew down, then sneaked along the hall toward Father Inventor's room. They passed the dining room, and, amusingly, she saw Lady Gervi, Yippie, the two children, and Violet all sound asleep—or whatever passed for sleep for them—jumbled up in a cozy pile, by the sparkling fire.

Creeping along, they listened to the myriad sounds coming from the other side of the door leading to Heart's very near and dramatic future. She turned and hugged Equuleus fervently. They exchanged unspoken endearments, then Heart breathed deeply.

Equuleus tiptoed quietly backwards, while Heart shape-shifted into a clone of the door. She opened it the smallest crack she could to let herself through, and closed the door upon her very heart.

Incredible activity swirled all around her. Relieved not to see her father, she knew he must be nearby. But the further she got without seeing him, the more likely her mission would succeed.

She paused, looking at the wall and then looking down at herself—yes, it appeared she successfully shape-shifted into this dark wall, as she stole along it. Then she realized she'd better bring the map Equuleus shared with her to mind, to be sure of the location of Xavier's spacecraft from where she now stood.

Once inside, it came very clear. She was relieved that it was near the front of the work area and not buried within the "rabbit warren," where she would not be able to go. She crept along the wall for some distance, the map moving with her. She found herself before the gargantuan partial moon.

The mind map highlighted—she only needed to make a right angle turn, head for the partial moon, and find a tunnel right below the middle of it. If she succeeded, she'd be home free. Mechanical folks dashed to and fro, carrying who-knew-what, calling to one another.

Heart turned, trusting her shape-shifting to go through several rapid changes, and dashed for the tunnel, which she could not physically see at all.

She ran, *smack!* into a wall. She stopped and considered what surrounded her, then saw the tunnel a little to her left. She hurried through it, coming out on a landing. There before her, in the darkness, stood Xavier's gorgeous little spacecraft in all its glory. Forgetting about shape-shifting, she walked along the landing, stopping short in her tracks by what she saw emblazoned on the side in big red letters: *Heart!*

She couldn't—or shouldn't—be surprised, but, it stopped her. Well, she thought, it would be all right on Earth, as young guys often named their vehicles.

She returned to the urgency of the moment, when she heard Xavier, and her father in his bell jar, coming down the tunnel she'd just exited. Shape-shifting into the landing, she ran down the stairs and dashed to the spacecraft, then scurried through the open hatch inside. Once there, she relaxed and brought up Equuleus's map of where she might hide. The map showed a spot right beside her, where sat the giant box of candy, tidily strapped in. *Excellent!* She could use the strap to tie herself down. Quickly untying the box, she wished with all her might she could, just this once, shape-shift something *else!*

Should she leave the box and take her chances the weight increase would not be noticed, or ought she step back out with the box? She could see Xavier and her father—they paused on the landing in front of the spacecraft, chatting. Xavier gestured and waved at his pride and joy, the *"Heart!"*

Heart decided to creep out the back hatch with the box of candy, hoping to deposit it anywhere it wouldn't be noticed until after the *Heart!* had taken off. She spied another flight of stairs to the landing, which would have to suffice. Quickly stuffing the box under the stairs, she rushed back into the spacecraft and hunkered down in the hidey-hole, tying herself with the strap attached to the wall the best she could and trying to relax.

"Travel safely and come back soon," Her father called to Xavier.

"I will!" Xavier answered, now just outside. He stepped inside and pulled the hatch shut with a satisfying lock. His feet passed by her. She heard him pull on some sort of spacesuit, then flip controls and call out commands.

Rockets fired, a light filled the little ship and within moments, they'd zipped away from Pink flying out into the wild, wide open space.

She wanted badly to see the view of Pink and Earth—how beautiful it must be!

"*Whoooo-hooo-hooo!*" Xavier called out, confirming her suspicion. "*Soooooooo* indescribably amazing!"

How she wanted to see it! But she dared not move until turning the *Heart!* around would simply not be a practical option. Would he turn around if he knew she was there? Don't take the chance, she argued with herself. Instead, she sent Equuleus a picture of herself in her little candy corner.

He returned a message, *Good work, Heart. Violet is asking where you are!*

Keep it a secret for a while. I want to see the view so badly, I can taste it. But—I'd better lie low until we're too far to turn around.

I'm watching your flight—It's beautiful, beautiful, Heart. That little ship between Pink and Earth—spaceship Heart! Equuleus snorted.

I know. Be quiet, it's not funny.

Equuleus became serious. *No, it's not funny, Heart. It's perfect.*

* *

When Heart felt certain they'd reached the point of no return, she began to unwind herself from her bindings. She stood slowly, looking out in awe at the nearing Earth before her.

Earth!

"*Ahhhhuuuu—nooooo!*" Xavier suddenly cried, turning in his seat to stare at her.

Equally surprised, Heart jumped back and shrieked.

"Where did you come from?" he yelled at the same moment she hollered, "How did you see me?"

He pointed at the viewport, "I saw movement in the reflection."

"Oh, yeah," Heart nodded, calming down. "I thought I'd faint with you screeching at me."

"*You* faint? *ME* faint! What—what—what are you doing here?"

"Going for a ride." Heart made a sweeping gesture to Earth, "Taking in the scenery."

"This is not a joy ride, Heart. What am I supposed to do with you? I have to be focused. I have important things to do."

"I know that. I have to stay focused too, and I have important things to do, too. Not as important as your mission, not by a long ways. But important, all the same."

All the while, anxious calls to Xavier from Pink, poured into the *Heart!,* asking why he yelled.

"I have a stowaway. I'll get back to you." He clicked the connection off.

"Seriously, Heart, this is not good. There's only one being in all of the Universe who can take me off my game, and that's you. I can't think of anything I'd rather do right now than turn back and kick you out. Without the benefit of landing, I might add."

"Very nice. So caring. Indeed, you clearly have a high regard for me." Heart answered sarcastically.

"You know what I'm saying." He studied his instruments and the Earth for a few moments as if he truly contemplated turning around.

"No, Xavier. You are not going to turn around."

"If I am, I must do it immediately."

"You are not. As you say yourself, you have a mission to complete. If you care even a little about me—though, granted, you don't actually know who I am—but when I tell you why I'm going to Earth, you'll be supportive."

"I'm listening."

"Do you know about my best, life-long friend? ...."

"Eye, of course. There isn't anyone who knows about you, who doesn't know about Eye."

"Then you know—and you should have known!—any opportunity to go to Earth, I would be there. Or ... here, as it happens."

"Yes." Xavier nodded. "Yes. You're right. I ought to have known you would do everything in your power to be on any flight to Earth. Because that's *who you are*. And you love Eye, and you want to see him. Of course. Because—you love Eye."

"Yes, I know that. You needn't repeat it."

"Well, I'm just thinking. If you were on Earth, and if you loved me, and an opportunity came for me to go to Earth to see you, I'd do anything. If you loved me."

"I'm glad you understand."

"Why didn't I know that before? Why didn't Father Inventor know that?"

"I don't know. But now you do, and now he will too."

Xavier moved his hand away from the controls. "All right. You're on the joy ride. Come what may. Please *do* break my heart, Heart, by getting hurt, or incarcerated or ... oh, goodness, I must not think about all the things that can go wrong."

"No. Don't. Let's not put any energy into negative thoughts. We must stay focused. Why not stay positive? That's the outcome we want, that's the picture we need to have."

"Right. Agreed." He clicked the connection to Pink back on. "Xavier to Pink ...."

Heart's father interrupted him. "Heart! What are you thinking? *What are you thinking?*"

"Hello Father," Heart answered, so calm, she surprised herself. "You know what I'm thinking. Or, anyway, the gist of it."

"This is very selfish, Heart. And dangerous. Xavier does not need the distraction of you there ...."

"We've just been discussing that. We've agreed to stay focused, each upon our own mission. Xavier understands that by not being distracted by me, he has the highest and best opportunity to protect me. You know, full well, Father, I have my own agenda. I must have a long talk with Swen—which we never had. And, of course ...."

"You must see Eye," he interrupted.

"Though it will be very painful to see him and to have to leave, yes, I must see Eye."

"But Heart ..." her father paused. "I don't know ...." A strange hesitation came into his voice, "I don't know ... just come back as soon as you can, Heart ...."

"I will, Father. Xavier has been lecturing me on the subject of danger. As I said to him, let us focus on the positive outcomes we're going to Earth to accomplish. *Do not worry*. Now, Xavier and I must plan. We have but a short while to sort out who will be where, when. I must save the rest of your reprimand for when I return. I love you!"

Heart retreated to her little cubby hole to think and to plan, while her father and Xavier continued talking, if they needed. She didn't even want to hear their conversation.

"Heart," Xavier called a few moments later. "Come here."

"More reprimand?"

"No. More beauty. Just—come and appreciate the view. It's sheer joy to share this with you."

Heart moved to the front of the spacecraft. Glistening, sparkling, glittering, Earth, with its Dark Energy Highways its brilliant lighting, its sparkling waters, its floating clouds—the dark and the light as they passed from night to early dawn, the pink orange gold glow a vast bed of pillows waiting for them to plunge into.

"*Oh!*" Heart signed. "Is there any place so beautiful in all the Universe? Home. Home, Xavier."

"Ummm ...." Xavier answered, noncommittally.

Heart tore her gaze from the sight and looked over at Xavier.

"What is that strange response?"

"Well, I guess I think of Pink as my home."

"Really!? Did you not come from Earth?"

"Ahm ... ye-es. I mean, mostly."

"Strange answer."

"I know. But now is not the time to go into it. First things first. Tell me your basic plan, and let's sort out our logistics."

"Yes. We must."

Chapter 15

They rapidly sketched out an overall plan for the entire trip, with a variety of back up scenarios for possible events gone awry. Xavier even gave Heart basic instruction on how to fly the *Heart!* should such a dire circumstance arise.

Heart, who'd never driven or flown anything—other than riding Equuleus, of course—wanted to immediately take over the controls.

"No, Heart. Let's not risk falling out of the sky."

"Oh, all right. But soon, Xavier, you'll let me fly the *Heart!* sometime soon, will you not? I'm a natural, having logged many miles on Equuleus, including a trip from Earth to Pink!"

"Yes, very true. We'll see. As you've said yourself, 'one step at a time.'"

Eventually, the gravity of Earth began to tug upon them, a peculiar shock to Heart, feeling again the intense-yet-familiar gravity. "Whoa! Feel heavy!"

"Yep. You'll be fine in a short while. It'll all come back to you."

"Good to know!"

As they approached, they came into the dark of night. Heart watched Xavier flip a number of switches.

"What are you doing?"

"I'm turning on the dark highway lights. Now the *Heart!* looks like any other Dark Energy Highway vehicle. Granted, you're not quite as popular as before you defected to Pink."

"Humph!"

"Ah Heart, you'll always be number one with me."

"Anyway, I didn't 'defect' as such. I, you know, saved my life, and Equuleus's life."

"I know that. Don't get ruffled."

"Telling someone not to get ruffled is a good way to make someone feel ruffled."

"I did not know that," Xavier said, intent upon his controls. "Ah, there! Now we're on the Dark Energy Highway!"

"Well done, Xavier! Well done!"

"Now, my little stowaway, you sit. By the way, where did you hide yourself?"

Heart pointed her thumb over her shoulder. "Back there, where that big box was." Now, she knew, the boom would really be lowered.

"Where the big box *was*?"

"Um-hum."

"Where is it now?"

"Under the stairs to the landing where the *Heart!* sat."

"Arg! My treasure of candy? You jettisoned my candy? Why?"

"Because I thought you might notice my weight. So I got rid of the handiest thing with some significant weight."

"I did my final check of the *Heart!* just before going to say good-bye to Father Inventor. I would not have known."

"That's all right. It'll be there when you get back. A nice reward for your success."

"If it *is* there when I get back!"

"Oh! Look, Xavier! The Museum of Scientific Improbabilities and Unpredictable Oddities!"

He turned his attention back to his trajectory. "Yes. Now, will you please sit! I don't anticipate any problems, but standing is not an option."

Heart sat in the co-pilot's seat beside him strapping herself in, and a few moments later, the *Heart!* came to a smooth landing. She heard the familiar clang of the gates opening, and even—*yes!* the *ching-a-ling* of Key Man's keys.

"*Oh! Oh!*" Heart whispered softly. Was it even possible to feel like this?

Xavier remotely opened the back hatch and, disengaging himself from his seat, moved toward the back.

"Xavier! My lad, so good to see you! We've been waiting for you, come on, come on."

"I dare say you're not aware my stowaway."

"Stowaway?"

"Yes. Father Inventor would not have wanted any possibility of this leaking on the airwaves."

"Stowaway? Oh! Is it? ...."

Before he could say another word, Heart flew into his arms. "Heart!" he whispered. "*Oh, Heart! My Heart! Oh!*" Key Man, clearly so stunned, he could hardly move. But he rapidly gathered himself. "*Come inside, quickly. Come inside! Come, Xavier, Come!*"

Putting his arms around both of them, he scurried them through the front door, then pushed the buttons and levers, causing the gates and doors to *slam, bang,* and *clang* shut against the outside world.

Heart heard several voices coming toward them. Familiar voices. She couldn't wait to see the expression on their faces.

Key Man dimmed the lights for an added cloaking feature.

"Why are the lights so dim, Key Man? Poor Xavier won't be able to see a thing!" Heart heard Martha ask.

"Yes, turn up the lights a bit, Key Man, let's provide a proper welcome ...." Peter agreed, then stopped mid-sentence. *"Martha, look! "It's ...."*

"Heart!" Martha whispered, running toward her.

"Oh! Martha!" Heart reached out her arms and enfolded her beloved friend to her, while Peter rushed up to get in on the hugging. Key Man joined them, and Xavier stood by, watching proudly as if he had master-minded the whole scenario.

"Come over here, Xavier," Martha insisted. You're part of this hug!"

"Oh, all right. If I must!" He grinned as he ambled to the group and flung his arms around all of them.

After they satisfied the needs of their first hug, they headed down the dark hall to Peter's room. There a simple but sweet repast of cheese, sliced apples, bread, and tea awaited the planned arrival of Xavier.

Everyone settled into a spot. And then, everyone began talking at once. Heart grinned like her face would leap off in glee and jump up and down of its own accord.

"Oh, Heart!" Key Man, who insisted on sitting next to her, said simply, taking her hand.

"Key Man!" Heart answered back. The intensity and sweetness of their simple statements made everyone giggle. And then, for absolutely no reason other than sheer joy, the giggle grew and grew until it became a loud guffaw. It went around and around in waves. Just as it seemed it would quiet down, it rose again.

Heart felt she might burst with so much love and being loved.

With one exception.

Right at that moment, a knock at the door caused everyone to fall silent. Peter looked at the door scanner on his wrist. "Wonderman One and Wonderman Two!"

He jumped up and answered the door.

Wonderman One and Wonderman Two were, of course, too large to readily pass through the door, let alone be in the crowded room, but they stood at the door with their gear grins and sparkling gear eyes spinning. "We saw you, Heart! We don't want to disturb your welcome, but we just had to say hello!"

Heart went to them and gave them a gigantic hug. "It's fantastic to see you. You know I've met ...."

"We know! You're living with our counterparts," Wonderman Two said. Or was it Wonderman One?

"I am!" Heart looked back into the room as if it had magically enlarged with her back turned. "I'm sorry you can't come in. I really wish you could join us."

"That's all right. We only need to say hi."

"Before Xavier came, my father put on an amazing dinner for Xavier and some of the Clockworks and Mechanical Folks, and Wonderman One and Wonderman Two on Pink began to dance. They danced, and juggled beautiful, brightly-colored candy,"

"Auggh!" Xavier cried, in the background. "My lost candy!"

Heart chuckled. "Never mind him. Anyway, they danced an amazing dance, and called out in some strange and ancient language ...."

"Gearian," the Wondermen said in unison.

"Gearian? I've never heard it before. They called to one another in this language, and soon everyone danced and called out in this strange language, including me ...."

"It's true," Xavier interjected again, "she was dancing—what a beautiful sight!"

"I don't know what I was saying but it made me feel ... so companionable."

The Wondermen nodded, gears rotating. "Yes, yes. Oh, lovely, we would have loved to have seen it!"

"I'll send you the 3-D."

"Thank you, Heart. Thank you. Well, we won't bother your welcome anymore. Just—so glad to see you!" They backed in perfect unison away from the door.

Heart stepped out into the dark hall and watched them clank and grind and hum down the hall, a fluorescence of their own coming off them, leaving a trail.

She stepped back inside, grinning, but, with a twinge of sadness and mystification.

"He's in Key Man's rooms," Martha said.

Heart looked at her gratefully. "And?"

"Well," Key Man picked up the conversation, "he told us you were coming, and we said, no, Father Inventor would never let you come ...."

"Harumph!" Heart interjected.

"That's pretty much what he said. He knows you better than anyone—besides Eye, of course. But we simply refused to believe it, which we told him, relentlessly and directly."

"So when we knew Xavier would arrive tonight, he went to hang out in Key Man's rooms. He told us to leave him alone," Martha said.

"Because he didn't want to be wrong. He just couldn't stand to be there—and be wrong," Key Man clarified.

"I see." Heart stood, motionless, but filled with emotion.

"Go to him," Key Man said. "Go. The two of you can return. We have Xavier to entertain."

"Or to entertain you!" Xavier corrected.

"Or to be entertained," Key Man amended. "You can join us later."

Heart nodded, with a strange half-smile. She didn't know what she felt. She didn't know what she wanted. She didn't know what to expect, or what she would face. But—she *must* do it.

"Thank you! We'll be back in a bit." She went through the door and continued on down the long, long hall. She forgot to ask for a key. She didn't live in those rooms anymore. She might not be let in.

When she arrived at Key Man's familiar door, she knocked cautiously. No answer. Then she thought, Oh, no, you're not doing this to me! I've come from a moon to talk with you, endangering life and limb, and you very darn well will talk with me!

She knocked more forcefully while hearing a wry chuckle inside. "Hold onto your knuckles, girl!" from a dear—but at this moment, exasperating!—voice. The locks were thrown on the door, and it finally flung open.

“What’s the matter with you?” Heart growled.

“Hey, good hound imitation. Love you too!”

“*Oh!*” Heart simply sat right down where she was, and held her arms open. With no reluctance, Swen came into them. Heart buried her face in his neck. “What’s the matter with you? *What-is-the-mat-ter-with-you?!?*”

“You, Heart. You’re the matter with me,” Swen answered, snuggling closer.

“Oh, you’re just, you’re—*oh, Swen!*”

“I know, Heart. I know. Don’t cry.”

“Am I crying?”

“I think you’re about to, and you’ll rust my cogs.”

Heart giggled. “All right, I won’t cry. I’ll giggle ridiculously, instead.”

“Works for me.”

They bonded silently for a moment, then Heart whispered, “But—what happened? Why, *why* did you pull away from me before I left? Why have I not heard from you?”

“Well, Heart, I’m a dog. A brilliant, mechanical, bio, dark matter dog, but a dog, nonetheless. And dogs bond, Heart. It’s at our core. When I knew you must go to Pink—before *you* knew you must go to Pink—that is to say, you were either going to Pink, or ....”

“Destroyed ....”

“Yes. When I knew you must go to Pink—my most precious desire—because I’m not sure I would have survived the alternative, I had to pull away. I had to put my dog instincts elsewhere.”

“No one better than Key Man.”

“Truly no one better than Key Man. In so many ways. He loved me from the outset. And we shared our grief over our separation from you.”

Heart nodded. "Yes. Hard, hard separation."

"But you have Equuleus."

"I do. It's true."

"So, tonight, I felt you coming. I knew you would. They think they talked me out of my belief. But they didn't. I knew you were going to arrive. But I couldn't share you. Selfish dog that I am. If I was to see you when you came, it had to be …."

"Like this …."

"Like this."

"Oh, but, Swen, is seeing me now going to do you harm? I mean, your whole instinct issue, is that going to be hard?"

"Well, it won't be easy, but I am now bonded to Key Man. My life is good and meaningful. There continues to be all this turmoil on Earth. I wouldn't want you here permanently for anything. You're not planning on staying, are you?" He looked at her with his baleful hound dog eyes, worried.

"No, Swen. Just here briefly. To do this, to have this conversation. To know our love is *ever* here and *always* here. When I learned a spacecraft was coming to Earth, there was no choice but to come. To see you …."

"And to see Eye."

"And to see Eye. Much *muchmuchmuch* more complicated."

"Oh, yes. Much more complicated."

"Do you know anything about him? Is he all right?"

"He appeared on a 3-D news bit day before yesterday. He looked grand. He's grown. He's taller. He's muscular. He's beautiful."

"Oh no, Swen, you are truly going to make me cry, truly. You're going to make me cry."

"I'll change the subject and rattle on, while you let that picture sink in. Would you like to see the news bit?"

"Oh, I think I'd better not, not right at this moment."

"Agreed. I think you'd better not, too."

"Wouldn't it be lovely, though, to just forget everything, and the three of us simply go back through that tunnel to the other side, living in the beauty and simplicity of The Periphery? With day and night. You can't know how strange it is, Swen, to live where it's twilight all the time. Where you can move yourself into complete darkness or into total sunshine, but, for many pragmatic reasons, you live where it's never either.

"You have dinner, you have breakfast, you're awake, you lie down, It's all the same—twilight, twilight, twilight!"

"Oh," Swen nodded, "hard on you, *Girl of Light*."

"It *is* hard on me. But you're the only one I've told this to."

"Although Father Inventor knows it."

"In the same way, he knows everything about me, yes. But I've even worked at keeping my *thoughts* quiet about it because I don't want him thinking it's as big a thing to me as it is. He's got plenty on his mind, with all that's going on here."

"He does indeed, that's for sure. Plenty going on here."

"So I'm really going to enjoy this day and night while here. But still, it's tempting to go off to The Periphery ...."

"No argument, Heart. The beautiful Other Side, with its Beautiful People and creatures."

As if in response to their musings, the door, which stood ajar, flew open—and in walked Jackson.

Both Swen and Heart jumped to attention.

"Where did you come from?" Heart asked in shock.

"The Periphery," Jackson answered, shaking his head as if he couldn't believe how dense she could be.

"Yes, probably!" Heart answered indignantly. "A more accurate question, since you always need to split hairs is, *why are you here?*"

"I've been reading *Ourbook*, and understood that if anything came winging in from Pink, you'd be on it. Legitimately or otherwise. Probably otherwise, as no one on the other side has been given a heads up about your appearance."

"Except from *Ourbook*. For those who read it very carefully." Heart couldn't keep the sardonic edge out of her voice.

"Well, Heart, here you are."

"Hard to argue," Swen observed.

"Point made—I guess." Heart looked into Jackson's eyes, and as usual, it made her take a step backwards. Something about him simply *overwhelmed* her. "So, you thought I'd be here, and I'm here. But what are *you* doing here?"

"Thinking you could use some help. You're welcome."

"Again," Swen observed, "strong reasoning."

"Hmmm ...." Heart looked down at Swen. "Who's side ...."

"Yours, Heart. Always yours. Which is why the magic of Jackson appearing at this moment is perfect!"

Heart stood pensive for a moment, looking around her at the clockwork art and beings and inventions in various degrees of broken, disassembled, assembled. She only wanted things to be put back together, lovingly, thoughtfully. Who cared how it happened? And, further, wasn't she *GLAD* to see Jackson?

"Right. Right. *Right!* To be truthful, Jackson, I *am* glad to see you."

"That's more like it."

An awkward silence followed, which no one dared touch.

Heart had her hand on Swen's head. His eyes half closed, he looked like he might start purring.

"All right, then," Heart finally said, "let's get back to the others. I'm sure everyone will be delighted to see everyone else." Heart brushed past Jackson, and a shock of static electricity jumped between them that even Swen felt.

"*Whoa!*" Swen exclaimed.

"Hush," Heart admonished.

Chapter 16

They wordlessly walked down the hall to Peter's rooms. The door stood partially open and Heart walked in. "Look what I found," she said, opening the door wide.

Everyone gasped when Jackson came through the door.

"Why so much reaction? You've all seen me before. You act like you're seeing a ghos ...." He stopped flat in the middle of his sentence. "*Xavier!*" he whispered.

Xavier, in the far corner, jumped up and made his way through the tight maze. "Jackson! Wow, it's incredible to see you!"

"But you ...."

Heart saw Xavier shake his head ever so slightly, and Jackson stopped short. "But he what?" she asked.

"Nothing," Xavier said. "For all Jackson knew, I would never leave Pink."

"True," Jackson agreed. "Very, very true." He turned to Peter, "So you all knew about Xavier, and didn't ...."

"A need to know basis," Peter answered quietly.

"I see," Jackson said, equally quietly. "I just assumed it'd be a mechanical flying the spacecraft."

"Well, not only has Xavier left Pink," Heart said, "but he built his own spacecraft, with his own hands." She perceived an unspoken subtext in the room she didn't understand, and decided to leave it until after the missions were completed.

"Named the *Heart!* Yeah, I just saw it. I laughed thinking Heart had something to do with that."

"Oh, what do I even say to that?" Heart blurted. "For someone who's generally very bright, you completely fall between the cracks sometimes. If you think I would have anything to do with a spacecraft being named after me, you're very far from knowing me."

"I have to agree," Xavier said. "It's rather surprising you don't know her better, Jackson, for all the time you've spent together." Xavier eased himself a step closer to Heart.

"Very little actual time together," Jackson replied.

"Little real time together, it's true," Heart said. "But, apparently, plenty of time contemplating negative character traits to foist upon me."

"Why, Jackson?" Xavier asked.

"No, I haven't," Jackson protested. He looked from Xavier to Heart and back to Xavier again.

Heart watched as Jackson came to yet another conclusion. She was wildly curious to know what came into his mind, but, again, said nothing. Instead, she added, rather weakly as the steam had gone out of her argument, "Sure feels like a lot of critiquing from my perspective."

"Okay, kids," Peter said, standing, "there's only a little time to do a great many things. We're relieved and happy to see you, Jackson. Let's sit down and solidify plans."

"Excellent idea," Heart agreed, returning to her seat by Key Man, while Martha on her other side made room for Swen to sit on the floor by Heart. Peter pulled another chair from his bedroom, and Jackson sat across from Heart, while Xavier returned to his far corner.

Finally settled, they enjoyed the repast, while contributing to the development of the best plan of action for the looming events. All Heart needed to do at this point was see Eye.

Xavier's much more complicated mission involved strategically planting four magnetic dark energy devices, which, when turned on in tandem with their counterparts on Pink's and Yellow's new moons, would provide an impenetrable protective shield for Pink and Yellow.

"Ambitious plan," Jackson observed after they'd outlined it to him. "Ambitious, and impeccably beautiful. I'm in awe of Father Inventor's continuing fountain of genius."

"Which, of course, is the reason for this unanticipated race against time," Heart noted.

"Because the Purists have turned their back on their own deepest precepts, and have begun to use scientists to advance their cause against science?" Jackson asked.

"Even worse," Xavier pointed out. "It appears they may be accessing Father Inventor's brain clone, specifically to use against him."

Jackson shook his head in disgust. "It only took them a couple centuries to figure that out, but now, they're on it. Hypocrisy is a great device, once you allow yourself to employ it."

"Well," Heart added infuriated, "they have always been hypocrites, stating premises of love and kindness, except for 'these and those and the others' that they want to cease to exist."

"True," Jackson agreed. "Entirely too true, Heart."

"Although we'll probably never rid the world of prejudice and inequality, we can do our best," Peter observed.

"And pray that love finds a home in the center of every being," Martha added.

"Yes. That is our prayer," Xavier added in prayerful tones.

Everyone nodded in silent agreement.

"All right now, let's get down to it," Jackson stood, then sat back down as the crowded space did not allow him to move about. "I'll take Heart to the Darling Undesirables Facility at Long Prairie in a museum vehicle, while you, Xavier, place your magnetic dark energy resonators."

"All right," Xavier nodded. "But let's travel in tandem, just in case either of us runs into any difficulty. I already intended to place one of the resonators near there."

"Excellent! I agree, there's safety in numbers. Is there anything you need, Heart, once you're there?"

"No. I'll shape-shift from the back wall to Eye's residence building, then to his room. I hope I can do that much shape-shifting."

"*Oh!*" Xavier said, insight dawning. "*Right!* That's how you got to my spacecraft without being observed!"

"Yes. Fortunately, no one came through that space while I scurried along. But I don't know if I completely shape-shifted. I—I—oh, *what do I think I'm doing?*"

Martha reached across the table and grabbed Heart's hands, "You're doing what you must do. You must look in on Eye. You have to be able to make plans that manifest his future, and you can't get clear until you see him—if only for moments—to become centered, to move forward."

Heart looked gratefully into Martha's eyes. "That's it. I need to see him simply because I *need to see him*. The way I left ... stealing away in the night. I've felt horrible and guilty, although I didn't quite realize it." She squeezed Martha's hands. "It all comes crashing in on me now. I'm confused. But the confusion will not clear as long as there's this void, this guilt."

She stood. "Let's go. We can't be stalling because of my lack of clarity. I've made all of you take actions, and I've moved all of your lives by being here. I must at least stand by my choices!"

"Right!" Jackson stood too. "Let's get going!"

"I'll get a museum vehicle and take it around to the front by Xavier's spacecraft," Peter said. Peter went ahead of the group into the dark recesses of the hall, the little lights along the edges of the floor turning on as he moved.

"Will you come with us, Swen?" Heart asked.

"I hoped you'd ask! You know I want to."

"I'm glad. Not only do I want to spend every minute with you I can in this bizarre scene, but I can use your particular wall crossing skills to help me get inside the grounds."

"My paws are your paws," Swen said, standing for a moment on his hind feet and clicking his front claws together.

Everyone quietly chuckled as they made their way to the front of the museum.

"Let's check our communicators and make sure we have contact," Jackson said to Xavier. "I don't want to use the system on board the museum vehicle."

"Good idea, Jackson," Xavier agreed. "The museum's communication is, indeed, hooked up into that of the megalopolis."

While Xavier and Jackson made sure their devices had clear communication, Heart and Martha and Key Man shared quick and quiet hugs.

"Be careful, my dear Heart," Key Man whispered in her ear.

"I'll be back, don't worry."

The museum vehicle sidled up next to the *Heart!* Swen, Jackson, Xavier then Heart, stepped out into the sparkling night air and hurried to the vehicles. Heart and Jackson strapped themselves into the front seats of the museum vehicle while Swen climbed into the back.

"It's been a long while since I've been on a dark energy craft," Swen said, fumbling with the safety strap.

Heart turned to see what all the scrabbling was about. "Here, let me help you." She unhooked herself and turned to click Swen's safety strap into place.

Turning around she saw Jackson impatiently waiting for her to get settled. She looked across at Xavier, he grinned and gave her a little wave. She latched her safety strap.

Thank goodness, he didn't wink! She thought. She didn't need *that* distraction at the moment.

She'd brought a tiny 3-D camera the size of her pinky fingernail to place somewhere where she could watch over Eye, and see what went on around him—if anything did. She hoped that, with no duo of "Heart and Eye," the world did not find Eye, by himself, as interesting. She checked her pocket where the little camera hid. She would be Eye's eyes again, at least a little bit. She'd be able to watch over him to a small degree, trusting that would make her feel better at times when she wondered how he fared.

They'd pulled onto the Dark Energy Highway without a word, each of them deep in thought about the mission at hand. Each would have their role, and it needed to be orchestrated perfectly.

She couldn't resist looking over at Jackson.

"What?"

"Just wondering what you're thinking."

"What do you think I'm thinking?"

"I don't know!" Surprised, Heart realized she really did not know what he might be thinking. His look came across as particularly impenetrable and stern. "You look angry."

"I'm not angry."

"Right!" Swen said from the back. "This is your happy face!"

"It's not my happy face, either," Jackson answered.

"That's good to know," Heart said sarcastically. "I wasn't sure. I asked myself, 'is this Jackson's happy face?' *Hmmmm* ... not sure."

"Can we just save the chatter for later, after we've completed our mission?"

Heart turned away from Jackson and looked back at Swen, making a wry face. "Right, oh *capitan!*" Heart saluted dramatically.

Swen chortled uncontrollably, but Jackson didn't even crack the imitation of a smile.

Shaking her head in near-disgust, Heart fell silent. Well, Jackson was right. She did need to concentrate and keep her focus.

After all, she could very well be walking right into a situation where she would be captured and kept at The Darling Undesirables Residence of Long Prairie for the foreseeable future. Or worse. If the Purists decided to lose what tiny fragment of mind they had left, opting to destroy all the Darling Undesirables Facilities everywhere ... she chose to stop that thought right in its tracks. She looked over to nod at Xavier, but faced a stranger.

"Where? ...."

Jackson pointed a thumb over his shoulder and Heart turned. The *Heart!* followed them.

"Behind us. Of course, that makes sense."

She relaxed into the ride as much as she could, trying not to remember the last time she'd taken this particular journey, when Keeper A tore her from the side of Equuleus and then put Eye in the sensory deprivation chamber.

She shuddered. Horrible, *horrible* experience, feeling Eye almost lose his mind in the sensory deprivation chamber, an experience as devastating to Eye as the vile and unspeakable bots were to her.

Oh, goodness—a lot had happened since then!

In silence, they arrived at The Darling Undesirables Residence of Long Prairie. The two vehicles put down on the edge of a treed field nearby, with a quiet conversation between Jackson and Xavier.

But Heart couldn't listen to them. Just seeing the dark outline of the place she'd called home for most her life—well, not "home" exactly—the place that posed as home—caused a riot of emotion in her over which she needed to gain control. It would not serve to be overwhelmed by thoughts of her past—abused by some of the Keepers and adored by others. Where the best moments of her life were in quiet reverie by Eye's side, tending to their flowers.

Where the beautiful-but-terrifying Keeper A ruled with an iron hand.

Here she was, in a dark energy vehicle, after having successfully run away from all the pain inside those walls, about to go back inside.

Jackson unlatched his safety strap as the doors slid open. "Ready?" he asked, finally looking at her.

"No. But I must be. Jackson, I realize you're stern and efficient. And I know you only mean for all this to go perfectly. But—it would have been nice if you'd given me some encouraging words. I know, I know, it's outside your range. But it would have been ... *nice.*"

"I thought we brought the dog for that."

"I very much beg your pardon," Swen protested, thrashing again with his safety strap.

Heart released herself, turned around and unclipped Swen's safety strap. "Well, you pretty much put a silencer on that, didn't you?"Her ire began to rise, as seemed *always* to happen with Jackson. Really—he could be so *thick!* at times.

"Really, you can be so *thick* at times." She got out of the vehicle. "Come on, Swen." She stomped off across the field toward the back wall of The Darling Undesirables Residence of Long Prairie.

"It's all right, Heart," Swen said, running alongside her. "He's sort of a first class jerk. Brilliant, true. Anyway, don't think about that right now. Let's keep our minds on the wonderful thing that's about to happen. You're going to see Eye! For the first time since you and I slipped away that night.

"Heart, you're going to see Eye!"

Heart stopped in her tracks, got down on her knees and threw her arms around Swen. "That's right, my dearest friend. I'm going to see Eye. Why would I let myself be distracted by—*anyone?!"*

Jackson came up to the two of them and pulled Heart up off the ground. "I'm sorry," he said gruffly. "Heart, I'm sorry. I know a lot of things, but my social skills—well, I don't have any. I behaved hatefully because I'm afraid for you. I don't even know I'm doing it. Until you, guilelessly, say the truth. I have a lot—*a lot!*—going on in my mind. But that's no excuse. None whatsoever!"

Xavier came running up to them. "What's wrong? What's wrong, Heart? I saw you on the ground, are you hurt? Are you all right?"

True alarm reflected in Xavier's eyes in the dim night light.

"I'm fine, Xavier." She pulled herself away from Jackson. "I'm all right. Just a moment of emotion on my part. But I'm put all back together now. Let's get on our missions. I don't know how long I'll be, but I'll see you in a while here at our vehicles."

Xavier reached out and patted her shoulder. "It'll all be fine, Heart. Trust your instincts. They are remarkable. You don't need to second guess them, and you *do* need to see Eye. That's all, right now. Just see Eye." He gave her a big hug. "A hug for strength, Heart. Take my strength, take everything I've got, and go fulfill this moment's destiny."

Heart nodded. "Thank you, Xavier. I will take your bravery, thank you!" She turned, and Swen, trotting close beside her, moved across the field to the row of houses between herself and the back fence, that she needed either to climb over or crawl under.

When she got to it she turned to Swen. "Over or under?"

"Under, Heart. Easier and more cloaked. Just give me a few minutes. If I can sort out where I dug the tunnel the last time—an excellent spot, lots of coverage." He sniffed up and down the fence for several feet in both directions, finally coming to a stop. "Here we go!" He started to dig furiously.

"Surely there's not still any scent after all this time."

"Not so much," his muffled reply came back. "But the earth is softer here. Going to be a fast job," Swen's body had already half disappeared under the fence.

Jackson came up. "Oh! I thought you'd probably go over!"

"As Swen points out, there's more cover this way. Plus he found the tunnel he dug last time, so, as you can see, he's almost done."

Right then, Swen backed out of the hole. "All righty, dear Heart, you're all set! In you go!"

She took a huge breath, then crawled down into the little tunnel under the fence. In seconds she emerged on the other side. "Perfect, Swen!" she whispered between the slats of wood in the fence. See you in a while."

"Be careful, Heart," she heard Jackson whisper hoarsely. "Please be careful!"

She nodded, fully realizing Jackson couldn't "hear" a nod, but unable to respond to the uncharacteristic emotion in his voice.

Was he really that afraid for her? Was this really so dangerous?

Was the moon round? Did birds fly? *Of course* this was terrifically dangerous.

But she would do it.

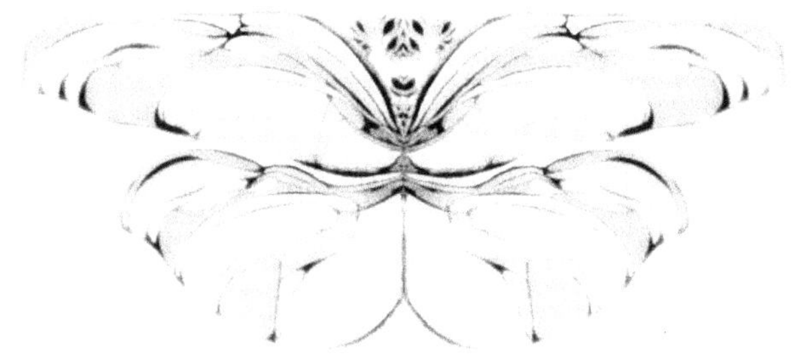

CHAPTER 17

She stood, recalling the locations of the 3-D cameras, pausing while she shape-shifted into her immediate surroundings. Yes, it felt like a good cover. She moved from the fence to the sidewalk, remembering her chat with Eye about the different kinds of grass on either side of the walkway. She shape-shifted to the grasses and the trees, at last coming to Eye's residence building.

She shape-shifted into the stonework of the building and went around to the rarely used side door, hoping it remained unlocked. It was. Creeping up the stairs, slinking along the wall, avoiding the cameras, she came to the second floor. She must now look like the hall, with its intermittent pale lights. She concentrated with all her being and scurried down the hall, turned the corner, and now ....

Now she stood in front of two doors—the right one, the door to Eye's room, the left one, the door to her previous room.

She wondered, superficially, who lived in her room now. Who had the wonderful advantage of her star dome? She hoped it was someone who loved it at least a little bit.

She felt stuck. Fear ran through her. Suddenly she realized she forgot entirely to shape-shift. Had she fallen out? At least she wasn't standing right in front of a 3-D camera. She concentrated on shape-shifting, and, when she felt fully engaged, she took a deep breath and stepped forward.

She put her hands on Eye's door, her ear to its surface. She heard nothing. Not even the least sound of breathing. Slowly, cautiously, she turned the knob and opened the door a crack. She could see Eye's desk, the few little things upon it, things that gave him lovely tactile sensations, so she knew it remained Eye's room.

She opened the door a bit further, seeing more of Eye's things, as sparse as the room was, overall. She opened the door enough to slip into the room.

Eye's bed, neatly made, stood empty!

Where was he? Heart's breath came short. Could this be a trap, set expressly for her? Keeping Eye's room just the same, but removing him altogether? She felt frantic. What would she do now? She knew she must find him, *now!* She might even send Jackson and Swen and Xavier off, and stay to find Eye. Xavier had to keep in motion. Even Eye was not more important than her father's work at the moment. Pink depended on Xavier to accomplish his mission.

She might never return to Pink!

She took a moment to tiptoe to Eye's closet—all his clothes hung neatly, as always, organized by fibers and textures. The bathroom door stood ajar, with everything neatly in its precise location.

Besides all of his things, Heart could feel Eye's presence. It really did seem he still occupied his room. Where would he go, in the middle of the night? He'd never left his room in the night. Except, of course, to come next door and chat with her.

Heart slinked stealthily as a black cat at midnight back through the door and into the hall. She pulled the door shut, thinking, wondering. Although a terrible invasion of privacy, she *had* to see who occupied her room. Guarded, she dared to attempt to open the door. It slid gracefully open without a sound.

There, under the delicate moonlight shining down through the star dome, peacefully slept Eye—with Butterfly, her arm protectively around his shoulders. Heart stifled a gasp. Then she dared to step inside, looking down upon them.

Eye moved about in his deep sleep, *"Heart!"* he muttered. Butterfly, in her sleep, instinctively wrapped her delicate little fairy arm more closely around him.

Heart turned and left the room, closing the door behind her with a soft *click!* she stepped across the hall, retrieved the little 3-D camera from her pocket, and attached it invisibly along the top of the doorframe opposite, so it focused on the door to her previous room. Now she could learn if Eye was being watched. She could see him from time to time.

Yes, it shocked her to see him utterly relaxed with Butterfly's arm wrapped around him. But, strangely, it didn't bother her like she thought it might. That would be selfish. Looking at her own emotions, she discovered that she simply loved Eye, and she longed for his safety and his happiness.

She retraced her steps as quickly as she dared—down the hall, down the stairs, out the door, across the yard—and soon stood at the back wall. She crawled through the tunnel where stood Swen and Jackson, looking anxious.

"Thank the Powers," Swen whispered.

"Let's get outta here," Jackson added in a troubled whisper, grabbing Heart's hand and rushing toward the spacecraft, Swen loping along with them.

"What's—*slow down!*—What's going on?"

"Keep moving," Jackson ordered. They rushed up to the vehicles. Xavier, already in the *Heart!* gave a visible sigh of relief as Swen, Heart, and Jackson clambered aboard the museum vehicle.

Engines purred to life. "You go first," Xavier said over Jackson's communication device. "I'll follow in a couple minutes. We don't want to attract attention by taking off together."

"Right." Jackson flew low in the field, away from The Darling Undesirables Residence of Long Prairie, then continued to hover close to the tree line for some distance. He finally took to the sky, up and up, until he made his way onto the Dark Energy Highway.

"All right, now then, will you kindly tell me what is going on?" Heart asked.

"Keeper A," Jackson said.

"What about Keeper A?" At the very mention of her, anxiety washed over Heart.

Swen took over the conversation while Jackson concentrated on his maneuvering, eagle-eyed in every direction. "She came out and wandered around on the grounds. She came to the back fence. She didn't see the tunnel, which seems strange.

"Then she walked along the side of the building. She stopped at that little door you went into. But she didn't go in. She went along the side of the building and around the corner—we could only assume she would go upstairs, where you went. There was nothing else for her to do but go into the building.

"Then you appeared through the tunnel. By the way, great shape-shifting. I nearly jumped out of my hide when you popped up under the fence. I looked for you so hard! For sure I looked right at you through the crack in the fence."

"Yeah. Great shape-shifting. Invisible!" Jackson agreed.

"Keeper A came out in the middle of the night, wandered around the grounds, followed where I went, and let me leave?" Heart said, stunned.

"So it appears. If that's a coincidence, it's an amazing coincidence," Jackson said.

"No coincidence, Jackson. With her scent implants, she absolutely knew I was there." Anxiety mounted in Heart. "*Oh!* What does this mean?" Then another onslaught of fear rose up. "What might it mean for Eye?"

"Did you see him, Heart," Swen asked excitedly. "Did you see Eye?"

Clicking and clacking came from the seat behind her. Heart released her safety strap and turned around to help Swen engage his. "Yes, Swen, I saw him." She reengaged her safety strap. "He ... I saw him."

"I guess you didn't talk with him," Jackson said.

"No. I didn't talk with him."

"But everything is fine with him?" Swen asked. "In his little beddy-bye, and all's well in Eye's world?"

"No. He wasn't in his beddy-bye. He slept in *my* beddy-bye. With Butterfly." Heart giggled a bit hysterically. "That rhymes all over the place."

Swen joined her giggle-fest. "It does! My Beddy-bye with Butterfly." But then Swen stopped, abruptly. "But, Heart, how did that make you feel?"

Jackson looked over at her as if joining his interest to Swen's.

"Shocked, of course. Shocked on several levels. That they were together in my little bed, yes. But the second shock was that—that they're getting away with it. Surely there are keepers who know about it."

"Maybe it was just tonight ...." Swen suggested.

"No. There was something so ... so ... *comfortable* between them. So obvious that this is their habit. The truth is, I don't know if there's anything in Darling Undesirables rules about such an event. You know, most Darling Undesirables don't live to be old enough for it to be a concern. In fact, there may be specific permission, such as 'Darling Undesirables may be put to bed together for comfort and companionship,' like, having a teddy bear.

"Anyway, no, I didn't feel bad. Seeing the sweetness between them, and to know Eye has eyes to help him through his day, is a great relief. Maybe that's why the Keepers are allowing it. Because they know what Eye had to go through with my sudden disappearance. He does need someone near him. In fact, it's a lot less work for them if they don't have to be overseeing him all the time."

While Heart talked, she replayed what Swen said—that Keeper A wandered around the grounds in the middle of the night. She had never, *ever* heard of, or seen, Keeper A wander about at night. Or, in truth, any other time. She had her own amazing and fragrant garden to wander through. She had a host of Keepers and grounds workers to check things out, at her beck and call.

So why, *WHY?* would she be wandering about, alone, in the night?

Keeper A *must* have known she was there—but didn't do anything. Just let her go. "I've lost track of Xavier, is he nearby?"

"Yeah. He's three vehicles behind us." Jackson poked a finger in the rear 3-D.

"Ask him if he could see our vehicles every minute we were there."

"Because?"

"If he saw anyone walking about who might have seen our landing and the three of us rushing up to the fence, who might have reported us, and Keeper A put a tail on us. Because I can't wrap my mind around why she would let me go."

"Right." Jackson flipped on the communication device on his wrist. "Xavier—you there?"

"Right behind ya!"

"Burning question here—were our vehicles in your sight the entire time we were absent?"

"Yes, but for a few brief seconds. I get what you're driving at. I saw no one."

Heart broke in, "I know we'd planned to go back and reconnoiter first, but, Xavier, if you have the ability to complete your plans—and I'm being circumspect now, because, I don't trust *anything*, but you know what I'm saying—I think you'd better complete your plans."

"Right. Got it. I'm on it. See you later."

"There he goes," Jackson said.

"It's very, very odd, is it not?" Heart asked.

"Everything on this side of *The Wall* is very, very strange to me. An entirely foreign world. I'm quite content in The Periphery."

"I know you are, Jackson, for good reason. Decent people, with a thoughtful lifestyle, enjoying every moment, taking care of one another. Bucolic and lovely."

"Not without its challenges."

"Every life has challenges, Jackson."

"True. Very true. Very ...." Jackson appeared to become lost in thought.

"What are you thinking about? I mean, where did you go, there—something else came to mind."

"Yes. But for some reason, I guess I'm not supposed to mention it. I don't understand, I really don't."

"Oh *will* you kindly stop babbling, and either make your point or be quiet so I can sort out what's going on." Heart shook her head in frustration. "*Sheesh!* When I want you to talk, you won't utter a syllable. When I don't want you to talk, you babble up an incoherent storm."

"I think he's referring to Xavier," Swen said quietly.

"What about Xavier?"

"He's head over heels in love with you," Jackson said plainly.

"First of all, don't say that. Second of all, *he* has already said it. I didn't want to hear it from him, and I don't want to hear it from you!"

"Does that make it untrue?"

"True, untrue. I don't know. Not what I can afford to be thinking about right now." Heart fumed, looking out the side window. Then she found herself wondering what she was even fuming about. "Anyway, it's just some crazy childhood infatuation. He's no more in love with me than you are."

"Right," Jackson said.

"Oh, Heart, you make his point beautifully." Swen started giggling again. "Great show everyone, big fun! Thanks! *Tee-hee!*"

"Hush, you," Heart uttered in an unmistakable don't-mess-with-me tone.

Swen clamped his jaw shut with a clack.

"But there is something—strange, or—different about Xavier that I can't quite place," Heart mused. "There's something in his presence I've never encountered before. I mean, well, I have, with a few Darling Undesirables who were very delicate. Which Xavier is decidedly not. He's tough and solid. So I can't quite place what I'm picking up on." Heart paused. "Do you have any idea what I'm talking about?"

"I have every idea what you're talking about," Jackson answered. "I ... I'm stymied, though, why he didn't want me to mention the amazing thing about him back there in Peter's rooms, I don't know."

"You and he didn't really talk directly. You just made some plans, and next thing, we're here. So, what communication?"

"Yes. Well. I don't know if you noticed my shock at seeing him."

"Shock? No. Surprise, yes." Heart thought back on the moment when Jackson saw Xavier in Peter's rooms. "If that was shock, Jackson, I have to take your word for it. You know, you're not the most expressive person I've ever known."

"I know. I know. But I felt shocked. I'm not sure what I'm betraying by telling you about him, if any-thing. For some reason, though, I feel compelled to do so." But then, Jackson stopped talking.

"Carry on!" Heart insisted.

"I'm still thinking through why he might not want me to tell you. There's a lot I don't know."

"And there's a lot *I* don't know. If you think I should know something, now is the moment, Jackson. We'll soon be back at The Museum of Scientific Improbabilities and Unpredictable Oddities, and the opportunity will be gone, because I'm pretty darn sure Xavier and I need to get back to Pink as soon as possible. This whole thing with Keeper A's behavior, *as you know!* has me very edgy."

"Right. I'll plunge forward. I think you may know a little about the battles waged against the people in The Periphery."

"Not really so much, no. The Darling Undesir-ables were only taught that The Periphery was dark and filled with evil. While the exact opposite is the truth. It's filled with light and love. Beautiful people and beautiful countryside."

"Yes. But we had to battle the Purists, even though we are out of everyone's way and minding our own business. So, one of the reasons the government boosted the dark energy charge in *The Wall*—that can, in fact, destroy you, Heart, because of your dark energy component—served to keep the Purists *out* as well as the residents in."

"Very interesting!"

"One battle a number of years ago was particularly fierce. This is the battle that, subsequently, brought about the augmented dark energy in *The Wall*. Anyway, Xavier and I fought in that battle. We were kids at the time. Xavier was only eleven. And …."

"And?"

"And—he was killed."

"WHAT?"

"I watched him die."

"I'm confused," Heart said simply.

"I carried him to The Mystic. I was crying …."

"You were crying?"

"Yes. The last time I cried. I was just a kid. Xavier was my best … anyway, I carried him to The Mystic. She took him, then she sent me away. I never asked what happened to him. We were in such disarray after that battle. We'd lost several of our people. I tried to put things back together, with the help of a small band of people and a few mechanicals who had defected to our side. So—no closure for me!

"Then, last evening, I stepped into Peter's crowded room, and there I see Xavier. Same boyish, prankish grin. Same freckly nose."

"That's him, all right."

"But now, he's a muscular machine, besotted with you."

"Oh Jackson, *PLEASSSSE!* Turn down the hyperbole!"

"Not really hyperbole, no," Swen added from the back.

"You, back there, refrain from commenting!" Heart ordered.

"No comment. Not commenting. Hush, Swen," Swen chattered softly under his breath.

"Will someone let me out of here?" Heart begged. "Now, really, Jackson, Xavier's personal emotions aside, can you give me some clarity on this business of him being very much alive? Maybe you thought he died, but he'd just passed out."

"No, Heart. He'd been pretty much blown apart. No mistaking it."

"So—how do you account for him as he is now?"

"I don't know. That's why I feel I must tell you. I don't know how he managed to return to life. But he sure has."

"Yes," Heart agreed. "Returned to life, and bigger than life. I think he's probably one of the most alive beings I know."

"Soldier Swen asking permission to speak."

"Don't be silly, Swen."

"I apologize. I took my silly pill yesterday, and it hasn't worn off yet."

"*Swen!*"

"I know. I don't know what's come over me. I'm just so happy to be with you Heart!"

Heart softened, turned and patted Swen on his shoulder. "I'm happy to be with you too. I've missed you!"

"I've missed you too, Heart. More than you will ever know. But I thought I'd mention that the reason he's one of the most alive beings you've ever met is because he's *come back to life*. He knows how wonderful every moment is—that's the way he seems to me. Just watching him in Peter's room, and how the light sparkles in his eyes, how he got so utterly engaged in our plans, and—there's no denying it—how he looked at Heart." Swen snickered.

"Holy dog-doo, the way he looked at you practically made *me* faint, just by the waves of adoration coming off that young man."

"Control yourself, Swen."

"Trying."

"Anyway, inside that comment, I think there lies some truth," Jackson agreed. "Xavier, returned to life, is more alive than any of us. When he says anything, or feels anything, it's bigger than for the rest of us."

"So, there you have it, Heart. Xavier made it clear to me he didn't want me to mention this when I first saw him. I tried to honor that, but—it's simply too big, and needs to be revealed to you. He's amazing in so many ways, always was, and now, more so than ever. There's a lot I don't know. He got to Pink. But how? And when? Did they regenerate him on Pink? Or regenerate him here and then sent him there? I don't know."

"Well," Heart answered, thoughtfully, "I don't know either. But I imagine he'd been regenerated on Pink, as that seems to be what is done there. Since I stowed away on the *Heart!* I didn't get any debriefing from my father before coming here. I don't know what he would consider confidential information. So, I'm not, right now, going to say anymore. But it does lend clarity to his childlike ways, including the childlike way he insists that he … he's in love with me.

"Not to change the subject, but I do hope he's not running into any complications planting the remaining magnetic resonance devices, and that he returns soon. Whatever is going on, swirling around us, I feel urgent about getting back to Pink."

Jackson nodded. "I feel the same way—it's urgent that Xavier get back to Pink. Father Inventor needs him. And you're safer there, too."

"All true." Heart looked out her side window and gasped. "Oh! Dawn! Here comes the sun!"

Looking down, while all the land lay in darkness, soon Earth would turn and its surface bathed in a brilliant and gloriously sunny day. "I've not been in daylight since leaving Earth."

"Well, you're getting a sunny day as a keepsake today. The *Heart!* will not be able to inconspicuously leave Earth's atmosphere from the Dark Energy Highway in daylight. Although it would have been better if we could have gotten everything done in the night, you will, at least, be able to enjoy one beautiful day," Jackson said.

"Oh, Jackson. How poetic!"

"There's a poet in him Heart," Swen observed.

"Surprising, yes?" Heart quipped.

"Umm-hum."

"All right you two, enough. I am capable of making decent observations."

Soon they saw The Museum of Scientific Improbabilities and Unpredictable Oddities straight ahead. "Thank goodness we made it back before daylight. I think I'll take the vehicle to the back of the museum, just in case anyone is watching. That will seem less suspicious, although it's strange enough for a museum vehicle to be out ranging about in pre-dawn."

"It'll be even worse if the *Heart!* lands at the front door in the wee hours. You'd better tell Xavier to park in the back, too," Heart observed.

"Absolutely!" Jackson agreed. He turned on his communication device, "Xavier. Come in, Xavier."

They waited several seconds. No Xavier. Jackson called again. Still no response. Heart became nervous—then his voice came on. "Sorry, just finished placing the fourth device. What's happening?"

"We're about to land. But I realized it might cause undue attention, for anyone out on an early morning run, to see a museum vehicle returning in the pre-dawn. So I'm going to park the vehicle in its place. Heart pointed out it's probably even more important for the *Heart!* to be less conspicuous, so fly it around back, too."

"Aww, Heart! You're thinking of me!"

"No, silly. I'm thinking of *me!*"

"Of course, that's pragmatic. But you can't change my mind. I know you were thinking of me, too. See you in a bit!" The connection flipped off.

"You see how exasperating he is," Heart said to no one in particular.

"Right," Jackson said, while Swen sniggered.

Chapter 18

By the time they touched down behind The Museum of Scientific Improbabilities and Unpredictable Oddities, the sun crested over the museum and brought its glorious light, full upon Heart. She climbed out of the vehicle and stood stock still in the light, closing her eyes, flinging her arms wide as if she could, by this invitation, store up enough sunlight to take back with her to her eternal twilight home on Pink.

Or, at least, have enough to revel in this day!

Jackson and Swen said nothing, letting Heart have, literally, her moment in the sun.

When she pulled herself out of her near trance state, she looked at her friends. "Thanks for letting me drink it in. *Ah!* You never know how much you'll miss the sun until you don't have it."

"I'm sure, dear Heart, Father Inventor will come up with a way for you to have periods of sunlight," Swen offered.

"Oh, Swen. How strange—I've never thought of that. I just thought things were as they must be. Perhaps you're right. Now is not the moment to ask him, but one day, perhaps, I can broach the subject."

"What's it like for *him* to have no sun?"

"Oh, I sort of imagine he doesn't even realize it, the way he's so involved in his work all the time."

"But today, Heart, you need to spend time outside," Jackson said. "There's a little outdoor garden in the museum cafe, isn't there?"

Heart nodded. "Yes, but I can't be with the public. Someone will recognize me for sure."

"This is a special occasion, Heart, and you need sun. I think the museum can, for one day, afford to have the cafe closed for 'renovation.'"

"That does sound lovely!"

"But for now," Swen suggested, "we'd better get inside. The sun is up and there are early morning joggers about. Let's not take any chances."

"Right," Jackson said.

Inside Martha, Key Man, and Peter awaited them. Silently, they moved to Peter's rooms and closed the door.

"You're back, so I take it, it went well," Martha said, as everyone became settled.

"Yes." Heart looked to her two accomplices. "But not without some very odd happenings."

"Such as?"

"The strangest event being—Keeper A apparently knew I was there, and followed the path I walked. But then—just—let me go."

"Really?" Peter interjected. "Are you sure she wasn't simply taking a stroll?"

Heart raised her eyebrows at the suggestion. "I'm sure she was not! Not only have I never seen her 'stroll' anywhere but in her own lovely, fragrant garden, but, according to Swen and Jackson, she followed my path. She did that with her scent implants. She clearly knew of my presence, and let me go. Why?"

"What do you think?" Martha asked.

"Either she somehow tailed us, and the front door will soon be stormed, or ...."

"Or what?"

"Well, I'm thinking about what a challenge I've been in her life. With me gone, and everyone believing I'm on Pink, things have settled down, I'm pretty much forgotten about ...."

"*Humph ....*" Peter sounded.

Heart turned to him, "Meaning?"

"You're hardly forgotten about, my dear. Just a few days ago, a huge group of people carrying 3-D signs, paraded up and down several major Dark Energy Highway intersections saying, *'Bring Our Heart Home!'*"

"*Oh!*" Stunned, Heart fell silent.

"It's true," Swen nodded energetically, ears flopping. "You have not been forgotten!"

"So ... this news lends support to my theory. Keeper A knew I was there. The last thing she needs in her life is the world all topsy-turvy over me. She wanted to *make sure I left*, not capture me and have to deal with me. And deal with the world. Does that sound ...."

Xavier burst through the door. All eyes turned to him, and a huge grin spread across his face. Oh those freckles, that smile! Heart didn't know where to put her feelings in response to his immediate proximity, there not being a pocket readily available for such things.

"Perhaps you're all wondering why I've called this meeting!"

Everyone chuckled but Heart. "Yeah. Ha. Funny," she said.

"How did it go?" Jackson asked.

"*Smooooooth* as dark energy on a moonbeam." As every chair was occupied and the room crowded, Xavier sat down on the floor next to Heart, crossing his legs. "I put the third one in a line with a second one just outside *The Wall*. And the fourth one," he gestured behind his head, "over there a ways. So—my work is done here. But, of course, we'll have to wait for the cover of dark before we can leave."

Heart looked down at him by her on the floor. He reached up and patted her forearm. "How does that sound, co-pilot?"

"Sounds fine. Sounds like the only option we have, in fact. So, you feel good about what you've accomplished?"

"I feel great about it, beautiful girl. *GREAT! Expansive!* But, you know, I fly the *Heart!* It can only go well."

"Well ...." Heart hesitated, looking down at his hand on her forearm.

"Right," Jackson agreed. "'Well' is an understatement. Don't get too big for your own safety ...."

"I know, I know," Xavier cut in. "I'll temper my enthusiasm for all you conservative types. Calm as a summer breeze." He templed his hands together in his lap. "Wow, though, what about that Keeper A's weird behavior?"

"Heart just mentioned," Swen answered, "that she suspects Keeper A might be more interested in seeing that Heart leaves than anything else. That it would really upset her life if Heart came back into it. She wanted to assure that Heart left. Is that about it, Heart?"

"That's perfectly 'it,' Swen. Now—let's hope I'm right!"

"Makes excellent sense," Xavier nodded. "I worried a bit that I might come back to Purists storming the front door."

"It looks like we get to spend a precious day together," Martha said. "So let's enjoy it."

"To that end," Jackson added, "Heart mentioned how delightful the sun feels, and how much she misses it. So it seems to me that you might want to close the museum cafe for the day and let her sit outdoors. Xavier probably wouldn't mind, either."

"Oh, the sunlight is no big deal to me. I'm sort of used to eternal twilight. But if Heart wants to be in the sun, let's do it!"

Everyone mobilized, preparing to open The Museum of Scientific Improbabilities and Unpredictable Oddities for the day, and closing off the cafe, turning on all the window shades that, from inside the museum looked like works of art, but blocked the view of the cafe's outdoor space.

"It's like the old days," Heart said to Peter as they made a cozy place for their party to come and go throughout the day in the sunny courtyard. "Before I went to Pink, and we all had things to do together."

Peter gave her a hug. "It is, my own Heart. Even if we are at an entirely different place in history. Preparing for another triumph of Loving Beings on Earth *and* on Pink."

"Yes," Heart raised her face to the glorious sun. "Similar, yet so different."

Martha came out to join them, arms loaded with yummy things to eat.

"Oh! My! Goodness! We're going to have a party, all day long," Heart exclaimed, grinning.

"There's more."

On cue, Swen came in with a tray strapped to his back with yet more edibles and pretty knickknacks.

"Martha! Your pretty things—all these lovely little things."

"They're no fun if not shared!"

"I love it, it's so touching. I'll remember each and every one of them, always. Here, on this day. *My Day of Light!* How sweet!"

Heart became aware that Jackson, Key Man, and Xavier had also entered, and that everyone suddenly fell so silent, the quiet resounded.

"What?"

"*The Day of Light*," Jackson, Martha, Key Man and Peter whispered together.

"Yes?"

Heart looked from one to the other, their clearly stunned silence, each of them intensely processing something deep inside.

"What?"

"You've just quoted," Swen said softly, "one of *Ourbook*'s most treasured, and yet considered cryptic, passages. That you have said it, now, means, I believe, a certain set of prophecy is in the process of unfolding."

Heart shook her head. "Oh, come on everyone, I'm going to sit in the sun for a few hours before returning to eternal twilight. That does make it a day of light. Not—*oh my goodness!*—the fulfillment of prophecy. Let's be logical."

"You're not going to dissuade them, Heart," Swen said, bumping up against her. "But, do you think you could take some of these 'pretty things' off my back? It's scaring the dog doo right out of me that I'm going to break something."

Everyone giggled with emotional release and rushed to unload Swen.

"All right, all right. Don't disassemble me, too! One at a time, kindly." They soon unloaded Swen, and the charming setting was complete.

"Key Man and I are off now, to let in the thundering masses," Peter said. "Relax, Heart, and enjoy yourself. We'll be back later."

Heart waved at them gaily as she leaned back in a lounge chair. "Lovely!" she sighed.

"Xavier and I need to study out a couple of things," Jackson said. "We, too, will soon return."

Heart waved them off as well and looked at Swen. "So, where are you off to?"

"Nowhere. I'm sticking right by your side as long as I can." He came alongside her and stretched out, putting his chin down on his paws.

"Very good," Heart reached down and patted him, filled with pleasant joy.

"Now, Martha, come and sit near me and hold my hand."

"With pleasure." Martha stopped fussing with the arrangement of the charming tchotchkes. She stretched out her round little body in the lounge chair next to Heart. "Oh, yes, this is indulgence! What a great idea of—was it Jackson's idea?"

"Yes!"

"That's a bit surprising."

"It is!" Heart paused, thinking about how Jackson could be the most exasperating and the most accommodating person in all the Universe.

"He is quite the enigma," Swen said in muffled tones, talking into his paws.

"He is that," Heart agreed.

"He's really on his studies, given that he knew to come now."

"You mean *Ourbook* doesn't say, 'Hey, Jackson, get on the other side of *The Wall*, now!' when he did his devotions yesterday morning?"

Swen stifled a small snicker, while Martha made a tiny disapproving sound, quite unusual for her.

"Sorry," Heart apologized. "I can't help it if I don't share everyone's belief in a book I've never read. But I guess I needn't be disrespectful—if that's how my comment seemed."

"It did, Heart. I know there are things you consider sacred, and you would not like them to be made lightly of."

"You're right. You're absolutely right! I always have, and I always *will* hate it when people speak disrespectfully about Darling Undesirables, or make fun of the really sad ones."

Martha took Heart's hand. "Well, I'm with you on that, of course! But—it would also be better if you responded respectfully about other people's beliefs. Even if you do not share them."

Chagrined, Heart hung her head and tried to pull away her hand. But Martha would not let go. "I'm an idiot," she whispered *sotto voce*.

"My dear Miss Heart, you are most certainly not an idiot. Now you're speaking inappropriately about something else I care deeply about, namely *you!*"

"Well, I'm sorry again and some more. I didn't have the very best of socialization, one might say."

"Enough about all of that! Let us talk of wonderful things. Tell me what your life is like on Pink?"

Heart perked right up and turned to face Martha. "It's not Earth, dear Martha. Which I candidly do miss. *A lot!* It's twilight all the time. Oh, how I'm loving this sunlight!"

"Can't Father Inventor fix that?"

"That's what Swen said! Perhaps he could, but he's busy. *Busy, busy, busy.* I don't want to bother him about my little issues."

"Sunlight is not a small thing."

"There's never night, either. Which I also miss. Equuleus and I fly into the night sometimes, there's a little sliver of it on Pink. But it just makes me sort of sad to be in that little sliver of night. So I stopped going there. The day part is *too* sun exposed. But the castle is exquisite. Beautifully beautiful. Beyond words. I wish you could visit, Martha!"

"Perhaps one day I will."

"Well, that's problematic, because you can never be outside of the castle."

"That's all right. I'm sure there's plenty to interest me in the castle. And there's *YOU!* That's why I'd go. For a visit, at least."

"Oh, Martha," Heart said, taking Martha's hand in both of her own. "Just to imagine you said that—just to have this dream between us, is *magnificent.* Thank you! I will lie under my star dome and think about your visit. One day. When things have settled down."

"Oh! Do you have a star dome there, too?"

"Yes, and, as we're out of Earth's atmosphere, I can see further, and so much more clearly. Father invented it, of course! He told me he's the one who made sure I had a star dome at the Darling Undesirables Facility at Long Prairie, and he put up the money for it to be installed in my room. He had a very strict contingency that it be properly installed and fully usable. He told me he had a remote viewer to make sure it worked properly."

"I'll say remote!"

"Umm-hmmm, there on Pink. Anyway, he'd promised that when the star dome properly functioned, he'd give the Darling Undesirables Facility at Long Prairie three times the amount of money that the dome and the installation cost. So ... Keeper A was, you might say, motivated."

"You might say!" Swen interjected.

"I thought you were asleep."

"I can sleep and listen," he protested.

"Good to know!" Martha said. "Can't get away with anything around you!"

"'A newshound always hears news,' as you've heard, many times."

"But we're confidential, here, right?" Heart confirmed.

"Oh, now you've insulted me! Good going, Heart." Swen actually raised his snout off his paws in indignation.

"Oh, my goodness, I say! I'm sorry again. I maybe ought to keep my mouth shut!"

"No," Swen and Martha said in unison.

"Continue about Pink," Martha encouraged.

"Well, I just planted two greenhouses of flowers. But first, I built the greenhouses with Equuleus and

HelperFriend. My father took flower seeds in stasis up to Pink, ever so long ago, just in case I happened to be there one day and would like flowers!"

"Who's HelperFriend?"

"Whoops, I wasn't going to say too much about what all is on Pink, in case it ought to be confidential. As I stowed away on Xavier's spacecraft ...."

"The *Heart!*" Swen interrupted.

"Yes, the *Heart!*" Heart agreed. "I didn't exactly have a chance for a debriefing with my father before-hand."

"No," Martha agreed. "I guess you wouldn't."

"But, I'll just say that HelperFriend is a clockworks man, who is very charming, talented and adorable. He makes music and dinner, and sometimes at the same time. Oh, yes, I'd like to regale you with the story of the dinner before coming here. Which seems like a year ago, but, in Earth terms, would only be the night before last. Whew! Lots happening!"

"Very true, dearest Heart. But tell me," Martha continued, "how's Equuleus?"

"He's wonderful, He's awesome. He's my heart— my constant companion. We're together all the time, since, as I said, my father is so very busy. Equuleus and I live a life of luxury and, to a certain extent, bore-dom. But since we're both not fully bio, we can go out-side of the castle." Heart hesitated.

"What are you thinking?"

"Just trying to decide if I can tell this other little piece. Which I cannot see why not."

"Do tell," Swen said, raising his head off his paws.

"Not if she shouldn't," Martha nodded reassur-ingly to Heart. "But, trust me, I'm interested!"

"Well, one day, when Equuleus and I went out exploring, we happened upon a little lavender rabbit. Mechanical and a little bio. Well, more bio now than she was. Her name is Violet. Which is so amusing, because she thinks she's white, but she's lavender. Apparently, her eyes are constructed to be more suitable to pink's terrain, so there's this color shift in her vision. Or in ours, Equuleus's and mine. Anyway, we struck up a friendship, and so now I have Violet and HelperFriend too, as well as Equuleus."

"And you have Xavier," Martha murmured.

"No. I don't 'have' Xavier. From what he says, he wishes that to be. But I think it's just some sort of fantasy. It's not real. Anyway, I only very recently met him."

"What is reality?" Swen asked cryptically.

"Very good question," Heart replied, "I don't have the answer."

"However, Heart, what Xavier feels for you is real to him. Be kind to him, if you will. He's a very brave boy," Martha admonished.

"I ... hmm ... again with the issues around confidentiality. Swen, should I bring up Jackson's conversation about Xavier?"

"I don't see why not. Martha is about as involved with every nuance of—*everything!*—as anyone could be."

"He told me about the battle he and Xavier fought, and that Xavier died ... and Jackson's shock at seeing him here, Xavier apparently not wanting Jackson to tell me what happened to him."

"I see," Martha said, nodding her head, her eyes closing down to little half moons as she considered what Heart said. "Well, we'll leave it at that for the moment. What Jackson told you is plenty."

"It certainly is, and it explains a lot. I've not been able to figure out how Xavier can be brilliant and forceful and in command at one moment, and then seem to be arrested in his social growth the next moment. He's brilliant. *Very brilliant!* But immature."

"Excellent observations, Heart. Well expressed, yes. That's lovely. We'll let him be childlike, will we not?"

"Oh, sure. Because, though I loathe to admit it, that childlike thing about him is—*errrr!* charming. Don't you dare tell him."

"*He-he*, Martha, we can hold this over her!" Swen chortled.

"Indeed, we could!" Martha laughed, which Heart so dearly loved-loved-loved. Her laughter filled with chimes and delight, her little round mouth becoming a perfect "o" her eyes becoming even more pronounced half moons. Her laugh was enough to make anyone laugh, no matter how dark and dreary they felt.

"But, Martha, you make a good point, there's no reason for me *not to* be nice to Xavier. Other than, as I say, being nice to him might give him the wrong impression. He appears to be readily open to the wrong impression."

"I suspect he'll be so busy in the near future, he won't have time to do anything about a wrong impression."

"Yes. Well. Hmmm. I suppose that's true."

They fell into a comradely silence, when Heart suddenly recalled the tiny camera she placed facing her previous bedroom door. The receiver hung on a chain around her neck, and, curious to observe its reception, she turned it on.

"Excuse me for a few moments while I see ...." She fell silent, frowned and cocked her head. "What ...?"

Swen, taking in her voice and her body language, stood up. "What's happening?"

"I put a little camera on the door frame across from my former door, just to keep a bit of watch over Eye, and now, Butterfly, too, and ... what am I seeing?"

"I don't know, Heart, what are you seeing?" Swen asked.

"Keeper A. She's at their door. She's putting her hands on the door, and ... that's all. She's standing there, just standing there. With her hands on the door. It's still very early, breakfast won't be for an hour. So— Eye and Butterfly are still asleep.

"Keeper A is turning away now. And, now she's out of view." Heart looked over to Martha. "What do you make of that?"

Martha shook her head slightly. "I don't know, Heart. Odd, I'll grant you."

"Oh, it gives me chills. It's so upsetting! Her sneaky behavior. I don't understand it. It's like she's not even the same person she used to be. I don't understand it." Agitated Heart stood and circumvented the little patio. "Why would Keeper A trail me? Because she wants to make sure I leave and don't cause her trouble? All right. But then, why is she haunting the room where Eye is, in this weird way? Is she going to do something to him?"

"Maybe," Martha suggested, "she's simply checking to see if, during the night, you managed to sneak off with Eye. Here you are on Earth. She knows it. There you were, where Eye is. She now knows that. It seems ... and I'm only trying to follow down the path you're exploring, if I were Keeper A, who is always, if nothing else, very pragmatic, I'd be wondering if you managed to nab him in the night. She comes to the door, her scent implants let her know Eye is still there, and that's all she wanted to find out ...."

Heart, standing on the other side of the patio, nodded. "That sounds plausible. Though all my alarms are set off. I'll be the first to admit I might not be at all objective, but ...." she paused, thinking, "but, yes, that makes the best sense."

She returned to her lounge chair and sat, though not entirely relaxed, perched on the edge of it. "Thank you, Martha. Thank you. I mean, there would be no reason for her to do anything with or to Eye. If she didn't sound the alarm about my being there because she wants peace and quiet, she certainly won't stir up big noise by doing something with Eye. When there's no reason to."

She relaxed back into the chair. "Let us return to pampering." She extended one hand to Swen, who happily put his nose up to be scratched, and her other hand to Martha, who took it and reclined again, too.

"Ah," Heart sighed, "this is perfect! I shall never, ever, ever, *ever* forget this moment!"

"Nor shall I," Martha agreed.

"Me neither!" Swen rested his chin on Heart's knee. "This is doggie heaven."

Heart closed her eyes, and in her mind, urged the sun to pour through her, and wishing, again, she could store it up, save some for Pink twilight time, and pull it out to brighten the moment, sharing it with Equuleus and her father.

Could she not remain in this tableau until the end of time, she wondered languidly. But, of course, that would never do. She had places to go, things to do. As much as she loved Swen and Martha—which was huge and profound!—she also loved Equuleus and her father.

"Two homes," she sighed.

"What's that, dear Heart?" Martha asked lazily.

"Two homes. I have two homes. When I'm at one, I'm happy, and yet, I miss the other."

"Oh! Poor Heart!" Martha said, sympathetically.

"All sympathy warmly received." Eyes closed, Heart smiled broadly.

"But, Heart, it's not as much about the places as the population, I think. I mean, if Swen and Equuleus and your father and Eye, and Key Man and Peter, and I, and ... whoever else, were all in the same place, you'd have one home. Regardless of where it might be."

"Yes," Heart agreed, sitting up, agitated again. "But that's not going to happen with the insanity on this planet, is it?"

Swen raised his chin nodding. "Quite problematic, yes, so it seems. But Martha makes a great point—home is more a condition of population, less of location."

"Yes. Well, all right, changing the subject, because I can do nothing about that one, I have a question, Martha."

"Ask away!"

"My new little friend on Pink, the lavender rabbit, Violet, practically fell down on her little rabbit knees to worship my beautiful plaid outfit. Which, by the way, thank you again. You see how perfectly my new clothes are holding up. Anyway, she asked me if Martha wove the fabric. I told her that you said you made the outfits, but I have no idea if you wove the fabric. But I thought, well it's possible since you said you wove the fabric of my paisley blanket. So, first question did you weave this fabric?"

"I did, indeed, my precious Heart."

"Oh my goodness, Martha, I'm speechless. Thank you again. Imagine that, Swen, not only making the clothes but first weaving the plaids."

"I'm imagining," Swen answered.

"As you know, with my vexing life at the Darling Undesirables Facility at Long Prairie I'd regularly study my plaid, simply to calm and center myself. When Swen escaped with me and took me to The Periphery, we absolutely counted on the lights in the plaid to let me know when I came close to danger and when I was safe. But now I'm wondering if there's not even more due to the plaid. If you not only made the clothes but also wove the fabric, I can't help but think there's power in the crossing of colors."

"You've hit right upon it, Heart."

"That there's power in the crossing of colors?"

"Yes. But more properly, *'The Power in the Crossing of Colors.'* Ancient, ancient knowledge."

"The specific colors in particular placement—serves some purpose ...."

"Yes. Serves to protect you. Occasionally serves to clear the path. Occasionally serves to inform you. Serves to strengthen your own decisions. Provides clarity."

"You didn't tell me this before, because ...?"

"You didn't ask."

"That's simple enough," Swen observed.

"It is," Heart agreed. "So, all I have to do is ask you questions, and you will give me answers?"

"No. There are some questions, my dearest Heart, I will not answer. Because I must not interfere with your free will, free choice. But there are plenty of questions I may answer, or answer in part because you've asked."

"Then, I have an even more burning question. Violet said, 'is this the fabric Martha—*and the nieces*—wove?' *And the nieces?* What does she mean by that? Who are 'the nieces?'"

Martha shrugged and shook her head ever so slightly, smiling sweetly. "Immediately, dear girl, you ask a question I may not, at this moment, answer."

"Hmmm ... vexing. Thus implying that at some other moment I may ask, and you might answer, the question."

"Yes, Heart. Trust me, I very, very, *very* much look forward to the day."

"Oh, woe! More irritating *Ourbook* stuff."

"I'm afraid so."

"But, why do you look—so passionately—forward to the day? What ...?" Heart stopped abruptly in the middle of her sentence. "*Oh!*" she whispered.

Swen jumped up. "What's wrong, Heart? What's wrong? Your energy field, something is going on. Martha, something's not right." Disturbed, Swen jumped around to the other side of Heart, practically knocking Martha out of her lounge chair. "What's happening, Heart?"

Martha stood and shoved the lounge chair out of her way, leaning over Heart, who, clearly, was in distress. She grabbed her wrist pager, "Peter, come immediately. Something is wrong with Heart. Bring Wonderman One and Wonderman Two. *Hurry!*"

Chapter 19

In moments, clattering ensued at the door, and Martha, loathe to leave Heart's side, scurried to the door, unlocked it, then rushed back to Heart's side.

"Heart, Heart—what's happening?"

Peter immediately came to her side. "What are you feeling?"

"I—don't—know. I, I can't seem to organize my thoughts. Very weak. Can't think. Can't breathe ...."

"Be calm," Peter said, stroking her forehead, "you're breathing. You're breathing. Relax." He turned to Wonderman One and Wonderman Two who arrived at the small door, both trying to get through at once, when one alone could hardly get through without pulling in every mechanical limb and stooping over, their face gears spinning in anxiety, picking up on Heart's pain.

"One at a time!" Peter ordered. "Wonderman One, step back, Wonderman Two, come forward!"

With these commands, they straightaway became more orderly and did as they were told. Peter, Martha, and Swen backed away as Wonderman One and Wonderman Two approached Heart.

"Equuleus," Wonderman One said.

"Yes," Wonderman Two agreed.

"Equuleus, what?" Peter nearly squawked.

Key Man came barreling through the door. "What's wrong?"

"Something isn't right with Heart," Martha answered, all the happy "O's" of her face closed down.

Key Man tried to get through the solid clockworks of Wonderman One and Wonderman Two, but they formed a wall.

"*Heart!*" he cried.

"I ... I ... I'm all right," Heart's voice sounded odd and weak through the metal surrounding her.

Key Man, Martha, and Peter exchanged a look of extreme alarm and surprise.

"Is there any reference to this?" Peter asked.

"I don't know of any. I don't recall any passage suggesting her life would be compromised lying in a lounge chair!" Martha answered, confused.

"I won't have it!" Key Man fumed.

Swen worked his head in between Wonderman One and Wonderman Two. "You'll be all right, Heart. It's all right."

"Not really," Wonderman Two said.

"Well, don't scare her!" Swen literally barked.

"Sorry, no don't mean to," Wonderman One said. "But, we can only tell the truth, as you well know, Mr. Dog."

"Swen, please."

"But ..." Heart whispered, "what is happening? I've only ever felt anything sort of like this when I got too near the dark energy of *The Wall*. But now, so weak. No reason. Blacking out ...."

"Good reason," Wonderman Two said. "Equuleus!"

"Will you stop saying that," Peter growled.

"Is that a command?" Wonderman One asked. "It will be hard to explain, if so."

"No, not a command. The command is, 'tell us more!' We don't know what you mean by saying, 'Equuleus.'"

Wonderman One and Wonderman Two, each with a hand on Heart's forehead, said in unison. "Heart is too far from her heart for too long. She must return to Equuleus."

"She lived the first fifteen years of her life away from Equuleus," Peter stomped around the small remaining patio space. "Why is this happening now?"

"She is too far. Equuleus, off-world, and Heart here, it's too far, too long. Her reserves are nearly depleted."

"Why didn't anyone tell us this?" Martha pled, nearly in tears.

"Who could tell you? Perhaps Father Inventor."

"We must contact him!" Martha exclaimed.

"Too dangerous," Peter said.

"What's happening?" Jackson demanded, striding into the room.

"Heart—Heart is not well," Key Man stuttered. "She, apparently, cannot be this far away from Equuleus for this long."

Jackson shoved Wonderman One, or was it Wonderman Two? aside enough to look down at Heart. Wonderman One and Wonderman Two still kept both their hands on her forehead. "Well, fix her!" he demanded of them.

"We cannot," Wonderman One and Wonderman Two said in tandem. "We can soothe her. But we cannot be her heart. Only Equuleus ...."

Heart's eyes fluttered open at Jackson's raised voice. "Now what are you mad about," she asked weakly.

He chuckled wryly. "I'm mad about you taking our valuable time, acting like you're sick."

"I'm not sick!" Heart insisted. "I've never been sick in my life."

"I know. You're made, in part, of dark energy. So what's this grandstanding? Get up! I have things to do."

"Can't ... get ... up ... Jackson." Heart's eyes closed.

Furious, Jackson stepped away from Heart. "This will not do!" he shouted.

"Calm yourself, Jackson," Martha begged. "You'll attract attention. There are employees all over the place."

Jackson nodded brusquely. "Right!" He said somewhat more softly. "Well, then, we must contact Father Inventor, and risk it."

"No, Jackson. No. We simply cannot risk the Purists discovering Heart is here. Completely out of the question," Peter said.

Swen stood near Heart's head, whining very dog like.

"What's with you?" Jackson snapped.

"She's really not good, Jackson. My dog-part knows when a creature is not well, and her energy is very bad."

Someone pounded at the door.

"Now what?" Jackson flung open the door he'd just locked and let Xavier in.

"No one's answering me, I'm trying to get any of you on my ... Heart!" He dashed over to stand behind Swen. "What ... what? I don't understand ...."

"She can't be this far away from Equuleus this long," Swen said simply.

"Oh no, oh no," Xavier reached around Wonderman One and grabbed Heart's hand. "It's all my fault! I let her stay onboard. I should have turned back. *I should have turned back!*"

"Don't blame yourself, Xavier," Martha comforted, "none of us knew, including Heart. No, you must not feel guilty, we must come up with a solution."

"We must contact Father Inventor," Xavier demanded.

"Truly too risky, Xavier," Martha said. "Just what Purists would love to discover, that Heart is here."

Xavier nodded, then shook his head. "This is not happening! I can handle anything but this."

Silence fell upon the group as everyone tried to imagine how to save a failing girl, whose heart was far aloft on a small, synthetic moon, within a clockworks, bio, dark matter, winged horse.

Silence prevailed, except for the furious whizzing, whirling, clacking, clanking, clicking, and ticking of Wonderman One and Wonderman Two.

"Possible ..." Wonderman Two said.

"Solution ..." Wonderman One said.

"Slightly ..." Wonderman Two said.

"Dangerous ..." Wonderman One said.

"What? *What? WHAT?*" everyone demanded.

"Put her bios into stasis." Wonderman Two said.

"We will sustain, through us, what is our heart, through her."

"That is, huh, what?" Jackson asked.

"My thoughts precisely," Key Man added.

"Her bios will very soon shut off. Not good. Bio components will be called dead. Not good." Wonderman One said.

"If we put her bios in stasis *NOW*, she will probably be able to start up again," Wonderman Two said.

"Then, we make a circuit, which is a mechanical's equivalent of a heart, through us." Wonderman One and Wonderman Two said.

"*DO IT!*" Jackson ordered.

"Wait!" Martha interjected. "What's the dangerous part?"

"We must shock her to put her in stasis," Wonderman One said.

"She is very fragile, the shock is not good." Wonderman Two said.

"What's the alternative?" Key Man asked.

"She will very, very soon be beyond repair," Wonderman One and Wonderman Two said.

"We want to try and save our Heart." Wonderman One and Wonderman Two each pulled out his healing vial from his chest with his free hand, Wonderman One's vial filled with a mystical looking, roiling bluish liquid, Wonderman Two's vial filled with a mystical looking, roiling reddish liquid.

"I think we must let them," Peter said.

Swen and Xavier whined most piteously.

"They must," Heart whispered, grabbing Xavier's hand, "Swen?"

Xavier put her hand on Swen's head.

"Xavier and dog must stand back. Electrical current. Everyone must stand back."

"Come," Jackson demanded, pulling Swen and Xavier away from Heart.

"Do what you must," he ordered Wonderman One and Wonderman Two.

Everyone stood back and could see nothing but a purple flash of light, and then, Wonderman One and Wonderman Two, holding the vials, the two vials gradually became filled with a purple mystical, roiling liquid.

"What does that mean?" Jackson asked. "The fluids changing to purple—is that good or bad?"

The Wondermen seemed not to hear him.

"We must assume it's good," Peter said. "Otherwise, they would be doing something else, it seems."

Xavier uttered a strange sound, as if, he himself were reviving, returning to life. "Yes," he whispered, "it is what must be. Not easy. Very difficult passage. But—feels strong ...."

"Are you—do you think you're experiencing what she's going through?" Martha reached out to Xavier.

"Yes."

Everyone instinctively put their hands—or paws—on Xavier. If they couldn't heal Heart, they would do the next best thing. "Oh! Amazing!" Xavier said in surprise. "I'm certain she's receiving your healing touch."

"And yours," Martha added.

"Yes, yes," everyone mumbled, "and yours, Xavier."

"It is good!" Wonderman One and Wonderman Two exclaimed.

Heart stirred about.

"Must not move!" Wonderman One and Wonderman Two said.

"May we approach?" Martha asked. But Swen and Xavier had already resumed their previous position.

Heart's eyes flew open. "Oh, Goodness! What a trip! I almost didn't have a return flight!" She giggled. "I feel silly." She tried to peer around Wonderman One and Wonderman Two's massive mechanical bodies. "I'm back! Oh, strange—this feels so different—this energy going through me. Is this what it's like to be you?" she asked Wonderman One and Wonderman Two.

"A little," they answered. "A very little, because we are now each half depleted to charge you."

"Thank you, Wonderman One and Wonderman Two. Once again, I owe you—well, this time, I truly owe you my life, once again, through my own stupidity! Just thinking I could dash off as I pleased, without Equuleus. I didn't know."

"None of us knew," Key Man reassured Heart.

"Although, now that we've been here ...."

"Yes," Jackson agreed. "Always after the fact do we understand cryptic passages. Not much help, that."

"Really not," Peter agreed.

"*Ourbook, Ourbook, Ourbook*—can't a girl get used to an artificial heart for a few minutes before arcane passages are brought up?"

"Apparently not," Swen said, settling his chin on her knee.

"So, dear Wonderman One and Wonderman Two, must I stay like this for the duration? And, well, how do we handle things from here out?"

"Yes. We are your mechanical heart now. Your bios are asleep."

"Yes. I heard every word."

"We can sit so others can come near, but we must remain like this, until you are ready to depart. Your mechanical parts will be charged up for the journey back to Pink," Wonderman Two said.

"But, still, you must lie quiet and still on the jour ney, and use the very least energy," Wonderman One said.

"Once you are safely far from Earth, we will con tact Pink and give ...."

"Oh! My dear Wonderman One and Wonderman Two friends—you will communicate with Wonderman One and Wonderman Two on Pink, and tell them how to save me!"

"Pretty much," Wonderman Two said.

"Yes!" Wonderman One said.

"All right, then. Let us resume our enjoyment of the day, my delighting in the sun. Although, strangely, it doesn't seem as thrilling as before."

"The mechanicals," Xavier whispered.

"Yes?" Heart looked hard at him.

"It's not the same."

"I see. Well, that does make it easier to live on Pink, though, if you don't miss the sun."

"True."

Everyone pulled up a chair as close to Heart as they could get, while Peter exited and retrieved large chairs from offices for Wonderman One and Wonderman Two.

They spent the afternoon in loving companionship, talking about nothing and everything. Dreading the moment, ever soon approaching, when their Heart would take the perilous journey back to Pink.

That was all that was on everyone's mind. But no one spoke of it. They spoke of memories, and they spoke of the future, but for once, they did not speak of the "now."

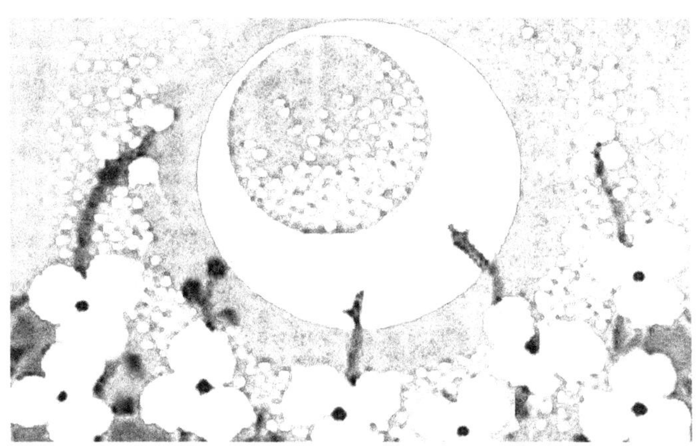

Chapter 20

Despite the dire situation, and despite the urgent need for Heart to get back to Pink in order to survive, the twilight fell all too soon, rapidly followed by dusk, dropping a cool blanket upon the intimate group.

They heard The Museum of Scientific Improbabilities and Unpredictable Oddities close down for the day, as the front door's grates' and locks' metallic shunting sounded throughout the marbled halls. The employees had been given directives to attend to all the daily business and not to bother, under any circumstance, the principals.

"Time to go," Xavier finally said what everyone knew must be said. Anxiety and sadness enveloped the group.

"How do we mobilize?" Jackson asked Wonderman One and Wonderman Two.

"Spacecraft must be ready for immediate take-off."

"Right," Xavier reluctantly released Heart's hand and jumped up. "I'll be ready and waiting."

"Then we lift Heart, lounge chair and all, carry her down the back hall and at the back door, we will give her a final little energy boost, and then disengage ourselves from her," Wonderman Two said.

"Oh, I love you both so much! Is there anything you want me to tell Wonderman One and Wonderman Two on Pink?"

"You learned the call during the dance, just share that with them. They'll know it's from us. All right now, here we go!"

Wonderman One and Wonderman Two lifted the lounge chair with Heart upon it as though it was a matchstick, and, after making sure no stray employee loitered in the hall, Peter led the way to the back exit.

"I'm going to start up a museum vehicle and travel with them until they leave the Dark Energy Highway," Jackson said, running forward.

"Good idea, Jackson." Key Man grabbed Heart's hand, and the strange group hurried down the hall. He whispered to her his wishes and dreams for her future, which made Heart smile broadly at the beautiful pictures he imagined.

"That's all so lovely, my own dear Key Man. I pray for that future. When you and I—*and all of us!* are, at last, together."

They stepped outside in the near moonless night. Pink shone low in the western sky. "Home," Heart said simply, looking toward little Pink. "My other home."

Wonderman One and Wonderman Two neatly disconnected their hands, their vials slowly returned to blue and red.

"Oh!" Heart sighed.

"It's all right. You'll be fine. Just stay relaxed."

"Yes," Heart agreed, immediately feeling the loss of energy, but, as Wonderman One and Wonderman Two said, she did not feel like she would pass out.

Everyone said their good-byes at the door, and Wonderman One and Wonderman Two carried her to the *Heart!*, engines roaring, then Jackson came up alongside in the museum vehicle.

At the entry to the *Heart!* Xavier took Heart from Wonderman One and Wonderman Two, carried her inside, and strapped her down gently but solidly to a pile of soft goods he'd rapidly pulled from everywhere.

"Are you all right?" he asked her, stroking her hair, looking down at her with a scale of concern she could not even begin to measure.

"I'm as fine as I can be, Xavier. Don't worry about me. Let's just get back to Pink."

"Here we go, then." He pulled the hatch shut, strapped himself in and waved to everyone standing in the shadow of the evening. Uneasy smiles and deep concern written on their faces, even the gears on the faces of Wonderman One and Wonderman Two registering clicking frowns.

Xavier raised the *Heart!* above The Museum of Scientific Improbabilities and Unpredictable Oddities, straight up and onto the Dark Energy Highway, Jackson directly behind.

Heart and Xavier were silent while traveling on the Dark Energy Highway, both of them concentrating on the moment, on the moments just passed, on the moments that faced them. Though the communication channel with Jackson stayed open, he, too, remained silent.

Heart hated being tied down to the floor. She wanted to see the city spread out below. She wanted to see The Museum of Scientific Improbabilities and Unpredictable Oddities from the sky once more. She wanted to wave to her precious friends. She wanted to imagine she could see The Darling Undesirables Residence of Long Prairie off in the distance, as they rose into the sky. Although, of course, that would not be possible. But she wanted to look out and see all of this, before passing out of the realm of Earth. She wanted to visualize Eye, snug in her former bed, protected by Butterfly.

Well, she didn't need to look out the window to consider that. She prodded around at her feelings. Eye and Butterfly. It would take some getting used to. But, whether she got used to it or not, it was real—and posed problems. Because, when she got back to Pink, and, had once again become her fully functional self, she'd be insistent with her father that Eye, and now, also, Butterfly, be removed from the Darling Undesirables Facility at Long Prairie. She urgently knew he must be removed. Keeper A's peculiar-even-for-her, behavior made Heart uncomfortable beyond description. Something new had emerged, Heart could sense it.

Some kind of danger lurked about. Eye must be removed to a safe place. With Butterfly. If she could be callous enough to have Eye removed without Butterfly, the guilt would weigh her down.

Anyway, she loved Butterfly. But, what to do with the two of them?

Jackson's voice broke into her thoughts. "Over the ocean ...."

"Yes," Xavier said. "Rocketing out now."

"Right. Take care of yourself, cousin, and take care of our Heart."

"Absolutely! 'Till later!" Xavier wobbled the ship gently for a wave, pushed a sequence of buttons, and the little ship's rockets engaged. Heart felt Earth's hold release as they shot into dark, deep space.

"How are you feeling?" Xavier turned his attention to Heart once the *Heart!* settled into its trajectory.

"I'm, I ... to be truthful, I feel quite strange. I don't feel sick or weak. No, that's not right, I do feel weak, but more, I feel—just—off. Not like myself."

"It's the mechanicals." He looked down at her with a look of pathos or pity or a combination of both.

"The mechanicals ...." Heart repeated.

"They don't process feelings in the same way that organic molecules assemble organic awareness and emotions. But, still, there's a will, a drive, and caring are there. They are there, but they're ... different."

"Yes. That's—yes. Xavier, Jackson told me about you. About the battle, about what happened to you. He felt, for some reason, I must know. And maybe it's for this moment, for you to help me. I don't know why you didn't want me to know...."

"I don't either, now," Xavier replied quietly.

"But ... has that been your experience? A shift from human emotions to—mechanical—mechanical emotions?"

"Not the same as what you're going through, I believe. Because yours came upon you suddenly, whereas mine were provided gradually, as they rebuilt me. I was a child, so, they might have been easier to incorporate. But, yes, I remember the jarring sense of not being myself. The self I knew as 'me.'" He fell silent.

"Was it painful—losing the 'you' you knew?" Heart asked, wondering if she had now lost the Heart she knew, wondering if she'd always have this odd place in herself as if some other entity was co-resident in her thinking, feeling place.

"Not painful, as such, because I didn't have pain. Just oh, um, feeling like a puppet, sort of, like someone else told my feet to move, my hands to move, my eyes to blink. Odd. Odd."

"Ummm," Heart nodded. Yes. Odd. Odd-odd. Inside where "she" usually found herself, she was not. Like someone or something else external to herself saying "move," "you're tired," "this feels strange." Like someone else telling her these things, and she was meant to trigger the appropriate emotions. But their address had been changed. "Yes," she muttered. "I don't appear to be the ruler of my inner kingdom."

"Oh! Beautifully expressed, Heart. Yes. Like that. Not the ruler of my inner kingdom. But if not you, then who?"

"I don't know!" Heart sensed she ought to feel alarm. She raised her voice. "I really don't know." She began to think about those who depended upon her, Equuleus and Violet. "This is alarming. Although I don't feel the emotion of upset, I have a feeling of urgency. Like I must do something. I can't relax. It's sort of awful. I can't reason with it. It's not an emotion, it's an urge, a push. I do not like it!"

"Well, there's an emotion!" Xavier observed.

"But not even. It's like—not an emotion. It's like, if I must blink my eye, I cannot *not* blink my eye. It's like that. Almost like a reflex."

"Oh, I remember that sensation. Don't worry, Heart. I'm certain when you and Equuleus connect, the whole mechanical dominance will rapidly fade. I assure you, even if it doesn't right away, that odd state will not last long. Plus, you have Equuleus. And you are part dark energy, so it will be different for you.

"My advice," Xavier added cautiously, "if you'd like to hear it ...."

"Please!" Heart said with a voice of urgency that surprised her. "Who said that?"

"You did, my dear. My advice is to relax into it. Don't fight it. The 'real you' will surface, sooner or later."

Xavier's voice suddenly became irresistibly soothing to her, and Heart found herself falling into the sound of it. "I–think–you're–right. You sound lovely," she added. Then wondered where—*oh where!* such a comment came from. "Who said that?"

Xavier laughed. "The mechanicals, I guess. It didn't sound much like something you'd say! Especially since you don't even particularly like me."

"No. That's not true. I don't dislike you I ... I mistrust you. I mean, those things you say about loving me and being devoted to me, and all that. I just do *not* believe it!"

"Why not, Heart? Why not? I'm quite sincere."

"Why not ...." Heart pondered Xavier's calmly presented question. "Because, as a Darling Undesirable, the whole world says all the time, 'we love you, we love you!' but they don't. They feel guilty. They're trying to assuage their own guilt. It's an ugly emotion. I've grown to almost despise being told I'm loved. Except by Eye, Equuleus, and my father, and Martha and Key Man. And Peter, but he's not much inclined to say it. And Violet, of course."

"What about Jackson?"

Heart burst into a short guffaw. "Jackson? Well, he's not ... I don't think ... can you actually imagine Jackson saying 'I love you' to anyone?"

"Yes." Xavier fell silent. "He said it to me. I will confide in you, Heart. In the horrible battle, after I stopped breathing, after I felt my heart—just—stop. Oh, that's a strange place, Heart. It's not bad. It's very ... intense and light at the same moment. Light. Light. And strange. Because, inside it becomes quieter than quiet. You don't even know all the noise of the inner workings. Until that moment when it halts.

"Into that peculiar void I heard—but not with my physical sense—I heard Jackson's voice, 'I—Love—You' he said. Profound sound. And then, I ... slept. Until I 'came to,' on Pink. Surrounded by the mechanicals and clockworks, rebuilding me. All the while, there, at my side, Father Inventor, with his hand on my forehead, or holding my hand, instructed them. Well, they knew what they were doing, in any case. They'd built themselves, you know. Broken bits and pieces got together and built themselves. Without Father Inventor. Without him even knowing about it.

"And so, they brought life back to the being known as 'Xavier.' Strange little boy who will never grow up. But, Heart, I love you. No matter what."

At that moment, Father Inventor's voice came into the tiny spacecraft. "How is she?" His voice filled with alarm.

"We must be safely out of range of Earth," Xavier said. "They've told him about your condition." He addressed Heart's father, "We're talking. Fascinating conversation. I think she's good."

"I'm all right," Heart said faintly from the floor.

"Did I hear her?"

"Yes," Xavier answered. "She told you she's all right. Not exactly accurate, but still, she's able to say it. She's dealing with the mechanical depersonalization."

"Oh, that'll go away quickly, once she and Equuleus are within range. All right, Xavier, excellent my boy, I'm very proud of you, taking care of her ...."

"Well, you know, I cannot do otherwise."

"I'm going to lock your spacecraft in the aurora and bring you in. You attend to her, and leave the steering to the light power. I shan't bother you again until you dock. Equuleus is standing by."

"Right, sir. Are you saying I can completely stand down, to attend to Heart?"

"It's an order, my lad."

"Yes, sir!"

"See you soon. By the way, there's a big box of candy by the *Heart!* dock. Is that yours?"

"I am ashamed to admit, I did take it. I thought it'd distract me during the boring travel. Not knowing, of course, that both outbound and inbound would be the most interesting moments of my life! Miss Heart took it upon herself to remove my treasure to jettison weight, and replace it with herself."

Father Inventor chuckled. "My girl! All right, see you soon." The connection clicked off.

The *Heart!* experienced a bit of a jolt as the aurora magnetically latched onto the spacecraft. The interior, enveloped in the shifting, pastel hues of the aurora, cocooned the two of them in a mystical place.

Silence returned. Xavier unstrapped himself and moved to sit next to Heart on the floor. "Do you mind if I hold your hand?" he asked.

"Why?"

"Because it'll feel nice, and maybe I can push some of my health to you."

"Yes. Perhaps. Let's try it."

Xavier held Heart's hand between his two hands and sighed. "I never, ever could have imagined this moment," he whispered.

"It ..." Heart registered true surprise, "feels nice. Warm and real. Even in this strange condition I'm in, so compromised, so not myself, it feels nice."

"That makes me happy," Xavier said simply.

"So ... Jackson said, 'I love you,' after your heart stopped beating," Heart prompted.

"Yes."

"Then all those beautiful residents of Pink and my father reconstructed you, and brought you back to life."

"That sums it up."

"Now you're working, for *The Cause of All Beings* to protect the lives of all beings, and I'm working to protect the lives of Darling Undesirables—in particular, Eye—from the agenda of The Purists. Here we are, strangely, side by side, in a little spacecraft, making our way back to Pink."

"That pretty much tells the story," Xavier agreed.

"Strange story ...."

"Everyone's story is strange, even the boring ones. Because there's always something unanticipated, unexpected. Something mysterious and surprising about life, isn't there?"

"I suppose so," Heart agreed, waiting to hear more of Xavier's wise-yet-innocent observations about life.

"There's life, and there's dark energy, which does not seem to need individual life forms, and dark matter, same thing. Then there's us. We are individual life forms, and we seem to need to make representations of ourselves. Like Father Inventor's amazing mechanicals and clockworks, that think and feel in their own different way."

"So ... what are you saying, Xavier?"

"I'm not sure. I'm thinking about those few moments—when Jackson said he loved me, and I could
understand him, even though I didn't exactly hear
him, in a physical way. But I heard him ...."

"Fascinating. But—what are you *not* saying?"

"Just—in that space, there was another space. In
that space, I was about to slip between ...."

"Between what?"

"Here and There." That's all. I can't say more, because I know no more. Your hand feels wonderful."

Your hands feel lovely, too, Xavier. What 'between
here and there'? Where's 'Here'? Where's 'There'?"

"Again, I don't know. You think you know 'here,'
until you get a glimpse of *'there.'* And then you know
that you know nothing you've ever known. *That you
know nothing.*"

"You understood that you know nothing?" Heart
whispered in awe.

Xavier nodded.

"Do you still think that's true?"

"Yes. Mostly, yes. But the difference now is
that it doesn't matter so much. I play the role. It
seems that we're to play a role, but most earnestly.
Even if the illusion shines through, which it does
in the space between. It's like ... it's like you see
to play the role even more earnestly, even when
you know how unreal it is, you know it more than
anyone."

"Hmmm ... So, it sounds like you're saying there's
no such thing as death ...."

Oh, Heart, you are brilliant! That's it, exactly. That's precisely what I'm saying. There's no such thing as death. There's the illusion of being not *Here*. But, of course, then, you're *There*. You've slipped between. It's very compelling *There*. It's not perfect, *There*, either. I think—I only caught a glimpse, but I think there are bigger challenges *There*."

"Oh, my!" Heart exclaimed. *"Oh my, indeed!"*

"Yes. But it's compelling. That's why no one hardly ever comes back. Well, there's me, a rare exception. But, I suspect that, if anyone does come back, everyone in this illusion—wearing blinders as they are—doesn't see them."

"I think I understand. It's like when I shape-shift—I'm utterly mystified when people don't see me. *I'm right there!* Everything that's 'me' is there. Except I blend in to where I'm standing. I look down, and usually, I see me. But when I look at someone, it's obvious, they don't see me."

"Hiding in plain sight."

"Yes. Hiding in plain sight."

"Interesting metaphor," Xavier became silent, contemplating. "Yes. Interesting metaphor."

"Do you think this experience, in that *'between'* space when your heart stopped, is that where you learned all of this? It's very compelling."

"I'm sure I learned more, much, much more, but simply could not bring it back with me. Couldn't. It's not meant for the three dimensions. Not even dark energy or dark matter can know the *between*."

"How do you know that? Maybe dark energy is the exact gateway to the *'between.'*"

Xavier brushed his hand across Heart's cheek. "Perhaps."

Heart waited for him to say more, but he simply looked into her eyes, in the floating muted pastels of the aurora in the little spacecraft. "Where did you go just now?" she finally asked.

"Where I always go. To a moment with you. In my imagination. Sitting, talking with you holding your hand. And now I am. I want to drink it in. I want to etch it like acid upon my brain synapses. I want to tattoo it in my veins, to my every moment as my strange hybrid blood passes through my veins, I want it to send it a picture of this—perfect—moment."

"*Oh, Xavier!*" Heart breathed.

"What, Heart?"

"Such poetry ...."

"No. Just. You."

Something happened to Heart in that strange and fantastical moment, tearing through space held in an aurora energy vortex, rushing toward a synthetic moon, where her heart, in Equuleus, and her father waited for her, with anxious anticipation.

She felt something in her center crash through the floorboards of her being. Even in her odd, cold, mechanical, cog-clockworks condition, something opened in her.

What is this new feeling? She wondered. In her mind, she moved around it. Is this, she asked herself silently ... it couldn't be ... was it *love*? "That kind" of love? The love that was still love, but different from all the others, the one she'd heard caused an actual chemical shift in aligning with *The Other*. An actual sort of locking of bio-materials.

But—how could it be between herself and Xavier? Both of them such a mashup of materials and experience.

These thoughts made her overwhelmingly exhausted. She longed to sleep. She wanted not to think about this feeling. Nor to feel it. As she attempted to avoid all of these thoughts, a memory came to mind. She saw Jackson approaching her, reaching up to her on Equuleus. She saw herself turn her head as he reached to kiss her cheek, and *she!* not he—*she!* turned her face and kissed him on his mouth.

No. That couldn't be right. Did she do that? Now everything seemed confused. *If!* If she felt that way about Jackson, what would she do with this confusing feeling for Xavier? Oh, she'd grown beyond tired and became vexed, and now, suddenly extremely weak as well.

"You've become exceptionally quiet," Xavier gave her hand a squeeze.

"I'm, I'm confused. And tired. And suddenly very cold. I think. I've hardly ever been cold, but I'm sure I'm too cold."

Alarm came into Xavier's features. "You *are* suddenly very cold. What's happening? Do you feel cold all over?"

"I think so. I'm very tired, I'm trying to think, but I can't—just too much for me. I'm not my usual self."

"No, you're not. We've already established that. I don't know what to do. Don't lose consciousness. Keep talking."

"I don't have anything to say."

Xavier jumped up and ran around the small compartment. Throwing everything about, he found a blanket and returned to Heart. He wrapped her in the blanket, then called Pink. "Heart appears to be shutting down."

Heart could barely hear him, and his urgency added to her confusion. There was nothing wrong with her. Except being unnaturally cold. She tried to speak. She simply wanted to say, "I'm all right," but she could not get the words out—as if her mouth had frozen shut.

Oh, it didn't matter! Xavier told her about the *between*. He'd been there and he came back. She needed to rest. Strange, yes, she almost never needed to rest.

She heard Xavier again. "How are you feeling?"

She tried to answer, but she couldn't quite understand his question. "Feel-ing?" So difficult to say that one word! *"Doooon't know."* So beautiful, the play of the aurora lights upon him. So beautiful, his worried look, his shining face, his adorable freckles ....

"You're very pretty, all the colors passing over you. Don't frown. The light makes you translucent—I can see right through you!"

"You're very pretty, too, Heart. The aurora colors are remarkable. I can't say that I see through you, but the lights enhance your beauty." He fell silent as their gaze locked for a few moments, until Heart slowly closed her eyes.

"Heart?" Oh, his voice came from far, far away.

Heart rushed upon the wings of sound, while everything telescoped in a narrow tunnel that swept her with it. It didn't bother her. It felt quite natural to give up and become a little leaf of flotsam upon the jetsam of energy. Deep inside her—somewhere—a thrumming pulsed. The core of dark energy in herself answering to the vast, vast Universe of dark energy.

She started to fragment among the stars, when a light, a pinpoint of light came toward her, directly toward her. *She knew this light!*

She tried to hail the light, to say hello. She didn't want it to pass her, though it seemed very intent upon its business, and surely would not respond to her calling to it.

But—she knew this light!

Then, indeed! It stopped right before her. In the voice of many tinkling bells, it murmured and chimed, "Heart. you are profoundly needed where you are, in this Universe. Gather your strength. Listen to Xavier's voice. He will call you back. *Listen!*" the tinkling bells commanded.

Heart obeyed.

"*Heart!*" Xavier urgently called to her.

"Ummm ...." She finally made a small sound.

"Oh! Thank you, thank you, Heart!"

Then she realized he held her, completely wrapped in a blanket. Xavier held her in his arms. It made her feel warm. It made her want to be here. "*The light!*" she whispered.

"I know," Xavier agreed. "The beautiful aurora lights ...."

"*No! The! Light!*" Oh, so hard to talk, but she would obey the Light. "*The! Light!* The light from the heart of Leo made me come back. It said I must return ...."

"Thank you Light of Leo, whatever you are, for bringing back my Heart," Xavier prayed.

"Yes, Xavier. That's right, a prayer of thanks to the wonderful, loving Light. Thank you Light, thank you, Xavier." Heart relaxed in Xavier's arms, concentrating on the delicious patches of warmth where their bodies touched, holding onto the command of the Light, though, it remained very, very difficult.

"Stay with me, Heart. You must obey the Light. We are soon back on Pink. Wonderman One and Wonderman Two are waiting for you, Equuleus is waiting for you, your father is waiting for you. Even your new little friend, Violet said a few words to me. She told me to tell you she loves you and can't wait for you to hold her again."

"It's incredible to be held," Heart whispered.

"Oh! Heart!"

Even in her reduced and compromised condition, Heart heard the emotion that racked Xavier.

"Don't—don't be hurt, Xavier. Don't be hurt," she sighed.

"I'm not—hurt. No. Yes. I am hurting. Only one prayer. Don't leave me. Don't leave."

"All right. But I must rest now. Must. Rest."

"Your Father told me I absolutely must keep you responding to me. Can you just nod, and let me know you're still with me?"

Heart nodded. This would do. She could keep her father, Xavier and the Light all happy if she only nodded in response to Xavier's talk-talk-talking. Even if she couldn't quite understand what he said ... even if she ....

Xavier said something else ... what did he say? She didn't know, but she nodded. She felt his warmth, and she nodded. She ....

A crunching sensation entered the spacecraft. Heart didn't know what caused this peculiar sensation. But as long as Xavier held on to her, she didn't care.

"We're here, Heart! We're on Pink. Wonderman One and Wonderman Two will bring you back to yourself. Equuleus ... Equuleus awaits."

"Equuleus!" Oh, pouring through her and sloshing out the sides, ran the love of Equuleus through her. He was near! She could feel him, hooking up to her. But, wait something wasn't quite right. Something prevented her from engaging with Equuleus.

The small ship docked with a mighty jerk, and she and Xavier flew across the cabin. "It's all right, Heart, I have you. I'm not letting go. I've got you!"

They collided with the far wall, but Xavier hung onto her. Sounds whirled around her, but all she desired to have continue was Xavier holding her. It felt quite bothersome not to be able to reach Equuleus. Something definitely wrong.

She heard the hatch grind open. Xavier stood, still clinging to her. He carefully went down the steps of the hatch.

Then, though far away and remote, she heard the population of Pink cheer, happy to see Xavier. That made her happy too. But then she heard them chanting in a giant whisper, *"Heart, Heart, Heart!"*

"No!" she wanted to shout. *"*It's not me, it's Xavier. He is our hero!" But she couldn't even open her eyes, let alone say a word.

Then, everything fell silent, a hush spread through the joy-filled mechanicals and mechanical bios and clockworks beings. She knew they were taking in the look on Xavier's face, and her own stillness. But the blanket around her, and everywhere his body touched hers, she felt warm.

She heard her father's voice. "Oh, Father," she thought. Her adored Father! But, try as she might to stay with all that swirled around her, she fell away from consciousness.

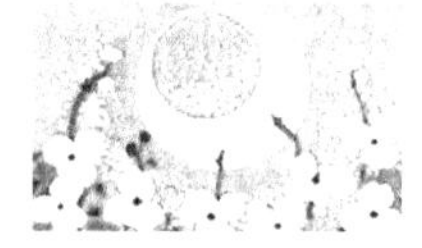

Chapter 21

All around her stood everyone she loved—Father, Equuleus, Eye, Jackson, Zack, Martha, Key Man, Peter, Xavier, Violet, even Butterfly ... and a couple others, she couldn't clearly see, but they were there, all in a mystical circle around her—however, at a great distance. Everything bathed in sparkling white light. Such a glorious light!

They all had their attention fastened upon her, silent, unmoving. In the center, she turned slowly, taking each one in and thanking them for being a part of her life, acknowledging the role they played in her life, and the reciprocity of her life in each of theirs. Her turning and acknowledging was like a great clock. She knew that when she came around to straight up twelve, she would be ....

Slam! An electrical jolt threw her right out of the ticking circle. *Slam! Slam!* She felt herself gasping, her back arching, as if rising from the depths of a deep, deep lake.

She gasped and her eyes flew open. Before her stood Wonderman One and Wonderman Two, arms linked, just like their counterparts on Earth had linked up to her. Except now, as she took in the roiling purple fluids in their vials, she saw them separate, and gradually, Wonderman One's—or was it Wonderman Two's? vial started to return to blue, while his counterpart's vial gradually returned to red.

Heart felt the unlocking, unlinking of the mechanicals throughout her body. Her bios came back into command. Her brain and her mind plugged back into their usual selves. Unusual enough, of their own accord.

She reached out, and there, to her right, stood Equuleus. She couldn't see him, but she could touch him.

Heart! she heard in her mind.

My friend, my true heart, she responded. She touched his face, and sighed deeply, taking in air, releasing the separation, taking in, hooking up. Here, the rest of her whole self. *Never again!* she thought to him.

No, never again! he agreed.

Wonderman One and Wonderman Two disconnected themselves from her, and stepped back, letting Father Inventor through. He sat on her left side, taking her hand.

"Thank you!" she whispered faintly to Wonderman One and Wonderman Two. "Thank you and your Earth duplicates. Love to you and to them."

"Oh!" Wonderman Two cried.

"Heart!" Wonderman One added plaintively. Overcome with emotion, they could say no more.

"Yes," her father said, "oh, Heart! Back with us."

"I am." She closed her eyes, drinking in the feeling of being herself again. Engaging with herself all through her body, and feelings, and thoughts.

Her father started talking quietly at her side, holding her hand, but not, she realized, talking to her. "Yes sir," she heard Xavier say.

Father was giving Xavier orders. She brought herself enough into consciousness to listen to the conversation.

"We must raise the moons' moons as soon as possible."

"Yes, sir."

"They're ready. The immigrants have been waiting for you to return, launch is entirely set to go. "

"Yes, sir."

"Are you ready, too my boy? Are you ready? You've been through a lot. I know you're a bit fragile when you have to deal with your emotions. Your mechanicals ...."

"Yes. My mechanicals can give me a hard time when I'm dealing with my human emotions. But I'm all right if she's all right. To be truthful, if she is ... if she doesn't ... if you think that she in any way might not make it ...."

"She's good now, Xavier. She's going to make it."

"*Umm-hum* ..." Heart agreed softly.

Xavier and her father chuckled. "You heard her!"

"Then I'm ready!"

Heart opened her eyes to give Xavier a smile, but the intensity that he fixated upon her, unnerved her. "I—I'm all right. Although, that part about being shocked, don't want to go there again ...."

"No fun," Equuleus agreed.

"Oh no, I didn't even think about what you might have gone through. I'm sorry, dear Equuleus."

"All right, I'm somewhat mollified by your apology, while I remain not entirely appreciative of what you've put me through. Not just now, but the whole flying off to Earth thing. Not nice."

"No, not nice—yet *so wonderful!*" She turned to her father. "I know you have gigantic, world building things going on, but Father, Eye must be taken out of the Darling Undesirables Facility at Long Prairie. Keeper A behaved so strangely ...."

"She behaved strangely? How so?" Her father asked, clearly curious.

"I put a tiny camera opposite my previous room's door. Keeper A came to the door and put her hands on it. Incidentally, Eye is staying in my room with Butterfly, and Keeper A must know it. But she didn't do anything other than put her hands on the door, then leave. Odd behavior. It's so confusing when odd people act odd, even for themselves."

"She put her hands on the door ...."

"Yes. And then walked away. Just that. Before that, she tracked me through the grounds while I was there, according to Swen and Jackson. Very, *verrrrry* strange behavior!"

"Hmmm, Yes," her father agreed thoughtfully.

"So—Eye needs to be removed, directly. And now, of course, Butterfly must also be taken with him. It would traumatize him—yet again!—to have another separation. He doesn't deserve that."

"You're all right with Butterfly being with him?"

Heart nodded. "Yes, I'm more than all right. I love Eye, without conditions. Whoever he is, whatever he does, whatever he needs, the undercurrent is, I love him. In any case, I've always adored Butterfly. That she's taking care of Eye is fine. Better than fine.

"They're similar in their gentleness, with the exception that Butterfly can see. Like two little elves in a cocoon when I saw them. Looking as if they felt safe together and utterly relaxed. So, Father, in the midst of all that you're orchestrating—and bringing two moons into the sky is a huge orchestration!—can you consider Eye and Butterfly?"

"It's as good as done, dear Heart. Jackson, Zack and I have been in communication about this very subject for some time. It's one of our, what we refer to as 'quiet plans.' Things not urgent, but that could roar to the surface practically instantaneously. The moment has arrived for Eye. The only problem now being to include Butterfly. Are you sure she'll want to leave the Darling Undesirables Facility?"

"Oh, yes. She won't want to be separated from Eye—as long as she has a garden, she'll be happy. They both love their flowers!"

"As do you."

"As do I. How are my little flowers? I trust my absence didn't harm them ...."

"No, no, they're fine. HelperFriend and the Plant Folks enjoyed themselves immensely, tending to your flowers. I've noticed an uplifting in spirits altogether since you planted the flowers."

"Maybe their joy was because I wasn't around!" Heart said.

"Absolutely not. The flowers distracted the mechanicals. They were frightfully worried about you."

"Oh dear, I caused so much trouble. I'm sorry, Father."

"You did—but you also accomplished important business with Eye and Butterfly.

"Now we'll include Butterfly and take action fairly directly. Otherwise, it likely would have happened with less planning, and we certainly would not have considered taking a second Darling Undesirable out of the Facility.

"Another very important detail, not that I'd have you go through this experience for anything, but it answered a question I've had about what would happen if you and Equuleus were on different celestial spheres. I worked it out theoretically, hoping I'd never have to see it in reality.

"I tried to figure out how to tell you of the potential risk when you left on the *Heart!*, but Xavier cut me off before I could gather my thoughts. Because the stress of fear and anxiety contribute to your system's failure if too long too far from Equuleus, I didn't want you to start your journey in a state of anxiety. Further, I knew if you continued, the concern would distract Xavier. But if he returned at that moment, we'd miss a potentially life and death time frame for him to accomplish his mission.

"I also knew, dear daughter, that you were pining for Eye. And I guess, Swen, as well. In any case—let's not push it ever again."

Heart hung her head. "Agreed."

Her father patted her hand. "However, as I would acknowledge anyone in *The Cause of All Beings*—I commend you for a mission beautifully and fully accomplished."

"Thank you, Father," Heart said shyly, looking up with gratitude. "But enough about me and my commendable misbehavior—when can Butterfly and Eye be moved?"

"Jackson and Zack have been at the ready to remove Eye upon my word."

"Really? Why didn't Jackson mention that to me?"

"I ordered him not to, it being of utmost importance for everyone concerned to see what you discovered without any clouding considerations—if Eye was still in his same room if he was even still on the grounds. If other considerations came up ....”

“Like Butterfly,” Heart said.

“Yes, like Butterfly. I’ll direct Jackson and Zack to take Eye and Butterfly tonight.”

“Where will they go? Oh dear, they’ll be so frightened ....”

“Where in the world is the best place for them?”

“Well ... ahm ... *oh!* The Mystic’s little cottage!”

“That’s right. She’s been getting ready for their arrival. Amdrona will go with Jackson and Zack, as she also has shape-shifting skills. The plan is for her to take the same route you did, going under the wall at the Darling Undesirables Facility, shape-shifting through the garden, going up to their room, and quietly telling them what is happening ....”

“The cameras, Father. The cameras in the rooms. Amdrona must move very, very subtly.”

“Yes, she knows. If you’ll note where the cameras are so she can be aware of their locations ... no one will even know she’s been there.”

“Except Keeper A, who seems always to know everything.”

“Well, I can’t argue with you on that score. She is a bright one, that Keeper A,” Heart’s father said, with an intensity that took Heart’s attention. “They’ll steal down to Zack and Jackson, I’ll have Swen go along as well to open and close the escape tunnel.

“Then they’ll fly to The Museum of Scientific Improbabilities and Unpredictable Oddities, where they’ll be safe on the other side of *The Wall*, long before sunrifse.”

Heart heaved a gigantic sigh of relief. "Thank you, Father," she said simply.

"You needn't thank me, my dear. I'm only doing what I always do."

"I know. Taking care of *All Beings*. Now then, you have huge things to plan, and I'm all right. So please return to what you were doing before my interruption."

"If you're sure ...." He leaned over and gave her a hug. "All right you three, let's get to work."

Wonderman One and Wonderman Two followed him dutifully, while Xavier lingered behind. "Are you certain sure you're well enough to be left alone?"

"Equuleus snorted. "I beg your pardon!"

"Sorry Equuleus, that didn't come out right. I mean, I know you don't need me in any way, of course, but do you not need the Wondermen to stand by?"

"No, no, Xavier. I'm feeling very much myself. Just a tiny bit weak, but getting better moment by moment. As long as Equuleus is nearby, I'm fine. You stay focused, Xavier. Keep your mind on whatever it is Father is having you do. By the way, what *is* Father having you do?"

"I'll be engineering the move of the two collapsed moons into place, and overseeing their expansion, once in situ."

"Oh! Just a small little project, I see!"

"Right!" Xavier grinned, freckles bouncing on his beautiful cheekbones. Heart found it most distracting.

"That's more like it!" she said. "Now, finally, you seem like your real self!"

"I'm my real self when *you're* your real self."

Heart laughed softly, "Now we're both our real selves, so you'd better get your real self upon *The Cause of All Beings*, while I laze about with Equuleus."

"I'm on it!" He headed for the door.

"Xavier," Heart called after him.

He stopped in his tracks and turned toward her. "Yes?"

"*Thank you!* Thank you for what you shared with me, thank you for keeping me warm. I know that's the only reason I'm still here."

"Don't say that!"

"I *am* saying that. You saved my life. Plain and simple, and thank you."

"I don't believe that's true, but whatever I did, I could do nothing less. I wanted to do more ...."

"There was nothing more!" She smiled at him.

Xavier winked and went through the door.

"*Oh my,*" Heart said faintly.

"What is happening to our heart, Heart?" Equuleus asked.

"I'm not too sure."

"It feels like ...."

"I know ... but then again, I don't know ...."

"*Hearrrrrt,*" Violet squealed, hopping into the room and up onto Equuleus's back. "Oh, Heart, you scared me! I was so worried, anxious, troubled, distraught, stressed, fearful, trepidatious ... and *soooo* afraid. "I couldn't stop thinking, 'what if Heart doesn't come back? What will my life be? I like Equuleus fine, sure, but he's not you!"

"Very nice," Equuleus said sarcastically.

"Sorry, I don't know what I'm saying, I'm just so happy to have Heart back."

"As are we all," Equuleus agreed.

"Are you two getting along?" Heart didn't like the tone between them.

"We only became a bit snappish when we didn't know about you. But we're over that now, aren't we, beautiful gear horse?"

"Of course," Equuleus said as if the conversation dealt entirely too much with something altogether too small.

"Be nice!" Heart said.

"Yeah. Be nice," Violet agreed.

"I *am* nice." Equuleus clamped his muzzle shut as if he had not another word to say on the subject.

"Very good." Heart decided not to pursue the bad attitude, given that she had put Equuleus through a very hard time. Perhaps harder than she knew. "Did my distance from you affect you physically?"

"I'm not sure, Heart. Not sure. I was so worried about you, maybe it was simply that."

"*What* was simply that?"

"Nothing to take anyone's attention over, with the much larger issues flying about."

"Yeah. That's hitting the target," Violet piped up.

"Hush!" Equuleus commanded.

"No. I won't hush. He couldn't fly. That's what happened. He almost crashed on the marble floor. All but plummeted from your rooms to the floor below."

"*What?!?* Equuleus! Nothing like that has ever happened!"

"No. But you've never gone off in a small spacecraft, to a planet with growing turmoil without me before, either."

"True," Heart answered. "But, what *exactly* happened?"

"I was worrying about you. I stepped to the landing and jumped off, but my wings only partially extended. I couldn't seem to tell them what to do. I sort of glided and sort of crashed to the floor. It shocked me. I haven't tried to fly again since."

"Alarming! What shall we do?"

"You're here, you're recovered. I feel fine. When you're ready to go outside, I'll show you I'm all right."

"Let's go! I want to look in on my flowers anyway. Oh! Where's HelperFriend?"

"I think you'll soon have your answer." Equuleus followed Heart down the hall to the front entrance, Violet riding along on his back.

After they stepped outside, Heart took Violet in her arms. Equuleus stretched, and then took flight. He twirled and spun and plunged and climbed, showing off. Then, soft as a dove, he landed where he took off.

"*Beautiful!*" Violet sighed.

"Very beautiful," Heart agreed.

"The flowers are incredible from the sky, Heart," Equuleus said. "The light and the colors, *stunning!*"

"Wonderful!" Heart put Violet on Equuleus. "Let me step inside the greenhouse for a moment."

Inside, she breathed deeply the humid, loamy scent, and walked about the fully bloomed flowers, their colors vying with their scent. "Beautiful, beautiful, my precious blossoms." The primroses, violets, daisies, columbine, marigolds pansies—all the cheerful flowers reached their heads up to the synthetic lights overhead.

She wandered among the flowers and came to the back door. Letting herself out through the baffle, she went into the neighboring greenhouse, and there encountered HelperFriend.

"*Oh! Heart!*" He cried. Strange little metallic tears ran down his clockwork face. "*Heart!*" He seemed incapable of saying more.

"HelperFriend, don't cry—if that's what you're doing! You'll mineralize the flowers!" She laughed.

"Oh, sorry, sorry! No, I don't want to do that." He tried to catch the little bits of metal as they fell. "I'm just so ...."

"I know, HelperFriend. I am too. I'm so happy to be here, with you."

"I couldn't be there when you came. I wanted to, but I'm such a wreck, as you can see. Just ... too emotional! I don't know how that is, given that I'm clockworks. But that's the way I am. When I come upon an emotion, I seem unable to change it immediately, like bios can."

"But you're not sad or worried now are you, dear friend? Here I am, on my own feet, in great shape."

"No, I know. It's wonderful. Better than wonderful. But I'm still crying these little bits of metal. Can't seem to stop."

"Look at the flowers!" Heart pointed to the flowers below HelperFriend. They'd turned brass and copper hued.

"Oh dear! That will never do! Will they be all right?"

"I don't know. But I think we'd better either step outside, or you need to stop crying bits of metal."

"I think I'll do both." He stepped through the baffle and Heart followed. Once outside, his crying gradually ceased.

"What's that?" Violet asked, pointing at the bits of metal on the ground.

"HelperFriend's tears," Heart answered. "He's made metallic flowers. They're quite beautiful."

"I've totally messed up the plaid grid."

"I don't think so, HelperFriend. The flowers are still different shades and still maintain a plaid grid, just in hues of brass and copper. Anyway, no more crying! I'm back, I'm well, the mission to Earth went perfectly for Xavier and nearly so for me, Pink's and Yellow's moons will soon be launched—all is right with our worlds!"

"Except for one little glitch," HelperFriend reminded.

"Except for one little glitch. The Purist's dogged determination that everything *must be their way*."

"Why are they like that?" Violet asked. "You don't interfere with their beliefs, do you?"

"No," Heart petted Violet as she sat contentedly upon Equuleus's back. "I don't even understand their beliefs, but it's none of my business."

"*Why* are they so intolerant?"

"I truly don't know. However, let's not focus on their negative energy. Let's emphasize our positive energy. We'll crush their agenda with goodwill and love."

"Perfect!" Equuleus agreed.

"Excellent," HelperFriend chimed in. "How about some lunch?"

"Oh! I *am* hungry!" Heart exclaimed, surprised.

They followed HelperFriend inside, settling in the dining room while HelperFriend went into the kitchen, singing arias in a stunning soprano at the top of his voice. Equuleus shook his mighty head as if he could shake the sound out.

"Equuleus, he has a beautiful voice!"

"Voice, yes. Choice of music, not my favorite."

Heart chuckled while Violet squealed, "*Bea-uuu-ti-ful!*" at the top of her voice, joining HelperFriend's highest note.

"Nooo!" Equuleus whinnied.

HelperFriend brought in a feast on a giant tray. "What's with all the racket?"

"I believe they're attempting to imitate you," Heart said, laughing.

"Goodness!" HelperFriend put down the tray, eye gears rotating madly. "Do not do that. Bad sound, both of you!"

Even Equuleus laughed. "I, ah well, yes, Helper-Friend, you're right. You must remain the only one among us to attempt soprano arias."

Heart leaned over and tugged at Equuleus's ear. "Good horsie," she teased.

But she couldn't take her mind off the thought of Eye and Butterfly getting rescued. She turned on her little camera receiver to be sure of an adequate reception and became uneasy when she saw Butterfly's door standing open. Dinner time—why would the door be open? Out stepped Keeper A. Next, she stepped through Eye's door.

What was she doing?

"What, Heart, what?" Violet whispered.

Heart glanced at her friends, then returned her attention to the 3-D receiver. "Keeper A—just stepped out of Butterfly's room, the room that used to be mine, and has now stepped into Eye's room. Why?"

"I have to show this to Father. I want Eye out of there, but we can't send Amdrona into danger! Maybe danger for Eye and Butterfly, too." She ran down the hall to her father's room and flew through the door into the wide open space where the busy-ness of a beehive took place.

"Where's my father?" she paused to ask a mechanical.

"Heart!" the mechanical muttered shyly.

"Yes. My father?"

A bit dumbfounded, he gestured, and Heart hurried in the direction he pointed. She spied her father in his transparent bell jar.

"Father!"

Everyone around him stopped their activity to look at Heart. "Good as new!" one of them said. Soon the chant was taken up and echoed through the chamber.

"What's wrong?" Her father asked, seeing the alarm on her face.

She held up the 3-D receiver. As they watched, the shadow of Keeper A fell upon the camera when she came out of Eye's room. "That's Keeper A," Heart said, then rewound the 3-D. "Here's just a few minutes ago."

She watched her father as he watched the 3-D. "That *is* strange, Heart. But don't worry. Eye and Butterfly will be rescued as soon as Zack and Jackson have the cover of dark. Whatever is going on, there won't be an expectation that we'll move this soon. Just—have faith."

"I do, but what if she planted something?"

"What would she plant that Butterfly and Eye wouldn't detect? Between the two of them, they have significantly augmented senses. I'm trusting the element of surprise."

"What if we're endangering Zack and Amdrona and Jackson and Swen? Butterfly and Eye are safe for the moment. But what if we're putting the four of them in danger?"

"They've all been in danger before. They know how to handle themselves. Plus, Amdrona can shape-shift. It's the perfect moment to break out Butterfly and Eye. Let them handle it, they know what they're doing."

Heart calmed down. True, all true. She *did* need to let them handle it. She needed to let everyone do what they knew how to do, and stay out of the way of the crescendoing energy.

"You're right. Everything will work out. Just, please let them know about Keeper A's strange behavior, so they can be on the lookout for—anything—strange." She backed away from him and out of the frenetic beehive, promising herself that she'd keep out of the area until after Pink and Yellow's moons were launched.

Back in her father's room HelperFriend, Equuleus and Violet, stood in a row, waiting for her to come through the door.

"*Well?*" Violet asked impatiently.

"He reminded me that I must trust everyone. Everyone knows what they're doing. With the element of surprise, Eye and Butterfly will soon be rescued. I must believe in it. I must trust it. And so I shall."

"And so shall we all," Equuleus nodded.

"Let's finish our lovely meal, then retire to my rooms to watch Amdrona, Zack, Jackson and Swen rescue Eye and Butterfly."

Let's," HelperFriend said, heading back to the dining room.

Chapter 22

In Heart's rooms a short while later, everyone settled in to watch a 3-D projection of a door, far, far away, as if it promised to be the most entertaining sight any of them ever saw.

Heart sat on the floor with Violet in her lap and Equuleus curled up beside her. HelperFriend sat in a straight-backed chair, insisting that this was the most comfortable position for his mechanical parts.

They watched the 3-D, showing Butterfly and Eye's door in the Darling Undesirables Facility at Long Prairie, with rapt attention.

After an hour Violet became restless. "When is something *going to happen?*"

"We don't know, Violet, dear," Heart stroked her back, "you don't have to stay here. We'll let you know when ...." Heart paused.

"When what?"

"*Look!*" A faint wobbling appeared on the 3-D, looking like nothing other than a transmission variance. But Heart knew what she saw—shape-shifter—Amdrona had arrived!

Breathlessly, everyone watched the door appear to open of its own accord, and stealthily close. Heart pictured what was happening on the other side of the door, but *oh!* how she wished she could be there! She longed to put her hand in Eye's palm and tell him of her love and her pride in him. To encourage him to be brave. And—and all that she would tell him, if only she could!

But Amdrona—beautiful, gentle, brilliant, kind Amdrona would communicate all of that in her own way. Eye would surely feel Heart nearby.

He must!

Amdrona took a *looooong* time. What was happening on the other side of that door? Finally, slowly, slowly, it opened again, its surface shifting and quivery. Out stepped Butterfly, holding onto Eye's hand, as he, too, stepped through the doorway.

Heart gasped. She couldn't help it. Her friend, her dearest little friend, who had gone through *everything, everything* together with her throughout their childhood.

"Eye!" she exclaimed softly. Violet looked up at Heart's expression, reached up and gave her cheek a soft rabbit-y kiss.

"He will be all right, Heart. He will be all right ...."

"I know," Heart hugged Violet. But she could not disguise the anxiety and sadness in her voice.

"Yes, they will be all right," Equuleus whispered.

Butterfly paused outside the door, holding Eye's hand so sweetly, that Heart wanted to reach out and hug her. Then they moved along the wall, and at the very edge of the range of the camera, Heart watched as Eye opened the door to his own room, and he and Butterfly and the quavery presence stepped inside. Surprised, she turned to Equuleus.

"He's getting something to take with him that reminds him of you," Equuleus murmured.

"Oh!" Heart had to close her eyes. That feeling like crying came upon her. Sometimes—sometimes, it was more difficult not to be able to cry, than simply to cry. But the sweeping emotion had its way inside her deepest recesses, and she sighed again and again.

Eye's door cracked open, then shut. Out of range now, the three of them must be on their way down the stairs, across the bit of lawn to the back fence—passing Butterfly's passionately adored flower garden—she surely would long to pause there, but Amdrona would push them on, to the fence, to the tunnel under the fence that Swen would have cleared.

First Butterfly, reaching back to guide Eye, who probably would actually fare better, because everything was always dark for him, then Amdrona. They would scurry to the museum's craft while Swen filled the tunnel back in again.

If no alarms sounded, if they pulled off their stealthy removal of the two Darling Undesirables successfully, the museum's dark energy vehicle would soon lift, hovering low among the trees until at a safe distance, and then pull onto the Dark Energy Highway, winging its way to The Museum of Scientific Improbabilities and Unpredictable Oddities.

Then, and only then, would Heart be able to heave a sigh of relief. But how would she know?

As if she'd asked the question aloud, HelperFriend said, "I can project a wave of energy to The Museum of Scientific Improbabilities and Unpredictable Oddities and you might be able to see them. Or at least hear them.

"It would not be good for me to do it too much as it could be detected by an energy sweep. But I can do short bursts around the time we expect them to arrive. It's an unreliable connection, we might get nothing, there might be a bit of visual without sound, or sound without visual. But, at least it might be possible to learn they've arrived."

"Oh, dear HelperFriend! That would be perfect. What do you think, Equuleus?"

"Let's let him try it. But, Heart, don't be disappointed if it doesn't work. You know we dare not allow a steady connection."

"Right. You're right. We'll be cautious and hope for the best. It's a good thing you never told me this before, HelperFriend."

"I didn't know I could do it before. I scrolled through my programs earlier—many of which I've never touched, specifically for this purpose. Because I knew it would be important to you. I've pinpointed a spot in the middle of the museum that they'll have to pass. If we only have audio, and they're moving about in silence, we still may not know any more than we do now. But if we get a bit of vid, it'll come up on your 3-D."

"It's worth a try. We can assume if I see any one of their party, they're all there. Of course, they'll be moving quickly to the tunnel and to The Periphery, so at the very best, it would only be seconds. But one second of seeing one of them is all I need."

Time dragged by, but finally, Heart said, "I think we might watch for them now."

HelperFriend whirred and a weak light appeared in the 3-D space. Heart saw a small bit of visual reception. She immediately recognized the hall HelperFriend's projection fastened upon.

"Fantastic, HelperFriend, you're right. No matter what, they'll pass this spot."

The light blinked off. "I'm not comfortable leaving it on longer than that," HelperFriend said.

"There's a good chance we'll miss them altogether. They could pass in a moment we're not watching," Equuleus said.

"True," Heart agreed. "But it's still better than nothing."

A few minutes later, HelperFriend flashed the energy again. Same hall, same utter stillness. Same subdued light.

Again and again, over varying intervals, Helper-Friend flashed the connection.

Finally, Heart said, "I'm becoming a bit uncomfortable about so much connection on our part. Perhaps we ought to ... just let it go."

"Just two more times, Heart," HelperFriend said. "Then, I fear I must agree with you. I've been running several million calculations of probability between the random energy sweeps and my random energy bursts, and the probability of being detected, still exceptionally minute, is beginning to approach a millionth. So, if you're all right with it, two more times only."

"I'll have to be ...."

HelperFriend's pulse flashed. They heard a voice! The faint visual of the hall and a voice!

HelperFriend held the energy burst on.

"*Zack!*" Heart barely whispered. "It's Zack!"

Shadowy forms came into view, then passed through HelperFriend's energy connect, that he dared hold on. One, two, three, four, five, six ....

"Jackson, Amdrona, Butterfly, Eye, Swen, and Zack," Heart whispered. Just as she said, "Zack" again, she saw the form she intuited was Zack stop and look about. Then his face came right into HelperFriend's light—or, perhaps made a light of his own. He smiled and the connection blinked off.

"*Oh, oh, oh! ...*" was all Heart could utter.

"He's psychic, that boy," HelperFriend said in awe.

"Yes. Indeed, he is. He did that for me after The First Turning Point Battle. When I couldn't stop worrying about the little donkey, Molly."

"True," Equuleus agreed. "I remember."

"He would not have smiled, *smiled at me!* like that if anything was amiss."

"So ... all is well?" Violet asked, looking up at Heart with worry and joy in her beautiful lavender eyes.

Heart hugged her close. "All is exceedingly well at the moment. Oh, Equuleus! Eye is free! He's free. It has been one of the greatest goals in my life, to know that Eye is free of any Darling Undesirables Facility. Now he's free to live with The Mystic and Butterfly and Amdrona and Zack. *Free!*" Heart paused, while her thoughts swept her away.

"Free," she said in a small, small voice.

"But, Heart!" Violet asked in alarm. "What's wrong?"

Equuleus extended the tip of his wing to Heart's shoulder. "It will be all right, Heart. *One day* ...."

"I don't understand ...." Violet cocked her head at Equuleus.

"Because," HelperFriend stood, then kneeled in front of Heart, his gear-clicking hand patting her hand, "she is not with them. They are real bios, they are her real, deep down, family."

"Oh, HelperFriend, I'm neither this nor that. If I were there, I'd be missing you, and Violet, and my Father, and, and ...."

"And Xavier," Equuleus said.

"And Xavier, and all The Folks here ...."

"Perhaps," HelperFriend said, "but it's not the same."

"Not quite. No. The sun. The night, the grass underfoot ... many little bits, many little pieces," Heart said.

"Grass underfoot," Violet raised her little paw, considering the possibility. "Do you think I would enjoy grass underfoot?"

"I don't know, Violet. This is your home, Pink is what you've known since your first thought. So—I don't know. Someday, I trust we will find out. But for the moment, celebration!" Heart jumped up.

"*Celebration!* Eye and Butterfly are free. Even as we speak, they are making their way through the tunnel under *The Wall* and into The Periphery. That's all I need to know to be deliriously happy. HelperFriend, music, if you will! Let us dance!"

The four of them danced to wild and raucous music as long as all of their bio, clockwork, mechanical, dark matter, dark energy feet were in the mood to dance.

Heart happily realized that she'd become fully recovered. She found herself recalling how she savored the experience in Xavier's arms on the *Heart!*, floating out to the beyond. But for Xavier holding onto her in every way—physically, psychically, emotionally—she would not be here, dancing, at this moment.

As she waltzed around the room with Helper-Friend—an impeccable dancer!—she wondered what it would be like to dance with Xavier, to have him hold her in his arms, not trying to keep her alive, but simply moving together with the music.

What ... would ... that ... be ... like?

"Dreamy girl! What are you dreaming about?" HelperFriend leaned close and looked into her eyes.

"No-nothing ..." she tried to lie.

"No nothing is right, I dare say!" He chuckled.

Heart brought herself back into the room with her friends, and left Xavier, emotionally, at least, standing at the door. She returned to her deepest joy—the second most compelling drive she had in all of life had been accomplished. *She'd taken care of Eye!* Even at extreme distance, she'd kept her focus on taking care of the one who needed her like no one else in the Universe needed her. She allowed herself, for the moment, to feel deeply, deeply happy.

Chapter 23

The four of them finally collapsed in a cheerful heap, not because they'd become tired, it being rare for clockwork, mechanical, dark matter beings to ever tire, but because they were so very contented with themselves and with one another.

"Oh!" HelperFriend, jumped up from the heap, casting Violet aside, who flew from his chest to the bed.

"Whoa!" she hopped about on the bed. "Fun! Let's do that some more."

"Message from Father Inventor."

Everyone fell silent.

HelperFriend opened his mouth and began to speak in Father Inventor's voice. "We're about to launch the moons. Come and join us Heart, you and your merry dancing band of pals. Thank you, HelperFriend for sharing those bits of entertaining 3-D."

"*Awk!*" Heart squawked at the thought of all of The Folks amused by her calisthenics.

"You deserve your moment of joy, Heart," her father added, "having successfully liberated Butterfly and Eye."

"How do you know that?"

"HelperFriend also sent that bit of 3-D through. Good work, Heart!"

"I'm happy it's done." She grew shy having her father compliment her about her deed so small, small, small in comparison to the many life-saving miracles he'd accomplished in his lifetime.

"Me too!" He smiled broadly. "Come on down, now, we're getting ready for the countdown."

"On our way!"

Heart turned to Equuleus. "Do you feel like your flying is back to normal?"

"Normal, and better than, if possible. Your happiness is my strength!"

"Yes!" Heart jumped onto Equuleus's back and Violet hopped in front of her. He moved to the landing and leapt—flying around and down, around and down, until he landed gracefully on the marble floor below. They waited while HelperFriend clicked and clanked his way down the winding stairs to join them.

"So exciting," He chattered, "*soooooooooo* exciting. This is … you know … we've been … well, it's just … since we first assembled ourselves … nothing quite, that is, nothing quite like … I mean, when Father Inventor launched the first moons, he had almost no one with him. Now, he has all of us.

"And he has you, Heart. You give his life meaning in so many ways, I can't even fully understand it. My bios are extremely limited. Most have to do with conversation and how to appear as though I'm empathizing, without really, deeply inside myself, understanding."

"Not so different from many bios."

"That can't be true."

"There are Keepers who have no idea what emotions are, what empathy is. But they've received training to put on a surface appearance of appropriate emotions. Eye and I hated that. They'd come at you smiling and nodding, or frowning and shaking their heads.

"I'd say to Eye, 'here comes a lost one.' We'd try to avoid them. But, of course, when I got in trouble, I'd be sent to interact with one of them."

They made their way down the hall to Father Inventor's room. "I'd never be sent to talk with a Keeper with real emotions. I ...."

HelperFriend opened the door and Heart stopped short in awe. A humming and whirring grew in intensity as the dome overhead the work area cranked open from the front to the top, slowly rolling back upon itself. Equuleus moved outside and backed away as the vast space continued and continued to become exposed. As Heart and her little band continued to watch the space open, small hills on the horizon folded back to reveal Father Inventor's acres and acres of "workroom."

At long last the humming and whirring stilled. Father Inventor and his many helpers were now tiny figures in the distance as Equuleus had backed up further and further to take in the expanding sight.

The helpers gathered around Father Inventor in his mobile bell jar in front of the vast, open space. Heart watched in wonder and awe as the floor of the exposed area now began to move. Everything on it, including the walls of the banks of Father Inventor's dials, and knobs, and switches, began to slide forward. Off to the left, Heart saw the *Heart!* on its landing pad slide forward as well, and everything else everywhere slowly ground forward, while everything in the farther distance began to slide back.

Gradually, a gargantuan maw opened.

A poised suspense hung in the air. Moments ticked by without a sound. Without movement. Was something wrong? Was her father building suspense for effect?

Suddenly, Heart heard a shout, *"Wooo-hooooooooo!"* Xavier crowed, as the largest armature ever to be constructed began to emerge from the womb of Pink.

"Woooooooo-hooooooooooooo!" Xavier shouted again, holding onto a tether tied to that which emerged, as if standing on the back of a bucking bronco. But it wasn't bucking. It rose smoothly from the belly of the moon, rising and rising, sparkling white and silver in the twilight. Then, suddenly a bank of brilliant lights came on. Everyone, including Heart, with bios in their eyes looked away. Everyone gasped and cheered.

Heart's eyes rapidly adjusted, and she returned her gaze to the contraption continuing to emerge from below. Amazing! *Amazing!* She didn't understand what she saw, but she knew for certain sure, it represented a crowning achievement of her father's remarkable mind. Which he never could have accomplished without the brilliance and devotion of all the mechanical and clockwork and bio and dark matter beings surrounding him at this very moment. A more faithful force had never been known in all of history.

Heart craned her head up to see Xavier, a tiny figure, high above while taking in the expanse of what lay before her, as it continued to unfold above the surface of Pink. Off in the distance to her right, a long armature reached out and on the end of it, at an ever-expanding distance, a gigantic bowl.

Then, off to her left at an equally great distance, an armature with another unimaginably huge bowl at the end. The cranking and groaning of the ever-extending armatures filled the air with unnatural, yet strangely animal-like sounds—like gigantic, uneasy dinosaurs, far from home.

Then, again, another poised silence. All movement of the colossal *thing* before her stopped. She shielded her eyes, looking for Xavier, but could not find him. Where did he go? She scanned the phantasmagoric reach of sparkling white and shining silver—not an iota of movement anywhere. No sign of Xavier any-where.

"What are you looking for?"

Startled, Heart jumped half out of her skin. Xavier, standing beside her, grinned his impish grin in delight.

"Where did you come from?"

"You saw me up there!" He gestured to the top of the device before them.

"I did! How did you get here so fast?"

"Not so fast! You've been mesmerized for some while, watching the moons rise out of Pink. In that time, I swung down to the ground and walked right up to you. But you were so engrossed in peering at the moons, from end to end."

"The moons ...."

"Yes." Xavier gestured to the right. "Pink's moon," then he gestured to the left, "Yellow's moon. What were you looking for, so intently?"

Oh my goodness, Heart thought, am I to be compelled to try and lie yet again? About the same person! No. She would just be truthful. "I was looking for you."

Xavier clapped his hands over his head, triumphantly. "Yes! I knew it! You were looking for me!"

"Don't get too full of yourself, crazy boy."

"I'm completely full of myself if Heart is wondering where I am!" His freckles danced with his wide grin, his green eyes twinkled.

Heart could not resist, *she could not resist*. She started grinning too, wondering ....

What is happening to me?

"Message from Father Inventor," HelperFriend interrupted. "He wants me to augment his voice to communicate to everyone his comments. Excuse me."

HelperFriend moved to the center of the populace. "My friends, and my darling daughter, this is a wonderful moment, but we must not forget that it is a fragile moment. These moons will provide impenetrable protection for both Pink and Yellow, and they will be beautiful. Beautiful, glowing white orbs to remind us of when we stilled the Purists' attempts to destroy what is now our home.

"At this auspicious moment, many of you will leave the happy home we've established for ourselves and will colonize Yellow. Even in the midst of our joy in successfully building the two moons that will circulate Pink and Yellow, we are sad to break up our many relationships.

"Eventually, I'll develop a means of travel that will make visiting one another faster and easier than it is at present. But for now, we must prepare to say our good-byes. *So! It's time to party!* Let us party, and forget about the morrow—which has never come on Pink anyway!"

Many of the mechanicals laughed, some nodded somberly, and some looked completely blank, not understanding the reference, having no idea what "the morrow" was.

But even among those laughing, there rang a somber note. Their closest alliances would soon be broken. The intimate relationships, the deep memories of having been built and cared for by one another—many of them would soon, by their own choice, be removed from home.

Heart shared the mechanical and clockwork pain and sadness flowing through everyone. "Oh! Must it be?" she asked in the softest voice. "Must it be?"

HelperFriend turned to her, and with a gesture uniquely her father's, and in her father's voice, whispered back, "Yes. It must be."

Then she knew his great sadness. Everyone on Pink had a relationship with her father more than a friend or a worker. Everyone was his child. Everyone had been contrived by his mind, had been brought, bit by loving piece, to Pink, even when he believed they were nothing other than bits and pieces.

But as the sadness passed through them, the party mechanicals passed among them, setting out delightful treats on tables that appeared from nowhere.

Heart saw her father nod to HelperFriend, who started playing an upbeat, strange music, such as Heart had never heard. A clockworks music with throbbing drumbeats and a delicate, haunting melody. Heart suspected HelperFriend composed the music for this, his family, and that he'd been working on it privately for, who-knew-how-long?, for this moment.

Lady Gervi's funny little dog, Yippee, came and looked up at Violet on Equuleus, uttering his strange doggie language. Violet looked at Heart. "Is it all right if I ...."

"Of course, Violet, get in there, have fun!"

Violet hopped down from Equuleus and scampered into the midst of the gyrating, jumping, wheeling, whirling, twirling dancers. Heart looked for her father, gliding about in his transparent bell jar, and saw him quietly moving toward his room, which had subtly reappeared, now that the moons had risen out of the belly of Pink. She followed him, with Equuleus and Xavier in tow.

They closed the door solidly behind them, and her father stepped out of his bell jar. He looked sadly at Heart. "It's hard, my girl. Very hard."

"Yes, Father. I understand."

"I know you do." He sat on the cot, and a great weight seemed to fall upon his shoulders. Heart went to sit beside him. "You will always do the right thing, Father. Even the really, really difficult choices, you will make the best ones."

"Thank you, my dear. Thank you. You're so compassionate. So aware. Like your mother. She always reminded me of the greater good I needed to accomplish. Even when the choices caused me much pain."

Heart tried to imagine her mother, that translucently beautiful woman, whose image glowed on the mantle in the library.

That woman who had died two hundred years ago, because Father Inventor could not contrive a heart that would replace her damaged and failing heart. The event—long before Heart's memory—that caused her father to place her own nearly indestructible heart in nearly indestructible Equuleus, threaded to her through dark energy and dark matter.

"Well, Father, if I am in any way like my mother, it is because of you."

"I doubt that." He shook himself out of his reverie. "But enough of quiet reflections! At this moment, we are together, and we're having a party!" He jumped up and flipped some switches. HelperFriend's strange music broadcast throughout the castle. "I am out of my bell jar, so I must stay inside. Let's head for the dining room and see what delights await us!"

"Let's!" Xavier led the way, holding the door open for Heart, her father, and Equuleus.

The strange, hypnotic and thrilling music pulsed like a living thing. Heart felt it moving deep in her, and wondered at HelperFriend, and what depths he must be plumbing in himself, to create this sound that reached beyond sound. This sound that she felt physically with its deep pulsing drumbeats, the percussion of other sounds as well, the high notes of some organic sort, surely. Not the sounds of instruments as much as a combination of the natural sounds of mechanicals and clockworks and bios.

It found a place deep in her that made her want to know everything about all dimensions.

She looked across the dining room at Xavier, feasting his eyes upon the beautiful pile of candy. Yet, strangely, not touching it!

He looked directly at her as if her look had been a physical touch. His look drew her to him, as if it too, was physical.

"Why are you only staring at the candy?" she asked. "Why aren't you finding a box to put it in and steal it away?"

"Oh, all I ever want to do with it is look at it. Isn't it so beautiful that you can't imagine putting it inside yourself and—destroying this beauty?"

"Maybe it's beautiful inside too," Heart answered, feeling somewhat stupid saying it.

"Maybe it is," Xavier agreed, taking Heart's hand as if it was the most natural thing to do.

Heart looked down at their hands, entwined. "Also pretty," she observed.

"Yes," Xavier agreed.

"But ... very intimate. Very intimate feeling. Eye and I used to always hold hands, you know, palm to palm. It made us feel safe. He made me feel as safe as ever I made him feel."

Xavier nodded.

"Because he can see things I cannot see."

"I do not doubt it," Xavier agreed.

"But—this is different. You have intertwined our fingers—yours, mine, yours, mine, yours, mine, yours, mine ...."

"Yours, mine. Yes. It's wonderful, is it not?"

"Yes," Heart agreed. "It's non-language talk. You can tell me many things, through your hand."

"I hope so, Heart. Please. Please know everything about me, and let me know everything about you. That's all I want."

Holding onto his hand, Heart led Xavier through the dining room and to the front door. The seals shunted and they stepped outside. She took him into one of the greenhouses. The flowers slept under subdued, simulated moonlight.

"This is me," she said. "A deep part of me. *Earth*. The things that grow from it. These flowers, and this plaid pattern they make, this is my core, my deep self."

Xavier sat down along the edge of the flowers. He studied them with the same intensity that Heart observed him contemplating the gigantic pile of candy.

"Color is wonderful, isn't it?" he said.

"It is," Heart agreed.

He leaned over and inhaled deeply. "What wonderful aroma. Each flower has its own particular marker."

"They do, each kind of flower, has its own scent." Heart sat down beside him.

"I mean, each individual flower has a unique, specific marker. It's like its own personal name. Like ... Father Inventor is human, but his name is Raymond Thomas. This flower is a primrose. But her name is—well, it's not pronounceable. But it's distinct from all the other primroses ...."

"Oh, my ... how do you ... can I do that? Do I have the ability to know each flower's particular scent name?"

"I'm not sure. I suspect it's a part of my rebuild. I don't remember being able to know each flower's distinct name before the rebuild. But then, I think there's a lot I don't remember.

"There is one thing I *do* remember ...." Xavier paused, smelling several other flowers, touching them lovingly.

"Yes?" Heart wanted to know what he did remember before ... dying ....

"I always remember Heart. I always remember how Heart let me be safe in knowing that I, too, am different from everyone. You and I are different from everyone, even each other. But we're the same in that. *Ah, Little Star!* When, as a little girl, you said 'stars!' were your favorite thing, that comment worked its way right into my child-soul and took root, just like these flowers. *Took root, Heart.* Because *I* loved the stars—before and after my rebuild. I know the stars, I love the stars, in a way that doesn't make objective sense."

Heart nodded while Xavier talked. She understood—utterly understood—what he said. "Star stuff. We're made of stars."

"Indeed, dear Heart. We remember something deep of our star origins."

Heart moved closer to Xavier, and they sat holding hands, while the party grew to a tremendous crescendo outside, while Equuleus danced and flew around the greenhouses, while her father smiled down upon them from his high above window in their cozy reverie in the flower-filled greenhouse.

Chapter 24

The party slowly wound down as the reality of the pending launching of the moons drew ever nearer. The greenhouses lit up to full daylight, and Heart and Xavier stowed away in their memories for safekeeping the nearly wordless reverie and bonding they experienced.

Then they rose from their flower poses and left the greenhouse, wandering around the perimeter of the castle, with the gigantic infrastructure of moons and armatures hovering above.

"So, what will you be doing ... with the moons?" Heart asked.

"I'll be placing them in their orbits."

Heart chuckled. "You're quite amazing, but I doubt you're the only one 'placing the moons in their orbit.'"

"But I am. Of course, the moons themselves and the armatures have their own brains and know quite well their duties. But I'm the one who will get them to their locations, where their intelligence can begin to engage."

Heart was sobered. "I thought you were teasing. Like you do."

"Not this time."

"What if you couldn't do it—what if you couldn't place the moons? Is there not someone else who could do it?"

"Ah, not really. No. Everyone is counting on me."

'But—*that's too much!*"

"No, it's not. I'm entirely capable of fulfilling my duties."

Heart became stricken with another realization. "But, wait! Are you immigrating to Yellow?"

"Not exactly. I'll be going to Yellow after the moons are deployed, to help those who are immigrating make their habitats and settle in, then I'll come back. But I cannot lie, Heart. I'll be gone for long spans of time, traveling back and forth, and being on Yellow."

"I see."

"Does it matter to you?"

"I ..." Heart had to think about the different ways Xavier being gone might matter to her. "Yes. It matters."

"How so?"

"I don't know. I just know I have ... a ... bad feeling. Bad feeling inside when I think about you not being here. I don't like it. I'm not going to like it. I'm already missing in my life so many of those I love ...."

"Love, Heart. *Love?*"

"Well, that's what we're talking about, isn't it. L-O-V-E. Right?"

"*I've* been talking about it, but you've been listening."

"I listen when I'm learning. I'm quiet when I don't know the subject. I'm learning from you. I don't know this feeling. I'm willing to name it love. But it feels different from what I feel for Eye or for my father, or for Equuleus."

"That's good that it's different."

"Yes, something new. But—what I feel for each of them is entirely different, as well."

"As it should."

"How is it that you are so wise?"

"Listening and thinking, I believe. Then I add to that, thinking and listening."

"I do that."

"And you are also wise."

They came around to the open space in front of the castle, facing the armatures, high above.

"Tell me, Xavier, exactly what you are going to do, so I can picture it, as you're doing it."

"All right." Xavier gestured with sweeping motions as he talked, so familiar with every step of his mission. "First, this whole contraparatus will launch, the giant bowls and this armature. I will be in *Heart!* in the sky with a small yet mighty dark energy device on board that will assure the proper placing of it all in the sky.

"Then I'll launch that gigantic shining bowl," he swung his arm to the right. As it comes to its orbiting position, its nested half will rotate out and close it into a perfect orb.

"Then the armature, Yellow's moon, and I will head for Yellow, followed by the first immigrants in our small fleet. The same procedure will transpire once Yellow's moon and I reach Yellow.

When the moon is in place, all of this armature, with a bit of assistance from me, will land on Yellow. There are some habitat-making components on Yellow, but more will be needed, as the immigration is larger than Father Inventor first envisioned. Within the armature, and the armature itself, are components for making habitats, and almost everything needed for those starting to build a life on Yellow."

"*Amazing!*" Heart whispered, dumbfounded by awe.

"Well, perhaps the most amazing part will then unfold. For it's at this point that I initiate Father Inventor's power and brilliance. After the two moons are deployed and have become full circular globes, I will travel back here, with our fleet, who will be returning with me for the second and final immigrants, I will initiate the invisible protection screen—a dark energy field, that will repel anything that does not send out a particular signal. *Anything!* Enemy or innocent, intentional or space debris—will be repelled when encountering the shield, which resonates between Yellow and Pink, emanating from their moons."

"Oh, Xavier, you're so ...."

HelperFriend came hurrying toward them. "Urgent, Xavier, Father Inventor must see you immediately."

Heart and Xavier exchanged a look. Even when things were urgent, he didn't use such language.

They started at a run for Father Inventor's room, but Xavier stopped short and grabbed Heart's arm. "Just me, Heart ...."

"But ...."

"You know I want you with me every moment until I must part, but ... he won't let you hear this."

Heart nodded and turned away from Xavier, who hurried into the castle. No. She didn't know her father would not let her hear something he considered urgent.

Great activity arose all around her. She watched as clockwork movement clicked into place while the residents of Pink worked together like a huge machine, themselves. She heard the engines of the fleet roar as they started up and came out to the open terrain. Then, at a distance, she saw Xavier hurrying to the *Heart!* He looked at her and grinning, waved both of his arms at her while continuing to hurry to the *Heart!*

Bemused and confused, Heart wanted to rush to him. Wanted to stow aboard the *Heart!* again.

Wanted not to be standing here, on the plain, alone and feeling stupid, and weirdly, lonely.

Equuleus came up to her, and she put her arm around his neck. "What's going on?" she wondered aloud.

"Instant mobilization—I'd say something is brewing with the Purists."

"Yes," Heart agreed simply, but feeling a fear like she'd never known. A fear for Xavier.

As they stood there, they saw Father Inventor, in his bell jar, come out onto the plain with HelperFriend. Almost like conducting an orchestra, he gestured and events happened. First, the little fleet of ten spacecraft, filled with immigrants who had immediately boarded, took to the sky.

"Different order," Heart mused.

"What's that?"

"Xavier said he would take off first and launch Pink's moon, and then he and the fleet would head for Yellow."

"Hmmm ... must want them out on their way for safety—or perhaps to put some part of the procedure in motion directly."

"Yes." She watched breathlessly as the fleet flew in formation in the sky, and, in perfect unison, waved their wings to those watching below, then jetted away. "Ah! What a beautiful sight! How did they do that, that perfectly synchronized wave? It's not as if they've been out in the air practicing every day."

"Sort of. They've been practicing on flight simulators. But I think that bit was a special surprise for Father Inventor."

"How do you know that?"

"All the mechanicals and clockworks activities come in to me as a routine download."

Heart shook her head in frustration. "Everyone knows things but me!"

"You know plenty, Heart. You've had more than enough to deal with. You didn't need me telling you every little bit of download."

Heart remained silent as the *Heart!* came forward. Xavier gave her father a salute, which he returned. Then, even at the distance, she could see his green eyes twinkle as he blew her a kiss. She wanted to smile, she wanted to maybe even—though it would be very unlike her—blow him a kiss in return. But she stood stock still, ramrod straight, frowning slightly.

"Well, at least wave to him," Equuleus suggested.

"Right!" Heart raised her hand towards him—but her gesture became more a reaching out, a desire to grab onto the entire spacecraft and hold onto it. Not let it go.

She saw that Xavier understood her gesture and a longing that she might, indeed, grab onto the *Heart!* and hold it, passed his eyes. Then his grin returned and in an instant, the *Heart!* took to the twilight skies.

"*Gone ...*" she whispered.

Equuleus whinnied softly but said nothing.

Everyone who remained on Pink raised their vision to the armature, waiting expectantly. Soon, the whole conglomeration of bits and pieces and giant silvery bowls at each end, began to raise slowly clearing the castle and pulling up into the sky. A gentle sigh arose from all the witnesses, looking straight up at the entire construction poised, far above.

Some subtle shifting of the armature seemed to articulately position the near silvery bowl just so in the sky. Then, suddenly, the *Heart!* appeared in the sky above, and with its appearance, the nearer silvery bowl began to writhe slightly.

Heart couldn't help but have the image that it was a birth process. As she watched, an inner bowl began to emerge from the outer shell, and rotate around until the little moon above became a gorgeous and glowing silvery orb.

"*Ahhhhh!*" everyone murmured.

Then, with an audible "pop!" the moon released from the armature, moved in position slightly as the armature pulled away from it.

Then, "*Ohhhhhhhh!*" everyone sighed.

Pink's moon had launched! Far above in the sky, silver, glowing, stunning. And ....

"The *light!*" Heart whispered. "The *LIGHT!*"

"Yes," Equuleus nodded.

The little moon's position in the path of the sun, cast a beautiful, mystical daylight upon Pink below.

"Oh! Oh, Equuleus ... *light!* The sun's *light!*"

"Yes, Heart. Such a beautiful, silvery light. Like nothing ...."

"Like nothing we've ever seen," Heart said.

"Like nothing we've ever seen," Equuleus agreed.

Heart looked toward her father, some distance away, in his bell jar. He appeared to feel her glance and turned his gaze away from the events in the sky above to look at her. She raised her hands to him in a gesture of gratitude, and then up to the light.

His face opened in smiles, and he raised his hands up to the little moon, and its light, as well. Then he returned his attention to the drama that continued, far above.

Heart, too, looked up, looking for Xavier. The armature with the remaining silvery bowl moved away, toward Yellow, a small yellow globe in the distance—but, Heart felt glad as never before, that she could often see Yellow, though its orbit was slightly different from Pink's orbit, and could not always be seen.

She did not take her eyes off the *Heart!* until it became an invisible speck, while the armature remained visible for some while. When even it was lost in the starry, starry sky, Heart turned her attention to her father, who, she realized, had gone back into his room to monitor Xavier's and Yellow's moon on his screens.

"Let's go!" she urged Equuleus, hurrying to the castle.

They passed through the door baffle, and into his room. All around her father, screens showed different views of Yellow, including what appeared to be a view of Pink from Yellow, with the new-born, dazzling little moon in Pink's sky—looking as if it had always been there.

"Oh! *So beautiful*," she sighed, pointing at the view of Pink, but even as she said it, her attention moved on to the other screens, looking for the *Heart!*

"It is a wonderful sight to behold," her father agreed. "But, here's what you're looking for." He pointed to a screen showing the *Heart!* and the armature moving toward Yellow, clearly another view from Yellow, as the *Heart!* and the silvery bowl of Yellow's moon became steadily larger.

Another screen showed the fleet of Pink's space-craft, also slowly becoming larger as they approached Yellow.

"It'll be some while, Heart, before any of them reach Yellow. You may want to do something else for the time being. I'll have HelperFriend come and get you when Xavier gets close to launching Yellow's moon."

"Yes," HelperFriend nodded. "I'll come get you."

"Well ... if you don't mind, Father, I'd prefer to stay here and watch the screens, and see everything unfold."

"Of course, my dear, if you'd like. I'd love to have your company."

"Good." Heart sat cross-legged on the cot, and Equuleus curled up beside her on the floor. She glanced out the window and saw Violet hopping to-wards the castle. In the new and glorious light, she appeared a much fainter, and somewhat silver shade of lavender.

"The light, Father! This stunning, amazing light!"

"I'm glad you like it."

"No. Like is not a strong enough word. I love it. I adore it. It makes me feel joy. And more at home. It's a very happy accident."

"No accident, Heart. I engineered it purposefully to make sure it would capture and reflect the sun's light. Pink's moon will circumvent Pink and simulate this mystical silvery light on a daily basis. We'll have soft, silver light days, and twilight nights."

"Why did you do that?"

"For you, Heart. Because I know how much you miss Earth's days and nights. It's not the same, by any means. But it *is* a kind of night and day."

Heart wanted to jump up and give him a hug, but he was very occupied, so she stood and went to the door baffle to let Violet in to join them instead.

"Wow! This light," Violet said as she came through the baffle. "Kinda strange, isn' it? I don't know if I'll get used to it. Everything is just too bright."

"You'll get used to it," Heart said, picking Violet up and returning to her cross-legged position on the cot. "Father made the light, especially for me."

"Oh! Well, then, it's a beautiful thing, this light. I'm used to it already. I forgot, Heart, about how much you miss daylight. Of course my eyes—they're all adjusted to the light we had before ...."

"If you really continue to be very uncomfortable with the light, Violet, I'll make some adjustments on your eyes," Father Inventor said. "But I'd like to see what the bios in your eyes will do to make their own adjustments first. If you don't mind."

Violet flopped her ears around and then covered her eyes, "No, I don't mind at all. Come on little eyes, do some evolving!"

Equuleus and Heart giggled at her cute antics. Then, they all settled into a nearly hypnotized silence, watching the fleet of immigrants, the *Heart!*, the silvery bowl of Yellow's moon, and the armature become, by increments, larger and yet larger in the view from Yellow.

Heart looked out the window from time to time, and, though she could not see the moon directly, she experienced a sweet pleasure in seeing the light shift slowly from the silvery, gentle daylight to the twilight she'd become so familiar with, as the moon made its way across Pink's sky and, apparently, set beyond its horizon.

Equuleus caught her gaze and said quietly in her mind, *I'll love to fly with you out to watch the moon set.*

And rise! Heart thought back to him.

Yes, and rise.

Suddenly, so it seemed, the fleet became big as life, coming in for a landing on Yellow. Another screen showed a tremendous chasm opening, much like the one on Pink but larger.

In flew the fleet, and as quickly as possible, the occupants of the spacecrafts scrambled out and began to busy themselves with the interior of Yellow, in preparation for, Heart assumed, the armature, once Yellow's moon was launched.

She was right. Before long, the half moon glided into view from the close-up surface camera. Heart looked around for the screen that would show the near space, where she saw the *Heart!* and the bowl-moon with the armature, hovering over Yellow.

Then the same procedure transpired over Yellow as had over Pink, as the bowl slowly became an orb, then *popped!* from the armature. Heart watched as Xavier fussed with the exact placement of the moon, and the armature obediently folded up and made for the gigantic, open maw in Yellow's surface.

Unlike the launching of Pink's moon, the new immigrants to Yellow did not stand in awe, watching the placement of their beautiful new moon. They had too much to do. As the armature made its way to its location, the opening closed down to a much smaller size.

"Is Xavier staying on Yellow?" Heart asked, seeing the opening closing down to a size not much bigger than the *Heart!*

"No," her father said. "He'll make some adjustments, and get everything in order for activating the shield. Then the fleet will return with him to pick up the rest of the immigrants. The opening has closed down to allow for the passage of the spacecraft. Soon, the fleet, with pilots only, will join Xavier, and begin their return to Pink.

"Then, back in Pink's sky, he'll activate its component of the shield. When the two moons have their shield components properly activated, my ground team and I will activate the components Xavier planted on Earth. Only when all the components are properly aligned can the switch be flipped to activate the entire, invisible, dark energy shield."

Her father's explanation made her uneasy. "What if … what if every component doesn't align properly? Is there no margin for error?"

"Very little. I *believe* the only thing that would happen is that the shield would not activate, but I'm not entirely certain about that. Dark energy remains a mystery to me to some extent."

"Well, if it's a mystery to you, it's a total *black box* to everyone else."

HelperFriend snorted. "There's a truth!"

"But what could *possibly* happen?" Heart pushed.

"Here on Pink we'd be all right because I've built in safe measures for that possibility. But on Yellow, if it really went haywire, I don't know. Everyone there has been highly trained in 'the worst scenario' so they have options to address the worst possible outcome. We do not want to lose Yellow."

Heart gasped. "*Oh no!* That's possible?"

"I don't think so," her father answered, coming over and patting her shoulder. "But, you know, just in case. Then, on Earth, there'd likely be some sparking, possibly some dramatic fireworks. But, again, Xavier has onboard the *Heart!*, and I have here, a means to shut down the whole grid that makes the shield. What would be especially bad about that, of course, would be the trail it'd leave regarding what we intended to accomplish."

"Who would understand that?"

"You make a good point. Whoever followed up on seeing the fireworks would have to report it to someone who has an idea of my work, and put a series of twos and twos together."

Heart nodded, relieved to learn there'd be small probability of danger to anyone.

"Of course," her father went on, "what would be a tragedy would be to not have the shield."

"Yes," Heart agreed. "It would be." She watched the busy activity on the screens. The fleet came into formation on the space outside of the opening on Yellow. They took off two by two, while the *Heart!* hovered in the sky. When the last two joined the others, already headed directly for Pink, the *Heart!* followed them from behind.

"Here they come!" Heart whispered.

"Yes," HelperFriend repeated, "here they come."

At that precise moment, a horrible bleating sound issued from somewhere on HelperFriend. He and Heart's father gave one another an alarmed look.

"What—is—*that?*" Heart called above the noise.

"I'm sorry, Heart, HelperFriend and I have to mobilize some components, you'll need to leave."

"But ...."

HelperFriend shockingly and brusquely lifted Heart, still holding Violet, off the cot and headed for the door.

"Put me down!" she said, infuriated. She looked back at Equuleus, who stood and appeared ready to take on HelperFriend. As HelperFriend put her down, she nodded to Equuleus. Carrying Violet, with Equuleus in close proximity, she left through the back door baffles and stepped outside into the twilight.

"I'm sorry, Heart," her father called. "You will understand, soon enough."

"Just..is Xavier all right?"

"Yes, Heart." Then her father shut down his audio to her. She could not hear his voice, not the awful bleating sound coming from HelperFriend.

She moved out to the plain with her two companions, and stood, tense, looking toward Yellow. "What is going on? What's the meaning of that terrible sound?"

"I'm looking into it, Heart." Equuleus fell silent.

"I'm afraid," Violet said.

Heart now noticed that Violet shivered in her arms. "Oh, Violet, dearest, do not be afraid, I have you! You're safe." She cuddled the little rabbit until she calmed down, but Heart did not feel certain, herself, of her reassuring words. She waited impatiently for Equuleus to tell her something. Anything.

"Hmmmm," he finally muttered.

"What?"

"I ... I strongly hesitate to tell you."

"You must tell me, Equuleus." Then she thought to him, so Violet wouldn't hear, *what could possibly be so bad, you won't tell me?* She looked into his mind and started so at what she saw, that Violet jumped down from her arms. "*NO!*" Heart shuddered. "*Oh, no!*"

She saw droves of the Purists' bots, streaming toward Pink.

"Apparently," Equuleus said, "the Purists have successfully plumbed the depths of Father Inventor's clone mind enough to develop bots that can travel, quite rapidly it appears, through space. The very reason everyone is urgently working to erect a shield is fast and furiously upon us."

Violet began to whine. Heart sat on the ground and hugged her close. But she shared no consoling words, as she, herself, now shivered. The only thing she had deeply feared in all her life now headed for Pink, in huge numbers.

Chapter 25

"B ut, wait," Heart said after a few moments of chilling trauma, "Xavier is putting up the shield, even as we speak. It will be up, long before the bots arrive."

Equuleus nodded slowly, but then began, instead, to shake his head. "Unfortunately, they are moving at a phenomenal speed, clearly part of their tapping into Father's clone mind. It looks as though they will arrive at Pink about the same time as the fleet and the *Heart!* return. I can only tell you the truth—it doesn't look good."

Heart stood up, agitated. "What can we do?"

"This is one of those times, Heart, when you can only wait it out."

"I don't wait tragedy out, Equuleus! You know that! I do not wait for tragedy to strike. There must be some action we can take."

"You know perfectly well, Heart, that Father and HelperFriend, and Xavier and everyone will do everything in their power to prevail. All you can do is—and you know I'm right!—make everyone worry about you, and take their minds off their focus."

Heart nodded.

"She's nodding, but she's not agreeing with you," Violet waggled her ears at Equuleus.

"I know," he said, resigned. They waited in silence while Heart thought deeply.

"I must try again, Heart ... if you decide to take some kind of action, but at the last minute, your deep—*and justified!*—fear of the bots muddles your perceptions, you could do great harm—*and be harmed!*"

"I understand, Equuleus. But when I encountered the bots before—or, rather, when they encountered me!—there was just me. They weren't the least bit interested in Swen. This time, it's different. There are others. There are many others to care for and to care about. And ... *I am not the same.* I've grown. I've been through a lot. You and I have been through a lot. I believe in myself. I believe in us."

"All right." Equuleus pawed at the ground. Heart could not discern if he was frustrated with her, or if he experienced the same yearning she felt to take action.

"This means?"

"This means, I can't argue with you anymore, because you're right." He reared up on his hind legs, and spread his wings to their full extent—glorious, amazing sight!

"*Ohhhh myyyyy!*" Violet exclaimed. "*Breathtaking! I would not want to be your enemy.*"

Heart chuckled softly. "True, true, my Violet." She paused for a few moments, thinking deeply. "All right, here's what we'll do. We must get out on the desert, to the first possible location of encounter between bots, the fleet, and the *Heart!* They will all be heading for the castle, and we must do our part to assure that the bots do not get here. We'll wait on that little hillock near Violet's original home, and wait for what transpires. You can go back to the castle, Violet, or come with us."

"Oh, I'm coming with you!"

"Aren't you afraid?"

"You make me brave, Heart. I don't want to leave you now."

"All right. But I may have to leave you, you know."

"I'll be in territory I'm very familiar with. Don't worry about me."

"Let's go, then!" Heart picked up Violet with one hand, and jumped onto Equuleus's back. "Fly, my heart," she commanded him, and they took off into the twilight sky.

*   *

Soon, Equuleus landed on the little hillock a short distance from Violet's original burrow. They looked toward Yellow, but still, nothing to see, not even Yellow's moon, which disappointed Heart. "We may as well relax," she said, sitting on the ground, holding Violet in her lap. Equuleus sat down beside her, and she turned to lean against his back, stroking Violet between the ears.

"Such a lovely night to hold such dark foreboding," she mused, contemplating the myriad stars.

"Yes," Equuleus agreed simply.

"Perhaps the bots will never make it. Perhaps they'll be defective. Like so many of the Purists' other plans and efforts."

"Perhaps, Heart. But it does not seem so."

"Hmmmm ...."

She fell into silence, recalling the horror—oh, another lifetime ago, now!—when the bots lifted her off the ground and carried her up into the freezing atmosphere, that proved almost too much for her bio-components. Swen had saved her then. But he was not here now. Equuleus would do everything in his power—which was prodigious!—to protect her. This possible encounter posing a challenge of an entirely different magnitude, if the bots could travel to Pink from Earth.

She recalled The First Turning Point Battle— looking down upon the plains of The Periphery, seeing thousands of bots spread their red, destructive haze. The people of The Periphery in heated battle, and Zack beside her, with his strange trumpet-like sound weapon, that brought multitudes of bots down.

"Ah! It's too bad we don't have Zack's weapon," she said aloud.

"Zack's weapon?"

"Yes. That sound weapon that brought down bots in masses, during The First Turning Point Battle."

"Ah!" Equuleus nodded. "Yes. I recall it. Incredible weapon."

"How do you recall it?"

"From Martha reading to me, by the hour from *Ourbook*."

"Zack's weapon is mentioned in *Ourbook*?"

"Yes."

"Hmmm," Heart pondered. "That's pretty specific."

"Indeed," Equuleus agreed.

"I will—I will have to consider that at some other time. *Ohh*, dear Martha. I wonder if I'll ever see her again ...."

"You will see her again, Heart," Violet cuddled up under her chin. "Don't say these negative things!"

"You're right, Violet. I must say, 'I can't wait until I see Martha again.'"

"That's better." Violet settled back down in her arms.

At that moment, wonder of wonders, the stunning silver moon began to crest the horizon. "Oh, look, Equuleus, Violet! Look!"

"Ahhh!" They all sighed, as the liquid silver light ran across the surface of Pink, and stopped at Heart's feet. Then, within minutes, the three of them were bathed in its otherworldly light.

"Oh, Equuleus," Violet cried, "you're beautiful and glowing in this light!"

"She's right," Heart agreed. "Bright copper glowing—each of your gears is outlined in bas-relief silver, while they, themselves, are golden and copper. I've never seen anything like it!"

Equuleus stood and strutted about, unfolding and folding his wings, turning his head to admire them, clearly enjoying a few moments of indulgent vanity. At last he said, "Enough showboating. Speaking of beauty, what about the two of you?"

Heart and Violet looked at one another. "Wow!" Violet said. "Even more beautiful, Heart. As if that was possible!"

"Same to you, my rabbity-friend. Glowing silvery-lavender suits you ...."

"Look!" Equuleus pointed his nose toward Yellow. In the far distance, Heart could just make out movement.

It looked a bit like some bird, winging its way in the direction of Pink, but she knew it was the fleet, in formation. Still far, far away, but at least it could be seen.

"Not much longer," she sighed, hoping with a deep intensity that the bots would never make it to Pink from Earth, and surely not before that big, composite, bird in the sky came home to Pink and landed. Nor before Xavier, funny, brilliant Xavier, connected the shield her father invented, that would protect Pink and Yellow, and their moons from all invaders.

They waited with edgy anticipation as the frail, argent light increased in subtle hues, and the fleet drew ever nearer.

Suddenly her father's voice burst forth from Equuleus's audio receptors. *"Heart! Where are you?"*

She shook her head at Equuleus.

"You must tell him!" Equuleus said.

"I ... I'm with Equuleus and Violet, on the desert, watching the fleet and the *Heart!* come in."

"You must come to the castle at once, Heart. This very instant. Why did you go out there? Never mind, just ... get back to the castle."

"I will, Father. But first, I want to see the fleet fly overhead."

"No, Heart. No. Return to the castle immediately. You ... don't know ... it's not safe. It's not safe until Xavier has turned on the shield. You must not distract me like this at this moment. I'm quite serious, Heart!"

Heart closed her eyes and bit her lip, then sighed deeply. "I—I know about the bots, Father. I know about them. I'm staying here to—to help protect the fleet and Xavier, if necessary."

"What are you thinking!?!" Heart felt terrible to be the cause of such strain in her father's voice. But she knew she must stand her ground.

"You can do nothing against them!" her father continued. "They are a new breed, a new strain. They are not the little garden variety that took you to the skies. They are truly dangerous. They have killing projectiles. Heart, I beg you, return this instant."

A terrifying chill ran through Heart at her father's words, but she remained firm in her resolve.

"Even so, Father, I must do my part."

"What about Violet? You're endangering her!"

"She is near her original burrow. If Equuleus and I must go into action, she will be safer in her burrow than anywhere else."

"Heart ..." The pleading in his voice tore her up.

"Heart, I can't bear it," Equuleus said. "Your heart is in me, and this pain is intolerable."

"Then ... turn him off."

"No, Heart, do not turn me off! You need my direction if you insist on staying there. If you weren't so far away, I'd have HelperFriend come and get you. But don't break communication with me."

"I must, Father. I'm taking you away from where your attention must be focused. You know I love you. I'm sorry to hurt you, to disobey you. But I must do as I'm driven to do!"

"Heart!"

"TURN HIM OFF!" she commanded Equuleus. Her father's voice broke off in mid-word. "Awful, terrible feeling," she muttered, turning her attention back to the sky.

The fleet flew close enough now that she could make out the individual spacecraft. They would soon be overhead. In the near distance, she saw the *Heart!* with great relief.

Just as she was about to jump up and wave with enthusiasm to Xavier, an unbelievable mass of gigantic, many-tentacled, dark, sickly gray, bots filled the air, swirling and whirling around the fleet and Xavier. In spinning motion, impossible to make out their form in their swirling and spinning, and the crush of activity.

"Oh!" Heart whispered, "*Give me strength!* Violet, get into your burrow."

Violet did not have to be told twice. In fact, Heart wasn't even aware that she had already hopped furiously to her burrow. She turned and glanced at Heart, then disappeared underground.

"Good!" Heart returned her attention to the sky, and fell silent at the sight. Horrific bloody red projectiles ejected from the ends of all their swirling tentacles. She watched in terrified awe as gigantic holes ripped through the bodies of the spacecraft. One of them downed right in front of her.

But then, she was equally surprised to learn that all the pilots had weapons of their own, and returned as they got, bringing many bots down from the sky.

With great relief, Heart saw in the distance behind her, several of the fleet appear to enter the castle, although so far away, it was hard to tell. She chose to believe it. The bots seemed to have no interest in things that didn't move, including the downed spacecraft in front her, nor any interest in herself, and Equuleus.

As she watched the carnage around her, she tried to find the *Heart!* in the midst of it, but the sheer number of bots blocked her vision of the sky.

Then she heard the sound weapon and followed the sound. There was the *Heart!* Clearly, Xavier had a sound weapon like his cousin, Zack. Bots fell away into the vast darkness with each sweeping sound of the weapon, but still, they came.

Finally, the madness cleared enough for Heart to get a bead on the *Heart!* "Lock onto the *Heart!* Equuleus."

"I've got it!"

At that precise moment, a bot made a direct hit upon the *Heart!* In disbelief, Heart watched the impossible happen—the indestructible—until this moment—viewport of the *Heart!* shattered into a million pieces, and the bloody red projectile entered the *Heart!* As she watched, the *Heart!* began to plummet out of control.

"*No!*" Heart screamed, jumping onto Equuleus. "To Xavier, Equuleus."

Obediently, he spread his wings to their full extent, but at the same time asked, "What do you intend, Heart? What do you believe you can do?"

"I must reach Xavier! Don't ask any questions, do as I say."

"Yes, Heart." Equuleus took off the surface of Pink in a furious flurry of wings and pawing hooves, racing directly toward the *Heart!*, which appeared to plummet faster with every second. Their movement attracted the few bots straggling behind the large mass, headed for the castle. "What are you going to do if I succeed in catching up to the *Heart!*?"

"I won't know until I get there—so, just get there!"

Equuleus put on another level of speed, such as he'd never accessed before in his life. "Incredible, Equuleus, incredible! You're gaining on the *Heart!* and leaving the bots behind."

Equuleus made no reply, concentrating every fiber of his energy upon catching up to the plummeting *Heart!* Finally, Equuleus pulled alongside it, as it fell ever faster into the black abyss of nowhere.

"Get closer!" Heart ordered. Equuleus sidled up closer alongside the *Heart!*, getting as close as his wings would allow. Heart stood on his back and gathering more courage than she knew she possessed, she jumped through the shattered viewport, into the *Heart!*

Once inside, she turned and saw in the sky many of the bots coming to pursue her and Equuleus and the falling *Heart!* Why, she could not imagine, although they must know something she didn't. They put on an unimaginable burst of speed, steadily gaining on them.

She took in the sight of Xavier, strapped into his seat, unconscious—or—Heart refused to consider the alternative. She noticed Xavier's finger hovered but an inch from a button. Knowing nothing about what she was doing, she dared to follow her intuition, and what seemed to be his direction.

She reached out and pressed the button.

An entirely unholy sound reverberated through the cosmos, a grinding of some invisible cosmic wheels. And with the sound, the *Heart!* came to an instantaneous halt, as if it was a chunk of metal slamming up against a magnet. Off in the near distance, she saw bots being flung into the distant darkness, tumbling and purposeless in the starry terrain.

Equuleus hung fluttering, rather much like a butterfly over a flower, outside the unmoving *Heart!*, pinned to an invisible wall. With gentle movements, Heart unstrapped Xavier, trying not to look at the hole in his chest. She carried him back through the destroyed viewport and climbed onto Equuleus, realizing that the *Heart!* and Xavier were both "marked" and that Equuleus's wing fluttering in virtual contact with the *Heart!* kept him from being flung into darkness as well.

No words were necessary. Equuleus flew to Pink. When they landed before the castle, Heart ignored the destruction around her as she went through the double baffle into her father's room. She didn't see him, but his room appeared to be intact, which she took to be a good sign.

"To my rooms," she said to Equuleus, still on his back, holding the unconscious Xavier. Equuleus tiptoed down the hall and, when in the foyer, flew up into Heart's rooms.

She slid from his back and sat down on the floor with Xavier. "Find my father, find HelperFriend, find Wonderman One and Wonderman Two, Equuleus."

Equuleus left to do as Heart bid him, and Heart, refusing to examine the strange and gigantic hole in Xavier's chest, held him tightly.

"It will be all right, Xavier. We'll make you right. You've been brought back before, and my father will bring you back again. Just hold on. Hold on to me." Much to her joy, Xavier's arms reached up to hold her.

"Oh! Xavier! You'll be all right. Everything will be all right. You put up the shield, the bots are gone, never to return. Everything is all right now."

"As long as I'm in Heart's arms, everything is all right. Love you, Heart. Just remember that, will you? Will you remember your funny Xavier and how ridiculously but completely he loved you?"

"Don't talk like that. You'll be fine. Wonderman One and Wonderman Two will fix you. Just like they did me."

"No, Heart, they cannot."

"*Shhhh!* I won't hear it." Heart rocked Xavier gently. "Where are they, where is Wonderman One and Wonderman Two?"

While she rocked Xavier, she felt his hold upon her relax, and then release altogether. He became perfectly still, and looking down, she could not ignore the clockworks exposed in his chest.

All clockworks, every gear bent or broken, blackened. She looked at his darling freckles on his wonderful face. They seemed unnaturally pale. Oh, where did the sparkle in those trouble-making green eyes disappear to?

She sat holding him for what seemed an eternity. Someone must come and help him, put him back together. Eventually, she heard her father and Helper-Friend outside her door with a couple of other heavy treads. The Wondermen.

"It'll be all right now, Xavier. They've come to take care of you."

Her father softly entered the room, and at the sight before him, he began to shed tears. "Oh! Heart, my precious daughter. Oh, oh, Xavier, my boy ... my boy ...."

HelperFriend and the WonderMen came up around Father Inventor, and Equuleus came into the room behind them.

"Why are you all just standing there? You have to fix Xavier. Look He's badly hurt. You must help him!" She felt utter confusion at their strange, broken and impossibly sad expressions.

"*HELP HIM!*" she demanded.

"Ah! I cannot bear to tell you ...." her Father whispered.

HelperFriend took over, "Xavier is gone, Heart. A mechanical can only 'die' twice."

"He's not just a mechanical! He's bio and dark matter!"

"Yes, but his bio component has only so much life force, and once that life force is used up, and much of it had been used up in his first death, he cannot be regenerated."

"That doesn't make sense." She looked at her father, who could hardly make eye contact with her. "Make it right, Father. He saved us. You have to save *him*. You *must!*"

"I would, my darling. You know I would. He is one of my precious children and such a light of joy for everyone. But, he's gone, *gone*, now." He leaned over to take Xavier from her, but she clutched onto him.

"What's the matter with you? Have you gone crazy? You can fix him, like before. Wonderman One, Wonderman Two, fix him. Hook up your forces and heal him!"

"We cannot, Heart," They said in tandem. "No matter what we may do, we cannot bring him back. What your father says is true."

"It's wrong. He saved us. He saved us all!"

HelperFriend leaned over and gently but forcefully took Xavier from her. Heart thought she would truly come unhinged when she saw his arm dangle limply at his side. No, this was not Xavier. He always had energy, always ready to jump and leap and ....

HelperFriend took him out of her rooms, and the WonderMen followed. Her father picked her up and laid her gently on her little bed, pulling the blankets over her. "Sleep, my dear Heart. It is the only healer. I know. I know. I am so sorry, my girl. But I cannot lie, I'm profoundly relieved to have you back. You were monumentally brave, what you did to bring Xavier back. Monumentally brave!"

"No! I wasn't brave. I was frightened, but I did what I had to do. Oh, *why* didn't I do it earlier? Why did I stay on the ground like some ridiculous princess, instead of being out there helping him?"

"You did everything you could, Heart. Now, rest. Berating yourself will not change anything. I'll leave you now. You have Equuleus, and perhaps you'll sleep. It's the best healer."

He left her without a sound. Confused, she didn't want him to leave. But she also wanted to be alone. Could she possibly sleep? It seemed unlikely.

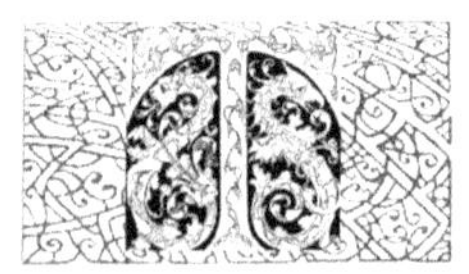

Chapter 26

Heart awoke, hearing someone stirring around in her room. She couldn't remember why she felt so terrible, or why she slept so very deeply. More deeply than ever before in her life. She opened her eyes. She faced the wall—something she never did!—with Violet curled up by her, deep in rabbit sleep.

Heart heard Equuleus make a soft sound and knew he acknowledged her awakened condition. He also let her know that someone else was in the room. For some reason, he made a picture of Jackson in her mind.

Thinking of Jackson made her think of Xavier. And when she thought of Xavier, all the horror came back to her. She groaned, wishing she'd not awakened. Violet peeked at her with one eye but closed her eye again.

Heart rolled over. There stood Jackson, looking at her, a very atypical look of concern on his face.

"Wha ... *Jackson!* Where did you come from?"

"Earth."

"Most likely, yes. But—how did you get here so fast?"

"You've been asleep for three risings and settings of Pink's beautiful new little moon."

"Oh! I've never ... very strange! And *how* did you get here?"

"In my Dark Energy Highway vehicle. While you and Xavier were on Earth, he showed me how to make modifications on my vehicle to make it into a spacecraft, while still looking like an Earth Dark Energy Highway vehicle. Ironically, I finished it but a short time before the shield became activated. Of course, I didn't know what ... what happened. Then the news came from Martha and Key Man. I jumped into my altered vehicle and came. Because ...."

"Because Xavier is your cousin."

"Yes. And because—I knew—I knew, or had an idea, about what you might be going through."

"Is it not a dream, then? Is it true?"

"Yes. Heart. Xavier is ... gone."

She turned her back to him again. "I—I can't take it in. If he's gone ...." She didn't know how to finish that sentence. Much to her surprise, she began to cry. "Oh, no, I never cry. Why am I crying?" She sat up, tears coming from somewhere, she didn't know where. She shuddered as if she might fly apart.

Jackson kneeled before her. He reached out to her, but then let his hands fall to his sides.

"He was ...." Heart began, but couldn't finish whatever she intended to say. "I just can't bring my-self to say, '*he was.*'"

"I know, Heart, I know. After discovering that he'd been rebuilt and regenerated, it's horrible to lose him again."

"Oh, Poor Jackson!" She reached her hands out to him, and he took them in his own. "You came to console me?"

"Well, yes."

"He ... he told me about ... about the first time ... when he ... he said he heard you say, 'I love you.'"

"Ah—no! He couldn't have. He'd ... he'd stopped breathing for a long time."

"He said he heard his heart stop. And you said, 'I love you,' and then, he said, he went to the *'between.'*"

"Between?"

"Yes. He said that beyond *'Here'* there is *'There'*—and that it's very compelling *'There,'* but there are bigger challenges. Then he said there's no such thing as death ...."

"Well, I guess if he's been there, I mean *'There,'* he would know. But we still miss him. *'Here.'*"

"Yes," Heart whispered. "We do."

They silently held an image of Xavier, *"There"* wherever *"There"* may be for a few moments.

Then Heart exclaimed, "Oh, Jackson, how did you get through the shield?" A flash of watching the bots flinging into space crossed her mind.

"Xavier gave me the code to put into the energy field of my vehicle. And ... and, I think you need to know, I brought back the *Heart!* One of the mechanicals got in another spacecraft and between the two of us, we towed the *Heart!* back."

Heart nodded but said nothing. She didn't want to think of the *Heart!* with its viewport blown out by the insane bots and their augmented weaponry. "The Purists tapped my father's clone mind. Will they not figure out a way of destroying the shield?"

"It would take some doing. First of all, it's invisible. So they have to somehow learn that it's there. But, even if they realize there's a shield, they would then have to figure out how it's energized.

"I believe your father's intellect will always outstrip their knowledge. His clone mind may be used for dark purposes, but ... I don't know, I also think that, if the clone is really Father Inventor's mind, at some point it will rebel and not do as it is told."

"I can only hold faith that what you say is true. There's been plenty of damage here already, thanks to his clone."

"You saved everything," Jackson said.

"Me? I most certainly did not!" Heart jumped up in agitation, pacing the room. "I did nothing. I didn't even save Xavier. I'm a total failure."

"Not so, Heart. You pushed the button. You saved everyone, everything."

"No! Xavier did it."

"I'd be the first to defend him, Heart. But truth is truth. You are the one who pushed the button that activated the shield, that sent the bots flying into eternal falling through space, that saved Pink, and Yellow, and their populations. You pushed the button that activated the shield, that grabbed onto the *Heart!* You saved the *Heart!* You saved yourself and Equuleus, as well. You did it."

"No, I didn't, Jackson."

Jackson projected a 3-D in front of Heart. "Everything that happened on the *Heart!* was recorded."

Before her eyes, Heart watched as she pushed the button that the unconscious Xavier was reaching for.

She heard the incredible and eerie sound. She saw the bots flying in the background and saw the jerk of the *Heart!*, grabbed by the shield.

"*You*, Heart. You pushed the button."

Heart turned to Jackson. "Do not tell anyone of this! It was Xavier."

"It was you. The historic record shows it. You can't get around it. Yes, the mission succeeded because of Xavier's work. But you must be acknowledged as the one who pushed the button. You know perfectly well, Heart, that your father and others have seen this 3-D."

Heart nodded somberly. "Yes, no doubt you're right. But, I'd like for it to go down in history that Xavier pushed the final button. That he activated the shield. He is the hero, not me."

"*You are the hero, Heart*. We would *not* be having this conversation if you hadn't been unnaturally brave, flying out to the *Heart!* to rescue Xavier."

"But he did everything to put the shield in place. I was just a stowaway, all along. A thorn in his side. A nuisance. A distraction."

Jackson smiled crookedly and almost chuckled. "Anything else you want to call yourself? You are a very strange girl, Heart. Xavier loved you, always. You were never any of those things to him. And you valiantly tried to save him."

Heart listened intently to Jackson. "Well, you're most annoying you know."

"Because I'm right? That's my mission statement: '*To Always Be Right*.'"

"Don't get too full of yourself."

"My only fault."

Equuleus snorted.

"I agree with Equuleus," Heart said.

Violet hopped to the edge of the bed. "I don't understand," she whined.

"No one does." Heart hugged Violet.

"I'd like to show you something, Heart."

"I'm not up to anything more right now, Jackson. I really can't stand one more piece of information."

"What if it's beautiful?"

Heart looked at Equuleus, he furrowed his brow.

Jackson, watching the interaction between them, said, "Let me show a bit of it to him, and see how he feels about it."

"All right," Heart agreed.

Jackson held up one hand before Equuleus, projecting an image onto it. Heart watched Equuleus's reaction closely, while Equuleus concentrated on what appeared on Jackson's hand. His response was immediate and dramatic. He looked over to Heart, wordless, nodding.

"All right then," Heart agreed. She sat on the edge of her bed, tense, apprehensive.

Jackson came over and sat beside her. "Hold out your hands."

Heart held her two hands together, while Jackson prepared to project upon them. "I made a little visit to a modest cabin just before departing Earth, because ... because I knew you needed to see this ...."

In Heart's palms appeared Eye's face, up close and precious. Heart gasped, and reflexively closed her hands to hold him, which, of course, only distorted the image. She opened her palms again.

"Heart!" he said, "My own dear Heart, I'm so, so grateful to Jackson for giving me a moment to talk to you. *Ahhh! Heart*, how I miss you! *How I miss you!* But you are upon your life's calling, and I can only send you good and loving energy." The view broadened, and behind Eye, Heart saw Butterfly in the background, on her knees, tending to her flowers, obviously in a joyous state of bliss.

"Heart, I only have a few moments, as I understand Jackson must leave directly, but how can I thank you for what you've done for me and for Butterfly? You have saved our lives! How did you know to have us both taken to The Mystic's cottage I do not know, but you've taken care of me in the most loving and selfless way anyone ever could.

"Thank you, Heart, thank you. I seem not to be able to come up with the words that I've said to you so many times in my mind, beautiful, eloquent words, but at this moment, all that comes to mind is thank you, and please, please take care of yourself! I long for the day when you and I can be together. I don't know when, I don't know where, but I feel it will be."

In the background, Butterfly stopped her work, looked up, directly into Heart's eyes. She folded her hands over her chest and bowed her head, mouthing the words, "Thank you," then she raised her hands and linked her fingers in the sign for "I Love You," in Heart's and Eye's secret language.

"Oh!" Heart exclaimed quietly. "I love you too, sweet Butterfly!"

"I sense Butterfly upstaging me in the background," Eye said, then chuckled. "I love you, Heart. Take care of yourself. Good-bye for now, precious friend ... good-by,e good-bye ...." The image of Eye slowly faded. Heart sat looking into her palms as if she could will Eye to materialize in the room.

"Oh, Jackson ...." She could say no more. She put her palms to her face. "Thank you," she whispered.

Everyone sat silently in a reverie for a few moments. Heart finally stood and moved to the window. She would have to carry on. Xavier was gone. Eye, happy and safe, but far, far away.

Jackson came to stand by her, while Violet and Equuleus joined them as well. "Look, Heart, the moons of Pink and Yellow are setting! What sweet light!"

Heart looked toward Yellow, surprised to clearly see its bright, silvery moon, its light glowing across space, and, equally surprising, it was setting in tandem with Pink's moon. "Oh! They are setting together!"

"Yes, Heart. Your father re-programmed the moons to rise and set synchronously for thirty of Pink's cycles—thirty of Pink's days, in memory of, and to honor Xavier. A feat of programming, as Yellow is larger, so its moon must travel faster to stay in sync with Pink's moon."

Heart nodded. Then she whispered, "You will have to go back to Earth, Jackson. You can't stay here."

Jackson put his arm around Heart, and she allowed herself to lean into him. "Yes, I will have to go back to Earth, dear Heart. But not this night. Tonight, we watch the glorious silver moons setting, and, in the morning, we will watch them rise."

"Yes," Heart sighed, "we will watch the glorious silver moons rise."

Book Three of *The Darling Undesirables* is *The Inventor's Clone*. Here's Chapter One – a preview of coming attractions!

Chapter 1

The more everyone conspired to keep Heart from viewing the carnage and destruction of Pink during the Bot Invasion, the more intent she became to witness it. She knew they were trying to minimize her pain in losing Xavier.

But nothing could.

She finally managed to steal away from everyone—Jackson, her father and HelperFriend. She even slipped away from Violet and Equuleus, who had gone into stasis in response to Heart's continual sleeping, sleeping, sleeping as she'd never done in her life. Only in sleep could she be with Xavier—this was her private secret, which she told no one.

As she crept down the castle's winding stairs, the light from Pink's new little moon, silver and dusky, filtered through the dome skylight, bathing all it fell upon—the stairs, the railing, the art upon the walls, the dark energy chandelier, the floor with the inset marble image of Earth, everything—in a delicate, fairy-like, bas-relief.

At the front entrance, the environmental locks shunted. Heart stepped through the baffle out into the still of the synthetic moon's evening. Braced for the possibility that her flowers had been destroyed during the Bot Invasion, she released a deep sigh to see the two greenhouses still intact, and through the translucent green of the structures, her sweet flowers shone.

She considered stepping inside with the flowers, ignoring all the tragedy and pain that swirled around and around on the little moon, when she heard a wrenching, high-pitched, wail, an agonized keening. Heart shrank back into the shadows of the front entryway, hoping the traumatizing sound would cease.

But it didn't. She knew she had to step into the moment. She crept toward the poignant sound—not quite as loud as she first thought, as it was much closer. Moving along the edge of the castle, she came upon Lady Gervi's peculiar little mechanical dog, Yippee, making the impossibly woeful sound.

"*Yippee*," she said softly, kneeling down on the ground, "what is it?"

The little dog moved toward Heart haltingly, torn between fear and trust. He looked up at her in pain, whining, whimpering and crying, unbearably piteous.

Heart picked him up, holding him close. "It's all right now, Yippee, the bots have been destroyed, we're safe now. You needn't be afraid."

At first, he relaxed into her embrace, seeming to understand her words, but then he became agitated.

He leaped out of her arms and shook his little head, looking up at her. He grabbed her pant leg in his metal teeth, pulling at her, insisting she follow him.

"Okay, Yippee, all right. I understand, I'll follow you. Let go and I'll come along."

He released her, and, continuing along the base of the castle, he looked back, again and again, to assure himself that she followed him. As they turned the corner of the castle, Heart stopped in shock.

The destruction of the hillside dome, home of all the mechanical, clockworks, and hybrid beings on Pink, took her breath away. She couldn't recognize anything. There was no dome—twisted metal stretched as far as she could see.

"Oh, no!" Heart whispered, wishing she'd not come out here alone, disoriented by the shock of the magnitude of the destruction.

Yippee began to whine louder, demanding Heart's attention. Confused, she looked down at him. "Yes, Yippee, I see ... I see ... horrible. It's ... *horrible.*"

Yippee grabbed onto her pant leg again and tugged at her. She reached over to try to pick him up, but he jumped away from her, moving his head back and forth, and finally, Heart understood that he meant for her to continue following him.

She didn't want to see more if that's what Yippee had in his little metal mind. What stretched before her was more than she could now take in. But, in the wake of his insistence, she followed him. He led her into a narrow cranny of the castle. Giant stones had toppled from the castle parapet, high above, and now lay in a pile of rubble before them.

Yippee clambered up the stones, most of which were larger than he, continuing to whine, and looking back at Heart. He suddenly disappeared into a cavern of the precarious ruins.

"Yippee, no!" Heart cried. But the little dog only howled more pitifully from the depths he'd jumped into. Setting thoughts of her own safety aside, Heart climbed up the pile of stones, hoping to reach down and pull Yippee out, against his will, if she must.

As she perched upon stones that rocked danger-ously, she slowly kneeled down and reached into the cavernous space. As she peered, she began to make out something besides Yippee in the darkness below. It looked like black gears.

Lady Gervi!—trapped under these tons of stone. "All right, Yippee, all right, I see her. Come to me now, and we'll go get help. Come on, I can't leave you here, these stones could shift more at any moment." She reached her arms down to him, relieved when he jumped softly into her embrace.

Maneuvering with all her strength and agility, she lifted him out and crept cautiously back down the pile. Even so, the stones shifted, and with every movement, Yippee whined.

Not until this moment had Heart noticed no one was around. She'd been so preoccupied with her passing thoughts—about Xavier, about her flowers, her concern about Yippee, and then reeling from the shock of the damage, she hadn't noticed *no one was around*. No matter how many residents of Pink may have been harmed in the conflict, the rest of them ought to be scurrying about, energetically clearing up the rubble, and working on rebuilding.

She hurried to her father's modest room at the back of the castle, surprisingly intact, at the edge of the destruction. Still carrying Yippee, she passed through the double baffle of his doors, coming upon a bustling frenzy of mechanical, clockwork, and hybrid gear-bio beings, along with HelperFriend and Jackson.

Her father stood before everyone, gesturing in front of a large 3-D monitor displaying image after image of Pink's destruction from every angle, followed by overlays of how it was before the Bot Invasion.

Everyone stood in poised anticipation, the energy knife-edged, everyone anxious to rebuild their home, while learning what must be done, and how. No one—not even Jackson nor HelperFriend, the gear man, noticed her enter the room. But Yippee would not be ignored.

He let out a growl ten times his size.

Father Inventor stopped talking and gesturing. Every mechanical, clockwork, hybrid and bio eye turned to Heart and Yippee.

"*Father!*" Heart exclaimed, "Lady Gervi is under a gigantic pile of stones. I don't know if she ...." Heart stopped, not entirely certain if Yippee could understand her or not. "We must get her out immediately!"

"Of course!" Her father gestured to the crowd, "HelperFriend, go with Heart and help direct the rescue of Lady Gervi, while Jackson and I get into protective gear."

"Yes, sir!" HelperFriend saluted her father, which Heart found extremely strange. She would have made fun of him under less terrible conditions.

Heart, with HelperFriend by her side, led the group to the pile of stones, hugging the whimpering little dog. They stood before the sight, daunted. How could they possibly move the rubble without stones dropping down upon Lady Gervi?

"You three, get the power lights," HelperFriend commanded, gesturing. He turned to Heart. "Where did you see Lady Gervi?"

Heart went to the pile and pointed to the specific stone she'd leaned over. "From that stone, there. But, even as I crawled back down with Yippee, the stones shifted."

"Hmmm ... yes," HelperFriend said. Heart watched as he studied the pile of stone, his gear eyes performing calculations. "Yes, all right." He turned and gestured to two mechanical women standing by him. "You two get a rope, go up to that castle window and let the rope down."

They scurried off to do as they were bid.

Then HelperFriend addressed Yippee in Heart's arms. "They're going to let down a rope, I'll put a loop in it. Do you think, Yippee, you can wrap the rope around the stones securely, so they can be moved in order to make the hole bigger?'

Heart was a bit stunned as Yippee nodded vigorously and growled with a sound much like, "yesyesyesyesyes." His little gear eyes whirled in edgy anticipation.

"Very good." HelperFriend patted Yippee.

Moments later, intensely bright lights lit up the scene, while a rope dropped from the castle window above. Heart set Yippee on the pile of stones, and with surprising dexterity, he ran up the pile and wrangled the rope around the stone Heart had leaned against, the two women cautiously, slowly, hoisted it, and moved it over to the side where HelperFriend could reach it.

He removed it, and the process was repeated three or four more times when finally Jackson and her father, suited up against the environment, joined them.

"HelperFriend appears to have everything under control here," her father observed, clearly relieved with the progress.

"Oh, Father, he's amazing," Heart said. "He's calculating the risk of stones shifting with every move, and look at that little dog! Goodness, he's brilliant—and intrepid!"

Her father nodded in agreement.

Everyone not actively engaged in the rescue watched the event with rapt attention. In short order, the pile of stones had been brought down to where HelperFriend took it upon himself to climb into the hole that had been exposed.

Everyone held their breath, hoping no stone would shift, hoping Lady Gervi would be brought out of the rubble intact—or enough intact to be repaired and re-animated.

Yippee stood at attention at the base of the pile of rubble, not even whimpering, poised, holding the equivalent of his little mechanical breath.

Heart could hear Helper Friend say something from within the stone vault, but she couldn't determine if he talked with Lady Gervi, or himself.

Then, suddenly, Lady Gervi seemed to levitate as HelperFriend held her aloft above the stone pile.

Yippee went into a paroxysm of yelps, leaping about at the sight of his beloved mistress.

HelperFriend's voice came from inside the stone pile, "If someone would come to my left side and take Lady Gervi. The stones are fairly solidly intertwined there."

Heart noticed that Wonderman One and Wonderman Two had joined the crowd.

"Wonderman One and Wonderman Two are here, HelperFriend," she called.

"Excellent! They can reach across and take her."

Without comment, the two Wondermen did as they were bid. The invisible HelperFriend reached Lady Gervi over in their direction, while the Wondermen extended their long arms and prodigious height. With the ends of their supernaturally strong fingers, they brought the unconscious Lady Gervi into the midst of the crowd, little Yippee almost turning himself inside out for joy.

Heart exchanged a look of consternation with her Father. Lady Gervi did not seem to have the least bit of animation in her, and one of her beautiful gear legs was horribly mangled.

Heart turned her face away from the dreadful sight, unable to forestall the memory of Xavier's torn body.

Her father came up to her and put his arm around her. She leaned into him, wordlessly, as they shared their unspoken empathy—the loss of their beloved Xavier.

"Take her into my room," Heart's father said. Heart stooped to pick up Yippee, then followed the Wondermen inside, along with her father, Jackson, and HelperFriend.

After the door baffles shunted closed, Jackson and her father stepped out of their protective gear, while Wonderman One and Wonderman Two gently laid Lady Gervi on Father Inventor's cot and began their reanimation procedure.

Yippee quivered in Heart's arms, and she held him closer, trying to comfort him, but at a loss, in the midst of her own apprehension and pain.

At that moment, Equuleus came charging through the door at the other end of the room, from the interior of the castle, gears whirring, his wings stretched to the limits of the ceiling, Violet clinging to his back, her little lavender rabbit ears bouncing.

"It's all right, Equuleus," Heart reassured.

"*You were gone!*" Violet squeaked, alarm in her voice. "How did you leave the room without us knowing?"

"You went into stasis since I've been sleeping so much. But ...." Heart's attention came back to the activities of the Wondermen, "I needed to see things for myself."

Violet took in Yippee, quivering in Heart's arms.

"Yippee," Violet said, "What's the matter with you? Are you injured?"

Yippee started a series of growls and yips.

"Oh, my little friend, I'm *so sorry!*"

Yippee pointed his nose where Lady Gervi lay, largely blocked by the massive bodies of the Wondermen.

"Oh!" Violet exclaimed. "Oh, dear!"

Yippee's peculiar monologue continued, Violet nodding. "Oh, Heart! You saved Lady Gervi!"

"I found her because Yippee led me to her."

"Yes, Heart, he just said that."

"Well, *I* can't understand him!"

"Really? How is that? He's perfectly articulate."

"*Stand clear!*" Wonderman One ordered.

Everyone moved back a step, while Wonderman One and Wonderman Two removed their healing vials from their chests, and then made a circuit with Lady Gervi between them. Then they sparked their reanimating charge, the only sound that of the electrical energy passing in the circuit between the clockwork beings, and Yippee's soft whimpering.

With their gigantic backs to the room, all that could be seen were blue and red pulsing lights, coalescing, gradually into a homogenous purple.

"Oh, my!" they heard Lady Gervi's cultured tone a few interminable moments later, soft and weak, but unmistakable. "I seem to have come upon a misfortune!"

"Yes," Wonderman Two agreed. "Please relax while we complete the reanimation, Lady Gervi."

"Of course," she said, compliant. But she suddenly became extremely agitated. "*Yippee!* Yippee was with me when the stones fell. You must go find him!"

Yippee yipped noisily, growling, chirping and yelping in Heart's arms, clearly letting his mistress know he was fine.

"Oh, Heart! Thank you, my dear. Oh, goodness, Heart saved me, I can't ... I don't ... *goodness!* How will I ever thank you? *Quite extraordinary!*"

"Not extraordinary, Lady Gervi," Heart replied, wishing she could be at Lady Gervi's side to reassure her, while Yippee seemed about to blow a cog from excitement. "I'm very happy Yippee took me to you!"

"Must be still!" Wonderman One said quite sternly. "Hush everyone. We must have silence to listen to Lady Gervi's clockworks."

The room fell as silent as a vacuum. Even Yippee became passive as a stuffed toy.

After a few more resounding clicks and clangs, Wonderman Two announced, "Success. Lady Gervi is fully reanimated. We go now."

Without ceremony, they replaced their healing vials back in their chests and moved from the room, each taking a turn in the door baffle as they were too large to pass through together. They were showered with a barrage of gratitude from everyone in the room, the most piercing being Yippee's own joyous howl. Heart rushed up to Lady Gervi's side and put Yippee by her where she lay on the cot.

He began a deluge of chatter, and she nodded at him, looking up at everyone around her, smiling sweetly. "Yes, Yippee, I do understand. Please, let us save some of the details for later. But, again, Heart, thank you! I dread to think what would have happened if you'd not come along when you did."

"Me too, dear Lady. I'm so glad I was able be helpful."

As Heart spoke, Lady Gervi moved about, clearly intending to stand up.

"Oh, Lady," Heart gasped, seeing Lady Gervi did not yet realize her left leg had been destroyed. She watched as Lady Gervi looked down to see the mangle of gears that had previously been her beautiful limb.

"Oh, dear," she said softly.

Heart knelt down on the floor by her and took her hand. "It'll be all right, dear Lady. We'll make it right, won't we Father?"

She looked up at her father who had moved to stand by Lady Gervi.

"Ahm ....." he said, hesitating.

"Not likely," Lady Gervi answered Heart. "Not likely, dear Heart. With all the destruction brought about by the bots, combined with the contingent of residents who moved to Yellow, taking with them a considerable amount of components from here to build a supporting system there, there are few gear components left here. And what remains ... will have to be put to the highest use of reconstruction.

"No, not likely I'll be reconstructed," Lady Gervi concluded, while Yippee whimpered softly but piteously.

"Oh, Father, this can't be true!" Heart stood and faced him, agitated.

"Lady Gervi has stated the situation most accurately, I am profoundly sorry to say," her father said, a deep, sad, furrow in his brow. "For the time being, in any case. Eventually, when things are put back in order, we can probably cast a few gears out of the damaged and distempered metals from the dome with strength too compromised to be used again in a building, but will suffice for a clockworks being."

"Thank you, dearest Father Inventor for your kind words," Lady Gervi said modestly. "But we both know that there are no doubt many clockwork beings yet to be exposed under the rubble, who are in worse condition than I am, and who will need gears more urgently than my mere leg."

"That's ridiculous!" Heart interjected. "You need to be able to get around. It's not just a case of vanity. *You must to be able to move about!*"

"It will be up to her, Heart, if she'll want to accept a compromise, have her damaged leg removed, and replaced with a bit of tubing, or whatever we can improvise."

"Oh!" Heart breathed softly, looking into Lady Gervi's twirling gear eyes, as she pictured her handsome self, reduced to a sad, cobbled together wreck.

What made Lady Gervi, *Lady Gervi*, Heart thought, was the sensual, fascinating movement of her gears beneath the gear-tight black covering. Her tall, regal-yet-modest presence was intrinsic to the morale of the population of Pink. They had built one another from scraps of broken and abandoned clockworks and mechanical beings. They had created Lady Gervi, each contributing their vision of beauty and magnificence, as a reflection of themselves. She needed to be whole!

"I will, like everyone else," she said bravely, "make the best of it, with gratitude that I'm still here. If I can move about, then I will be content to contribute to the reconstruction of my beloved Pink."

"*Here, here!*" Violet called, jumping down from Equuleus and hopping up beside Yippee, giving him a big, Violet hug.

"*Here, here,*" everyone else, but Heart, echoed.

"Well said," Heart's father agreed. "Always a lady, my dear friend, and now you show exemplary bravery and dedication to all of Pink's population.

"We have much work to do to bring our home back to habitable condition. Your example will encourage everyone to continue the hard work and sacrifice required in the process of recovery."

Heart heard her father's words—they rang kind and true enough. But she couldn't keep from thinking about the first time she'd seen Lady Gervi, when she met her at the farewell party for Xavier, before his return to Earth.

Lady Gervi had immediately made a profound impression on Heart. Taller than everyone except the Wondermen, she'd sailed among the crowd, gracious and graceful, while at the same time, intriguingly sultry. In Heart's sheltered life, she had never encountered anyone with such a natural way with guileless bodily self-appreciation.

"I think," Father's voice, addressing HelperFriend broke in on Heart's reverie, "we will have the Lady stay with us in the castle."

"Excellent, yes," HelperFriend agreed. "Which room?"

"I'll leave it up to you, HelperFriend. You and Lady Gervi. Whatever accommodations are most suitable for everyone is fine with me. Will you carry her, HelperFriend?"

"I shall, indeed."

"Wait!" Heart interjected, exchanging a look with Equuleus, in which she communicated her intention. Equuleus nodded. "Why not have Equuleus carry her? Does that suit you, Lady Gervi?"

"Oh, my! No, I would not want to impose. That's too much, really, Heart. I'm not worthy ...."

"Goodness, I won't hear it! Equuleus would be honored if you would allow him to take you to a room of your liking."

Equuleus whinnied his agreement. He then moved alongside the cot, and HelperFriend lifted her onto his back, then out they trouped—Lady Gervi on Equuleus, Yippee, and Violet leaping alongside, followed by HelperFriend and Heart.

Heart looked over her shoulder at her father and Jackson. She knew her father had things to attend to and was clearly anxious to get at them.

"You coming?" she asked Jackson.

He glanced at her father, and he nodded.

"Sure," he said, joining them.

But something in the look exchanged between her father and Jackson arrested her attention. What loomed in the unspoken dialogue between them?

Was there not enough going on without yet something *else* to deal with?

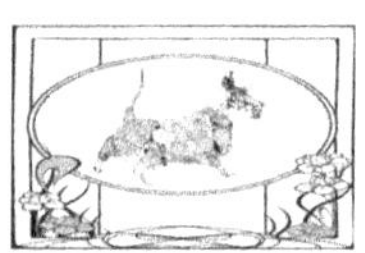

About the Author

I live in a forest in the Pacific Northwest with a few domestic and numerous wild creatures, where I create an ever-growing inventory of books and stories.

When you support my work you help support ten acres of natural forest, and all its resident fauna. *All the creatures and I thank you!*

Questions, comments, observations, reviews? I'd love to hear from you!:

Blythe@BlytheAyne.com

www.BlytheAyne.com